T0072116

ARKHAM HORROR™

WRATH
of N'KAI

JOSH REYNOLDS

ACONYTE

First published by Aconyte Books in 2020

ISBN 978 1 83908 011 1

Ebook ISBN 978 1 83908 012 8

Cover art by Daniel Strange

Distributed in North America by Simon & Schuster Inc, New York, USA

Printed in the United States of America

9 8 7 6 5 4 3 2 1

ACONYTE BOOKS

An imprint of Asmodee Entertainment Ltd

Mercury House, Shipstones Business Centre

North Gate, Nottingham NG7 7FN, UK

aconytebooks.com // twitter.com/aconytebooks

To Sylvie, for the support, and to Elodie, for the distraction.

PROLOGUE
The Shadow

It slept.

And in sleeping, it dreamed. These dreams were not true dreams, however, but rather flashes of memory. Moments in time, crystallized and left suspended in the blackness of its consciousness. As it slept, it analyzed every facet of these fossilized moments.

It saw again the offered sacrifice, and felt the old hunger. Heard the chanting of the faithful – a sound it had not heard in years.

It was the last in this place. It knew this, though it did not know how. It understood little about the world or itself. It had not been created to understand, but to serve. To watch and stand sentry through the long eons of geological waxing and waning.

The one who had created it had slumbered in the deepest of deeps; lightless places, where the welcoming dark stretched forever. It had been born in the dark, and found comfort in it. There was too much light above.

But the creator was gone now, as were the others like it. It did not know where, for it had not been allowed to follow. It had been left to patrol the long emptiness, and watch the dark for intruders.

It did not know why, only that it must. So, it had prowled the dark, ensuring that the deeps remained sacrosanct. Inviolate.

Then had come the chants. The prayers. Tiny sounds, filtering down from great heights. It had been drawn upwards, ever upwards, through abyssal canyons and red-lit caverns. Through the tumbled cities of those who'd once inhabited the depths and made obeisance to the creator, until something had put them to flight.

It did not perceive their absence, save as a vague hollow in its awareness. They had been there, and now they were not. Soon, it might well have forgotten that they had ever been at all. But then it had heard the chanting. The old words, calling it up out of the comforting dark, into the hateful light. It remembered again, and wondered.

Curiosity had compelled it more than any respect for the old rites. It had no understanding of the rituals of the ones above. They did not bind it, for it could not be bound, save by the will of the creator – or those of equal stature. Or so it had thought at the time. But it remembered the ancient days when those chants had preceded sacrifice.

So it climbed up and up, until it reached the tumbled cities, and that which was built above. Another city, larger than those below, and built by another race. It did not concern itself with the differences between such folk. Those of the lower deeps had been cold-blooded and wise. These were warm-blooded and so noisy.

It recalled an earlier time when these frail warmbloods had descended into the lowest depths. How they had screeched at the sight of it writhing in pain, pierced through by the horrid light they had carried with them. It had harried them up and up, as far as it dared go, chasing them back to their realm. Then it had returned to the safety of the dark, there to lick its wounds.

They had hurt it, though they had not realized it. And it had hurt them in return. But now, they were calling to it, as they had once done in time out of mind. Up it crawled, stretching itself higher and thinner, trembling at the dim radiance that infested these heights. But eager… oh so eager. The higher it climbed, the more eager it became.

It had been so long since it had tasted a sacrifice. Not since the days of the creator. It recalled now when the creator had departed. Not long after the warmbloods had descended into the dark with their stinging lights. They had come to find the creator, whom they worshipped, and in finding him, and his servants, had grown afraid.

It did not understand fear, save in the most basic fashion. It feared light, because light caused pain. But the creator did not cause pain. So why then had they been afraid? Such questions slipped its mind almost as suddenly as they'd arrived. It had no use for the answers, at any rate.

When it reached the city of the upper depths, it heard again the warmbloods' song of fear. Light sliced the dark, as shrill sounds split the silence. It avoided both, climbing higher still. And there, perilously close to the sky of stone, it found them, clad in the raiment of those who worshipped the creator. The servants of mighty Tsathoggua, the Sleeper of N'kai.

The sacrifice knelt at the edge of a cliff, clad in iron, marked with the sacred sigils. The warmblood struggled and made the fear-noises as it approached, but it was overcome by hunger and ignored this warning. Never before had the sacrifices shown fear. That this one did should have sent it fleeing back to the safety of the depths.

But it was hungry. Very hungry. Thus, it persisted. It slipped about the sacrifice, and inundated it with gentle grace, as was tradition. It filled the dark places of the struggling warmblood, slipping into its flesh and tenderly devouring the soft things within. So distracted was it by its feast that it did not notice as the adherents erected a cage of light about it. When it realized its peril, it had no place to hide save in the meat-husk of the sacrifice – even as they had intended. It burrowed in, retreating as the bars of light closed about it.

The adherents – the false adherents – spoke words it did not know, but understood nonetheless. Words of binding. Mnemonic chains to seal it away in the shriveled husk of the traitor-sacrifice. It made itself smaller and smaller, folding itself again and again, trying to escape the reverberations of those words and the light that grew ever closer. But it could not make itself small enough.

In the end, it huddled in the hollow belly of the husk, compacted to the size of a seed. The husk shook as it was removed from the place of sacrifice and taken elsewhere. Someplace dark, but stifling. Someplace forgotten.

It remembered all of this, reliving it over and over again in its long isolation. Trapped, it could do nothing else. Every time, it thought things might turn out differently. But they never did. It kept trying and failing. Trying and failing.

Eventually, it went insane. The seed sprouted, stretching, filling, trying to burst the bonds of withered meat that held it. But the chains refused to break. It could taste the marks the betrayers had carved into the husk. They stung worse than light. Sigils of binding older than the world itself, and too strong for a mere servitor to break.

Finally, exhausted, it slept.

It slumbered until something woke it. The rattle of shifting rock.

Muffled voices – voices unlike those of its captors, its betrayers.

Then, it was free and rising into the hateful light. It squirmed down deep into the hidden places of its prison, where the light could not reach.

And it waited.

CHAPTER ONE
Arkham

Rain streaked the glass. Alessandra Zorzi inhaled softly, tasting a tickle in the back of her throat from the cigarette. Her tablemate droned on, something about insurance. His voice, accompanied by the rhythmic clatter of the train, was dangerously soothing.

She exhaled a plume of smoke. "Fascinating," she murmured. She stubbed the cigarette out on her plate, smearing ashes through the remains of a subpar hollandaise. "But if you will excuse me, my stop is coming up."

He stopped mid-sentence, a look of surprise – and not a little consternation – on his round face. He wasn't bad looking, if a touch too American for her tastes, with close-cropped hair the color of ripe wheat and eyes like faded dollar bills. His suit was off the peg, but clean and brushed. He set his coffee down and gave a wan smile. "Of course. Sorry about talking your ear off."

Alessandra tugged on an earlobe. "Never fear. Still firmly attached, Mr...?"

"Whitlock. Abner Whitlock."

"Of course." She turned to leave the dining car and he coughed.

"Didn't catch your name," he said, hopefully.

She pretended not to hear him. A touch brusque, perhaps, but Abner Whitlock wasn't the sort of man to waste an alias on. In her experience, that sort was few and far between. He didn't call out after her, thankfully. Or try to stop her. Sometimes men couldn't take no for an answer. That often led to awkwardness. One reason among many she kept a loaded British Bulldog in her clutch.

The rain thudded against the roof of the carriage as she made her way to the sleeper car. It had been raining since New York. An inauspicious start, if one believed in omens. Alessandra didn't, and anyway, she liked the rain. It reminded her of home. Of the stinging bite of the Adriatic and the soft sway of a gondola as it navigated the narrow canals.

Of course, with those memories came the realization that she hadn't been home in years. She had been away from *La Serenissima* for longer than she had ever lived there, but it was lodged in her mind. The canals and bridges were an inviolate part of her mental map. Wherever she went, whatever she did, it was always there.

She was still thinking of Venice when she entered her compartment. It was small, but more importantly, it was private. Thus, when she saw the face – pale and wild, staring – she reacted on instinct. She had the pistol cocked a moment before the discarded clutch hit the floor. It took only a moment for her to realize it was her reflection in the compartment window, distorted by the lights in the passage.

She stepped inside, kicking the clutch out of the way, and shut the door. Leaning against it, she fought down the sudden knot of adrenaline. If a porter had happened along, or worse, one of her fellow passengers, she would have had some explaining to do. "Lucky little lioness," she murmured. Her grandfather's favorite term of endearment. It had stuck with her when most of his lessons had flown right out of her head.

She uncocked the pistol and tossed it on the bed. Fingers trembling, she retrieved her clutch and the pack of cigarettes. The pack was decorated with scenes of exotic delight, but something about the way the dancers leered at one another repulsed her in a vague and inexplicable fashion. She extricated one and stuffed it between her lips, not caring that she bent it slightly. She lit it and opened the window, suddenly needing the feel of the wind on her face. It wasn't a sea breeze, but it would do.

The damp air snatched the smoke from the cigarette's tip, and she blinked away errant raindrops. The clouds were like a spill of ink, and the sun was in hiding. She smoked her cigarette down to the nub and flicked it away into the rain. She closed her eyes, holding the last drag in her lungs for a moment before releasing it slowly.

A knock at the door. She'd already reclaimed her pistol and taken aim when she realized it was probably just the attendant coming to tell her Arkham was the next station. She lowered the weapon. "Yes?"

A muffled reply. She hesitated. "Thank you," she said, erring on the side of caution. She heard the creak of someone moving down the corridor and relaxed slightly. She shoved her pistol back into her clutch, wanting it out of sight and out of mind.

Marrakesh had left her jittery. She'd come close to being caught – closer than she liked. There was always a certain element of risk in her line of work, but having the French authorities pounding on the door to her hotel room at three in the morning was cutting it close, even for her. She supposed the esteemed Comte d'Erlette was still upset about the loss of his books.

As they'd busted down the door, she'd gone out the window. It wasn't the first time she'd done so, nor was it likely the last. The life of a gentlewoman thief was not for the faint of heart or the weak of limb. She had learned early that circumstances were to be endured, not controlled. One could not plan for everything, though one could easily go mad trying.

She began the laborious process of packing. Her suitcases were mostly for show. There was nothing in them she would be broken-hearted about losing. Indeed, she'd abandoned more than one wardrobe in her career. Clothes were just things, and things could be replaced. Often with nicer things, depending on the state of one's bank account.

Right now, hers was in worse shape than she liked to admit in mixed company. It was an expensive sort of life. That was why she'd accepted her latest client's offer. The theft of a few precious artifacts from a museum exhibition was easy money as far as she was concerned. All it cost was time, and she had plenty of that at the moment.

There were worse ways to live. She could have been married, after all. While she quite enjoyed a good party, she could think of no darker hell than the same face staring at her across the table every morning.

Her sisters had chosen marriage. They'd always been more upstanding sorts, with a keen appreciation for the largesse stability brought. On days like today, she couldn't say that they'd been wrong. When it came time to retire, she might have to find her own doddering old Milanese dinosaur to woo, wed, bed and bury. Possibly not in that order.

Of course, if the honorable comte ever caught up with her, she might not live that long. French aristocrats had distressingly long memories, and d'Erlette had deep pockets to go with them. That was why she'd decided to up stakes for the States for a year or three. Long enough for her picture to stop circulating through the cafes and souks of her usual haunts. Besides which, America was supposed to be a Land of Opportunity. And if there was one thing Alessandra Zorzi liked, it was opportunity.

The train was starting to slow. She left her luggage for the porters and shrugged into her coat and hat. She took a moment to study herself in the en suite's mirror. Tall and dark, with sharp features, wearing a cloche hat, short tubular dress, earrings hanging like fuchsias. Her stole was last year's fur, but she doubted anyone in Arkham, Massachusetts, would be able to tell. She retrieved her clutch and gave it a fond pat.

Another knock at the door. This time, she didn't give in to the impulse to go for her pistol. "Coming," she said, plastering a smile on her face. She stepped past the attendant with a nod, pressing a discreet gratuity into his hands. He beamed at her and tipped his cap. She wasn't so flush with funds that she could afford generosity, but she considered tips to porters, pages and housemaids a necessary business expense – it often kept them from remembering her clearly when the police came around asking awkward questions.

Outside the compartment windows, the station was visible. Bathed in a watery, orange glow, it was singularly unprepossessing – a crumbling castle from another time and place, looming over the dark, serpentine length of the Miskatonic. Further adding to this impression were the two great towers of stone standing sentry over the parallel tracks. Alessandra could imagine cauldrons of boiling oil being tipped over the parapets onto the invading barbarian hordes from Boston, Providence and Kingsport.

The train gave a shiver and slid to a halt. She fell into line with the other passengers and paused at the door only to adjust her stole. It was warm for autumn, despite the rain. She joined the rest of the passengers awaiting their luggage. Zamacona wouldn't have sent anyone to greet her. From what little she knew of her new client, he was as much a stranger here as she was.

Not that she knew much about him at all. She didn't even know how he'd managed to contact her – none of her usual connections had admitted to passing her name along. In her line, word of mouth was better than a business card. But most former clients were smart enough to ask permission before allowing a newcomer into their ranks.

The name was unusual – Asturian, she thought. Or maybe Galician. Regardless, she doubted it was his real one. Her clients almost always employed aliases, unless they were particularly foolish – or simply didn't care. Frankly, so long as his money was good, he could call himself whatever he liked.

Railroad bulls prowled the platform, trying hard not to look like undercover security men. She tensed, watching the nearest of them out of the corner of her eye. She'd been forced to flee through more than one train station in her time. If they were here for her, she intended to give them a run for their money. But none of them so much as glanced her way.

"Fancy meeting you here."

She turned. Abner Whitlock smiled genially at her. He had his raincoat over one arm, and his hat in hand. A heavy carpetbag rested beside his foot. "I meant to ask earlier… you wouldn't happen to be in town for the special exhibition, would you?"

"And why would you think that?" she asked, suddenly alert.

"No reason. It's why I'm here. My company is underwriting it." He grinned. "It sounds interesting, if nothing else. Imagine: an American mummy! Who'd have ever thought of such a thing?" He paused. "I'm sorry again, by the way."

"For what?"

"Boring you to tears over breakfast. It was rude of me to monopolize the conversation that way. I didn't even ask your name."

"No, you didn't."

He looked at her expectantly, his smile open and inviting. Whitlock, she suspected, was a man used to getting what he wanted. Though just what it was he wanted, she couldn't say. There was some threat there, but it wasn't the obvious one. Looking at him standing there, smiling, she had a brief impulse to stick her pistol into his belly and pull the trigger until she heard a click. Instead, she smiled prettily and turned away.

She heard him grunt under his breath. Not an obscenity, not even a word – more like a dog's chuff of surprise. As if she'd done something utterly unexpected. When she glanced back, he was gone, vanished into the crowd of departing passengers. She felt a flicker of relief. Men like Abner Whitlock were nothing but trouble.

She spied the station porter hovering about the edges of the crowd. When he noticed her standing beside her stack of luggage, he limped over. His smile was open and friendly. "Need a hand with your luggage, ma'am?"

"I would be obliged to you," Alessandra said, thickening her accent. "As you can see, it is more than I can fit in my clutch."

He laughed politely and nodded. "I think we can rectify that, ma'am. Let me grab a dolly, and we'll get you situated. Is someone meeting you?"

She hesitated. The question might be innocent. Then again, it might be anything but. "I will require transportation if it is available."

"Another thing we're happy to help with." He moved briskly

back the way he'd come, but returned a few moments later pushing a squeaky-wheeled dolly. Despite his limp he moved quickly, and loaded up her luggage without difficulty.

"Thank you…" she began.

"Washington, ma'am, Bill Washington. And it's all part of the service here at Northside Station. I…" He paused, his smile faltering as he turned. She turned with him, but saw nothing but the rain falling at the edge of the platform.

"What is it?"

His smile snapped back into focus. "Not a thing, ma'am. Thought I heard something, is all. To tell the truth, this old station has a bit of a rat problem." He pushed her luggage out of the station. A handful of taxi cabs waited along the sidewalk. Bill paused, as if looking for one in particular. He smiled and started towards one standing a bit away from the others.

He banged on the roof when he reached it. "Wake up, Pepper. You've got a fare."

There was a muffled yelp, as if someone had been startled. Then a gawky figure climbed out of the cab. "I wasn't sleeping," the cabbie said.

"Sure you weren't, Pepper," Bill said. "This lady needs a cab. You're it."

The cabbie – Pepper – stuck out his chin and squared off with the much taller porter. He was young – far younger than he was attempting to appear, she thought. He had thin, boyish features, without a hint of facial hair and a spatter of freckles across his nose and cheeks. He wore a battered flat cap, and loose clothes. "Only I say who gets a ride in my cab, Washington."

Bill's smile became pained. "You're embarrassing me, Pepper."

"Golly, wouldn't want that," Pepper said. He glanced at

Alessandra and stuck out his hand. Gingerly, she took it. "Pepper Kelly, pleased to meet you."

"An unusual name. I am Alessandra. Alessandra Zorzi."

Pepper whistled. "You want to talk names? I think you got me beat, lady." He paused. "You got a funny accent."

"My apologies." Alessandra smiled. She preferred honest rudeness to false bonhomie.

He shrugged and stuffed his hands in his pockets. "It's not a problem. Just thought I'd mention it." Something about the way he said it made Alessandra's instincts twitch. Her eyes strayed to the line of his jaw, the set of his face – the way he spoke and moved. Even his handshake. Like pieces of a puzzle.

Alessandra had always had a gift for puzzles. It was what made her a good thief. Being a thief – as opposed to a stick-up artist or a burglar – required the sort of cunning that few people possessed in abundance. She glanced at Bill, and saw the porter's jaw tighten.

Before he could speak, she said, "You know, in Paris, cab drivers get the door for their passengers."

The cabbie glanced at her. "We ain't in Paris."

"No. Just thought I'd mention it."

He thought about this for a moment, then laughed and made to open the trunk of the cab. "You're all right, sister. Hurry up and get out of the rain. I'll help old Bill here with your luggage."

CHAPTER TWO
Downtown

"So, you're what – Spanish?" Pepper asked. "Or Portuguese? Lots of Portuguese coming to Arkham these days." He glanced at her over one narrow shoulder as the cab wound through the streets of Arkham's Northside district. It was a crowded sprawl of factories, warehouses and processing facilities. The dark length of the Miskatonic was visible between the widely spaced buildings and the air smelled faintly of fish and industrial runoff.

"No. Shouldn't you be watching the road?"

"Only need one eye around here," he said, and was almost immediately forced to face front and grab the wheel in both hands. The cab swerved wildly for a few moments as a produce truck raced past, horn blaring. "Usually," he added, lamely. After a few moments of embarrassed silence, his curiosity reasserted itself. "France?"

"Morocco, actually."

"You're from Morocco?"

"By way of Italy."

"Morocco's in Italy?"

Alessandra paused before replying. "No."

"Huh. Didn't think so. So where am I taking you anyway?"

She looked out the window. The rain had begun to slacken. Tenements rose to either side of the street, and clotheslines stretched over narrow alleyways. So far, her first impressions of Arkham were not favorable. "The Independence Hotel. Do you know where that is?"

"If I didn't, I wouldn't be much of a cabbie," Pepper said, and gave a high-pitched laugh. He glanced at her speculatively. Alessandra, fully aware of the mercenary calculation taking place, straightened in her seat. "Lot of fares heading that way the last few days."

"Oh?"

Pepper nodded. "Yeah, some big exhibition is happening over at the museum. Is that why you're here?"

"You'll forgive me, but that is my business."

Pepper laughed. "I've heard that before, believe it or not. Arkham's that sort of town."

"Is it? It seems fairly innocuous at first glance." She glanced out the window. They'd left the tenements behind. Arkham was bigger than she'd thought. A city masquerading as a town. And still growing by the looks of it.

While parts of the city were caught fast by the previous century, the rest of it was happily embracing modernity. Revolutionary era brick buildings warred for space with French Huguenot architecture, and art deco facings peered out from among the older structures. Arkham, like the old cities of Europe, lived in a shadow of its past.

"Looks can be deceiving," Pepper said. He didn't elaborate and something in his tone kept Alessandra from pressing the issue. Instead, she focused on him. There was something about him that felt off somehow. Peculiar. As if he were hiding something.

Traffic was heavy. The narrow streets were full of automobiles, mostly delivery trucks. Several times Pepper was forced to aim the cab down sidestreets and blind alleys, through corridors of wood and brick that seemed altogether too tight for the vehicle to fit through. He kept up a steady stream of chatter the entire time, and Alessandra found she was warming to the cabbie despite herself.

"You keep looking at me," he said, suddenly.

"Do I?"

"Yeah. I got something on my face or what?"

"No. I apologize. It is just … you are young to be a cab driver, no?"

"No," Pepper said, somewhat pugnaciously. Alessandra realized that she had inadvertently insulted the young man.

"Ah. Again, I am sorry. How long have you been a driver, may I ask?"

"Why do you want to know?"

"Curiosity."

Pepper glanced back at her, his eyes narrow slits beneath the brim of his cap. "You ask a lot of questions."

"I am new in town. I wish to, how do you say, get the lay of the land."

"If you must know, I'm only driving this heap temporarily."

"Oh?" Alessandra prompted.

"Yeah. I'm really an entrepreneur." Pepper patted the wheel fondly. "This cab is my ticket to independent means. Just need a few big fares and then…" He trailed off, as if imagining his bright, shiny future.

"And then?"

He laughed again, but not so loudly or so cheerfully. "We'll see. I'm not the sort of person to go counting eggs before they're cracked, you know?"

Alessandra frowned. She'd always had a facility for languages. She was fluent in several, including English, French and German, and could make herself understood in half a dozen more. But the American capacity for idioms was almost more than she could handle. They seemed to have one – or several – for every occasion.

"There was a guy watching you back there, at the station," Pepper said, barreling on before Alessandra could reply. "Tall, sort of bland. Looked like a government man."

"Gray suit, blond hair," Alessandra said.

"That's the one. Old boyfriend?"

"No." She frowned, wondering what Whitlock's interest in her was. He had been unusually keen to get her name. She could ordinarily sense when a man was attracted to her, and she wasn't getting that feeling from him. It was as if he wanted something from her. Not a friendly feeling at all.

"Sorry I asked."

"Apologies are not necessary." She paused, considering her next words carefully. She'd finally figured out what was bothering her about Pepper. "So what is your real name, then?" The cabbie jolted in his seat as if she'd struck him. Pepper wasn't good at hiding his feelings.

"What?" he asked, as if he hadn't heard. His voice cracked slightly.

"The clothes are good. Someone hemmed them properly, or maybe you just found the right size by luck. The haircut as well. And you're either blessed with a boyish figure or you're adept at binding yourself." Alessandra sat back.

"What I can't figure is why a girl from Boston is driving a cab in Arkham."

• • •

Pepper pulled over and sat facing forward for long moments. Traffic passed them by, but she paid no attention. "How'd you know?" she asked, finally. She'd had nightmares like this off and on for the past year. Ever since she'd started the charade.

"I told you."

Pepper took a deep breath and turned in her seat. The woman met her glare with infuriating equanimity and did not look away. Pepper considered ordering her out of the cab, but wasn't certain she'd go. "Just my clothes, huh?"

Zorzi was silent for a moment. Then she smiled. "You talk too much. The more you talked, the more your voice slipped. If you would like some advice, the key to a good disguise is always simplicity."

Pepper was silent for several minutes. "I'll keep it in mind," she said, finally.

"What is your name?"

Pepper frowned. "Why should I tell you? Hell, why shouldn't I kick you out of this cab right now?"

"Have I offended you somehow?" Zorzi waved aside her reply. "If so, I can only ask your forgiveness. I did not mean to startle you. You are a long way from Boston."

"And you're a long way from Italy. People travel."

"Yes. You are avoiding thequestion."

Pepper hesitated. "Philippa. Philippa Kelly."

"I can see why you changed it."

Pepper stared at her, jaw set. "Funny. Are you going to tell anyone?"

"Why would I? It is no concern of mine. I was merely curious, as I said."

"Oh well, in that case, all is forgiven," Pepper said sarcastically.

"You got some nerve, lady, coming into my cab, asking all sorts of questions."

"There is no shame in it. I have pretended to be a man myself, on occasion."

Pepper looked her up and down. "Yeah, I bet you were real convincing."

Zorzi laughed. "What I really want to know is why you bother?"

Pepper looked away. "It's complicated."

"It always is. I assume Mr Washington knows."

"Why would you say that?"

"Experience and intuition."

Pepper took a breath. "Yeah. He knows." Bill Washington had been a friend of her father's, back before the war, but she saw no reason to tell Zorzi that. "He doesn't say nothing, though." She still wasn't sure why he'd never ratted her out, but she was grateful nonetheless. Washington was always careful to make sure she got a few fares every night, and he kept the other cabbies from stealing her spot in the line. Maybe he thought he was looking out for her.

"And neither will I. After all, who would I tell?" Zorzi sat back, the picture of refined contentment. Pepper looked her up and down again, with just a touch of envy. "Besides, I feel that this might be something of an opportunity for both of us."

Suspicious now, Pepper said, "Yeah? How so?"

"I am in need of a … well, a native guide, you might say. Someone I can count on to take me where I need to go, and not ask too many questions. I think that might be you, if you are up for it."

"You trying to muscle me?" Pepper asked, defensively.

"Not in the least. If you say no, I'll find someone else or do without. It wouldn't be the first time." Zorzi smiled again. "I can pay, if that is what you are wondering about."

Pepper frowned. She always needed money, but it seemed too good to be true. "I'd have to ask my boss…" she began, doubtfully.

"Say, twice your normal rate?"

Pepper blinked. "Then again, what he doesn't know won't hurt him." She turned back to the wheel and put the cab into motion, pulling away from the sidewalk with a tap of her horn to warn oncoming traffic. Brakes screeched behind them, but she ignored it. "So, what does a lady like you need a guide for?"

"I am in town on business, you might say. I find it easier to conduct my affairs when I do not have to consult a map or ask directions every few moments."

"I can see where that might be helpful here. It's easy to get lost in Arkham, even if you've lived here for a few years." Pepper shivered slightly, as she said it. She'd often found herself in the wrong part of town, especially at night. Arkham played tricks on you, if you weren't paying attention.

She'd often wondered why her father had wanted to return here, after her mother, Moira, had died. Patrick Kelly had been a big man, loud and friendly. At least before her mother's death. After that, he'd become taciturn. It was as if all that he was had gone into the ground with her. He'd retreated from the familiar, upped stakes and gone home.

It had been a shock. Arkham was nothing like Boston. And yet it seemed somehow bigger, as if it contained multitudes. The streets went on too long, the river was too wide, the buildings loomed like skyscrapers even though they barely topped three stories in most places. Even worse were the tales. It seemed like everyone had at least one.

But she'd gotten used to it quick enough, or as good as. You never really got used to Arkham, you just adapted. That was how her father had put it. You adapted. Learned what to look for – and what not to see.

She'd thought he was getting better, for a while. He was off the sauce and working. They'd had a nice place for Northside. Nothing fancy, but four walls and a good view of the river. Not that she wanted to spend much time looking at the river.

But then had come the war, and off he'd gone. There'd been a bullet with his name on it waiting for him on the Western Front. Or so Washington had said. But Bill refused to talk about it, no matter how much she pressed him. Maybe he thought he was protecting her, not telling her how her father had really died. Or maybe he was protecting himself.

Either way, she was counting the days until she had enough saved to get back to Boston and away from Arkham for good. She didn't belong here, and some days it felt like the town knew it. She glanced back at her fare. Maybe this Zorzi woman was the answer to her prayers.

Pepper smiled. Things might just be looking up.

CHAPTER THREE
Independence

The Independence Hotel was tall for Arkham. Eight stories of brick and mortar. It wasn't a patch on the Savoy, but Alessandra hadn't expected it to be. It towered over its nearest neighbors, rising from amid a stretch of storefronts and offices.

The lobby stank of self-conscious modernity. White and black checked tiles, black marble paneling, limned with gold. A colorful mural stretched across the domed ceiling, detailing a curious scene from what she guessed must be town history.

Alessandra glanced back over her shoulder at Pepper. The cabbie followed awkwardly in her wake, lugging several heavy suitcases. Alessandra herself carried the smallest of the lot and her clutch. "What do you have in here, bricks?" Pepper groused.

"One must come prepared with an outfit for all occasions. Remember to be back here at eight. I need you to take me to dinner."

"Lady, we just met," Pepper protested. "What, nothing?" she added, when Alessandra didn't reply. "Not even a smile?"

"Forgive me. I am still unfamiliar with your American sense of humor."

Pepper rolled her eyes. "Where are we going anyway?"

"I believe it's called La Bella Luna."

"What? Really?"

Alessandra looked at her. "Yes. Why?"

Pepper shrugged. "No reason."

Check-in was a long stretch of teak countertop set opposite a small restaurant. Behind the counter was an office and a coat-check. The clerk was a short, nervous man wearing a suit a size too large and a toupee a size too small. He smiled ingratiatingly at her. "Reservation?"

She returned his smile. "Regrettably not. I was hoping you might have a room available. Preferably something overlooking that delightful park across the street."

"Only the penthouse left, I'm afraid," the clerk said, somewhat apologetically. "All of our other rooms are reserved. There's an exhibition at the museum this week. Lots of folks coming in from out of town."

"I'm sure it will be suitable," Alessandra said.

"I should hope so. It has a fine view of Independence Square, for which this establishment is named."

"Is that supposed to be a meteorite?" she asked, as she signed her name to the register.

"Excuse me?"

She jabbed the pen upwards. "The mural. Is that a meteorite?"

The clerk nodded cheerfully. "Indeed it is, ma'am. The one that fell just west of here in June of… 1882 or thereabouts?" The clerk turned to the office. "Milo, you're the historian," he called out. "June of 1882?"

"Gardner Meteorite," Milo said, peering out of the office. He was a fresh-faced lad, dressed in a crisply pressed bellhop's uniform.

"Fell on the Gardner farm, just a mile west of town. Hence the name."

"How intriguing," Alessandra said, as she accepted her key from the clerk. "And whatever happened to it?"

The clerk frowned, and Milo coughed. Pepper, standing at her elbow, said, "Way I heard it, the thing melted away. And took the farm with it."

"Well, I'm sure I don't know about that," the clerk said as he looked at the register. "Milo, help Miss – oh my – *the countess*, I mean, with her bags." He simpered slightly. "Please let us know if there's anything we can do for you, countess. We at the Independence pride ourselves on our old world hospitality."

"I certainly will," Alessandra said. She glanced at Pepper, who was staring at her goggle-eyed. "What?"

"You're a countess?"

"Did I not mention that?"

"No!"

"Well, one doesn't like to brag. Remember, tonight at eight. Do not be late."

Pepper gave an awkward salute. "I'll be out front, like I said." She spun on her heel and slouched away, hands thrust in her pockets. When Alessandra turned back, Milo had finished stacking her luggage onto a wheeled rack.

"Ready, ma'am?" he said, dusting his hands.

"Countess!" the clerk corrected, sharply.

Alessandra nodded. "Lead the way, Milo."

"Don't mind the boss," Milo murmured, as he wheeled her luggage towards the elevator. "He's easily impressed."

"And you're not?"

"Depends on the tip."

Alessandra laughed. Milo called for the elevator. As they waited, she let her eyes wander. Something tugged at her attentions, and she turned.

Someone was watching her. She could feel it. Not Whitlock this time. She gave the lobby a surreptitious once-over, wondering if it was some dogsbody of her clients. But if that were the case, how would they have known she was here? Unless, perhaps, they'd followed her from the station. Given Pepper's driving, that seemed unlikely.

She saw no obvious observers. But when the elevator opened she stepped into the car with no small amount of relief. "You all right, miss?" the elevator operator asked. He was an older man, somewhat incongruous in his pressed uniform.

"A bit tired," she said.

"Well, you've come to the right place. This is the finest hotel this side of Kingsport. Ain't that right, Milo?"

Alessandra stifled a chuckle as Milo rolled his eyes. "That's right, Clancy."

Clancy patted a wooden panel with obvious affection. "Eight stories, ma'am. Bigger than any other building in Arkham. Hotel Miskatonic, over on West College Street, used to be the tallest at five, but we got them beat. Made the owner fit to be tied, way I heard it."

"Really," Alessandra said, only half-listening to the attendant's rambling.

"Oh yeah. There was a whole big to-do about it in the *Advertiser*. Real war of words, you might say." He grinned at her. "And then the *Gazette* got involved, and the mayor and…" he paused. "*The mob,*" he continued, in a stage whisper. "Protests, whole nine yards. We're living in interesting times, you betcha."

"Yes, I can see why that might be considered exciting."

The flow of anecdotes paused, but only for a few moments. "Really though, I'd wager this is the most modern building in Arkham. Tip-top, up-to-date, latest electrical generators. Even this elevator is brand new." Clancy gave the control panel another affectionate pat. As if in reply, the elevator juddered slightly. The lights dipped, for a couple seconds. He leaned close to the panel and murmured to it, as if it were a restive horse. He gave her an apologetic smile. "Still a few jitters. She's learning, though."

Alessandra raised an eyebrow, but chose not to take the bait. The last thing she wanted at the moment was to be drawn into a discussion on the probable gender of an elevator. She almost sighed in relief when the bell rang, signaling that they'd reached her floor. Milo opened the cage and helped her set her bags as the attendant wittered on, spilling historical tidbits by the handful.

He was still talking when the doors closed. Milo glanced at her. "The stairs are quicker, if you were wondering. And quieter."

She smiled. "I will keep that in mind, Milo."

He rolled her luggage down the hall, and stopped before a door at the end. "Penthouse, as requested." He opened the door and stepped aside, allowing her to enter first. The room wasn't as big as some she'd resided in, but it was substantial enough. Three rooms, including an en suite.

The large windows overlooked a park across the street, dominated by gray birch trees and stone pathways. Independence Square, she assumed. And beyond it, downtown Arkham. The rain had started up again, but the clouds had loosed their grip on the horizon. A pale gray pall hung over the town. She could even just about make out the dark ribbon of the Miskatonic, in the distance.

"This will do nicely," she said. She tipped Milo well, and he pocketed it quickly. After he had shown himself out, she set about unpacking in a desultory fashion. A set of men's clothes, including a cap and a shoulder-holster for the Webley stayed in the bags, as did a set of handcrafted German lockpicks, designed to her specifications. There was a weighted sap as well, for when the pistol wouldn't do. Also staying in the bags, hidden beneath a false bottom, was a handful of important documents.

Letters, telegrams, private missives – the keys to her hypothetical kingdom. They all insured that she was paid promptly and on time. Her client list was large and varied; the sorts of men and women with too much money and little common sense to go with it. She demanded exorbitant fees and received them. And when she didn't... well. That's what the letters and telegrams were for. Not that she'd ever seriously use them. Blackmail was an ugly business, and rarely worked out the way one hoped.

This particular set represented the entirety of her communications with her client. He wished for her to retrieve something and was willing to pay handsomely for her services. He'd even paid her fare to Arkham.

She picked up a newspaper clipping they'd sent. On it, the words GREATEST ARCHAEOLOGICAL FIND OF THE MODERN CENTURY were emblazoned in bold type. The grainy photo showed a group of men standing next to a wooden table.

Atop the table, something long dead squatted, its withered limbs tightly bound, head slightly bowed, chin resting on a sunken chest. He'd died sitting up, whoever he'd been, and wore a carved mask of curious intricacy. Despite the haziness of the photo, the mask put her in mind of the squashed features of a toad – or perhaps a bat. As she studied the picture, she again felt a curious sensation – as if someone were watching her. Instinctively, she looked around the room, but saw nothing untoward. Not even a bird of ill omen at the window. She looked back down at the picture.

A sudden chill raced along her spine and she hastily folded the clipping and put it away. She'd thought the dead man's head had been bowed. But she'd obviously been mistaken.

Instead, he was looking at her.

Abner Whitlock tossed his bags down onto the rumpled bed and looked around the room with a resigned sigh. Hotel Miskatonic had seen better decades. The wallpaper was the color of regret and the carpet on the floor was as thin as his patience. Still, the room was dry, and his bill was comped. That was all a man in his line could ask for some days.

Whitlock was an investigator for Argus Insurance, out of New York. Most of the time, he enjoyed his job. He got to go all over the world, from San Francisco to Shanghai, on the company dime. He was good at sniffing out the client's problems before they became the company's problems, and the company showed their appreciation by giving him a big expense account and not asking too many questions. Usually, anyway.

Not this time, though. This time, it was small potatoes. A favor for a friend of the board, and the company's best man hired out like a rented mule. Whitlock wasn't bitter, though. The smaller a job, the easier it usually was.

He ran his hands through his hair and looked out the window. The Hotel Miskatonic looked out over West College Street, which was a stretch of nothing in particular. Arkham was a one-horse town if he'd ever seen one. That's why this whole thing was so goddamn weird. A discovery like the one the company was underwriting ought to have made its debut somewhere bigger than Arkham.

Boston, maybe. Even Kingsport.

Mummies were still big business, though Whitlock didn't see the attraction. If he wanted to look at a stiff, he could just visit the local morgue. Other people didn't seem to agree. Eventually, the find would wind its way to more appropriate venues.

But for now, it was here, and that meant Whitlock was too. He stripped off his coat and loosened his tie. He had a few hours to kill before he met with the client and was officially on the clock. The trip had been long, and he was tired. He moved his bags and stretched out on the bed, uncomfortable as it was.

Sleep eluded him, however. Hands behind his head, he stared up at the water marks on the ceiling and played connect the dots while he tried to remember where he'd seen the woman on the train before. It had been bothering him all day.

He knew her. He was certain of it. She'd pretended otherwise, but he was good at remembering faces. He had to be, in his line of work. Maybe he'd met her at some function or other. This kind of thing brought the idle rich out of the woodwork in droves.

He paused. "Vienna," he said and snapped his fingers. That was it. Two years ago. Some jewels had gone missing during a fancy dress party and Argus Insurance had been on the hook for a wad of cash. He frowned. The case had been a funny one from the beginning. The jewels had been cursed – or so the owner insisted. Dyed in the blood of a hundred sacrificial victims or some such nonsense, everyone who'd owned them had suffered an untimely doom, that sort of thing.

Whitlock hadn't cared about any of that. All he'd wanted to know was how someone had managed to get in and out of a locked room without anyone the wiser and without using either the door or the windows. He'd never found out, though he'd eventually gotten a description of the thief – and a name to go with the face.

"Countess Alessandra Zorzi," he said, as the name slowly surfaced from the fog of memory. An alias if he'd ever heard one. The jewels weren't the only thing she'd stolen either. She was a career-criminal of the worst sort. And now she was here in Arkham. It wasn't a coincidence. It couldn't be.

Vienna was the only black mark on his record. He'd come close – but she'd managed to skate just in time. He wondered if she'd been laughing at him the entire train journey. The thought made him angry. "You won't be laughing for long," he muttered.

He sat up and went to the window. Across town, he could just make out the tall shape of Arkham's only other hotel. That was where she'd be. In Vienna, she'd frequented the best hotels, the best restaurants. It'd be the same here, he could feel it in his gut. A leopard didn't change its spots. Why would someone like her come here, if not to steal something?

And when she did, he'd be there to catch her red-handed.

CHAPTER FOUR
Zamacona

"Here we are," Pepper said, as she brought the cab to a less than smooth stop. "La Bella Luna." She turned in her seat. "This is where you wanted to go, right?"

"Yes," Alessandra said, looking up at the Italian bistro. Like many such places, it wandered dangerously close to stereotype – wire outdoor furniture, sitting in front of a glass display window with the eatery's name scrawled across it in gold lettering. Checked tablecloths, red upholstery and candles in green chianti bottles for the tables inside. As a Venetian, she found it vaguely obscene, in a tacky sort of way.

"You know this place is as Italian as I am, right?" Pepper said.

"I am not here for the ambiance, I assure you. Nor the food."

"They do make good spaghetti."

"I will keep that in mind." She made to climb out, but Pepper stopped her.

"Are you sure you know what you're doing? This ain't a place for decent people."

"Thank you for your concern, but I will be fine."

"It's run by gangsters," Pepper insisted.

"Many things are."

"Real ones!"

"All the better. Authenticity is important. You will wait for me." Alessandra paused. "Buy yourself some spaghetti, if you like." Pepper muttered something, but Alessandra was already climbing out of the cab. Pepper's concern was touching, if somewhat misplaced. She resolved to add a bonus on top of what she was already paying the cabbie – once this affair was concluded successfully, of course.

She entered the bistro and was immediately struck by the unappetizing smells of garlic bread and tomato sauce. A concierge stepped immediately into her path. "Do you have a reservation, miss?" he asked, politely.

"Indeed. My party is waiting for me in the private dining rooms downstairs."

He raised an eyebrow. "Right this way, ma'am." He turned, signaling furtively to someone just out of sight. Alessandra, no stranger to such operations, smiled politely and pretended not to notice. The restaurant was an obvious front, if you knew what you were looking for. According to what little her American contacts had been able to tell her, Arkham was no stranger to the criminal element. The town's position along the Miskatonic River, as well as its proximity to Boston and Kingsport, made it a potential hub for everything from smuggling to bootlegging.

The concierge led her through the bistro, towards a door at the back. Ostensibly, this led to the kitchens, but past it there was a second door, deftly obscured behind a corner. This door opened onto a set of wooden steps, winding down. From below came the muffled sounds of music and laughter.

"Soundproofed," Alessandra said, admiringly.

"Homemade," the concierge said, tapping the back of the door. Burlap sacks, stuffed with newspaper and insulation, had been nailed to the wood. "Go on down. Knock on the door. Tell them Sammy said it was OK."

"And what if I didn't?"

"Then you would have a very bad night. Enjoy yourself, ma'am."

Alessandra started down, hiking up her dress to avoid catching it on loose nails or jutting bricks. The concierge closed the door behind her, momentarily plunging her into darkness. As her eyes adjusted, she saw that there was a soft glow radiating from below.

The glow proved to be an electric bulb shrouded by linen shade. In the dim light, she made out a reinforced steel door set into the damp brickwork. There was a spy-hatch at eye level. She studied the hinges with professional curiosity. Unlike the door, they weren't reinforced. She ran a finger along one and it came away covered in mortar. She clucked her tongue softly. Someone must have been listening on the other side, because the hatch slid open with a loud clack. Alessandra stepped back.

"Sammy says it's OK," she said.

She heard a grunt of acknowledgment, and the sound of a heavy bolt being drawn. As the door swung in, the music spilled out. The soulful wail of jazz momentarily reverberated up the stairwell, before being trapped once more as the door was slammed shut behind her. The guard proved to be a sallow sort – narrow of face and frame, but dressed well, and visibly armed. He gestured and she spread her arms.

As he gave her a somewhat thorough pat-down, she took in the scenery. At first glance, the Clover Club was the epitome of what the Americans called a "speakeasy". More than a dozen circular tables occupied the floor in front of a small softly lit stage decorated with silver palms. Onstage, a torch singer crooned the latest jazz standard as a backing band played with stolid enthusiasm. In the corner, the bar was packed, its shelves sagging beneath the weight of bootleg alcohol.

Across the room, she spied the entrance to the card room. The clink of poker chips and the shuffling of cards was audible, as was the occasional shout of joy – or groan of frustration. Through another aperture she caught a glimpse of some sort of lounge, with large leather couches and mahogany furniture, before someone closed the door.

The guard stepped back, his no-doubt-arduous duty completed. He gave her a grin, and she smiled in return. Then, very deliberately, she dug the heel of her shoe into his foot. He gave a muffled curse and hopped back. Before he could respond, she was already making her way through the tables, hunting her quarry.

The place was crowded, though not so much that it was claustrophobic. She recognized a few faces from the train station, she thought, as well as a few from the papers she'd read on the way up. She wondered if the exhibition had brought in much out of town business. The American current obsession with teetotaling amused her somewhat – from what she'd seen, more alcohol was flowing in places like this than ever before.

Zamacona was waiting for her at a table opposite the bar. He was every inch the Spanish hidalgo his letters had made him seem. Tall and spare, with a face like the edge of a blade and dark eyes. His hair was fashionably slick, and his suit was expensive. But as she drew closer, she noted little incongruities. He was pale, as if he hadn't seen the sun in weeks. His wrists were thick, but his suit hung off him in places.

Her first thought was illness. Men like Zamacona were forever tramping through malarial wildernesses on behalf of their employers. But his eyes lacked a feverish sheen, and he seemed perfectly comfortable in the sweltering interior of the club. He tapped a finger against the rim of his glass, watching the singer. His gaze was… flat. Interested, but not in the way one might expect.

He glanced at her as she sat down. "You are late."

"Only fashionably. Have you ordered a drink?"

"For me."

Alessandra frowned. "Hardly chivalrous."

"I discarded chivalry, among other useless affectations, a long time ago. Besides, I understand you are a woman of particular tastes. I thought it safest to leave the decision to you." His smile was sharp and unsettling. The sight of perfect teeth always set her on edge. It spoke of money and vanity – but also pragmatism. He had not fixed the scars that pitted his cheeks or the badly healed break in his nose. Just his teeth. Alessandra adjusted her initial evaluation of the man, factoring these new observations in.

She signaled a waitress and gave her order. When she turned back to Zamacona, his attentions were on the stage once more. "I found your letters promising," she said. "But I'm not convinced."

He did not look at her. "And yet here you are."

"I'm certain there are locals who could do the job just as well, and for half the price."

"But not with your degree of… expertise." He took a sip of his drink. "It is not your skill as a thief that attracted my employers. Rather, it is your choice of target – such as the private library of the Comte d'Erlette, a few months ago."

Alessandra's drink arrived and she thanked the waitress without looking away from Zamacona. "You know about that?"

"We also know about the theft of a particular grotesquery from the cathedral of Vyones two years ago. And the pilfering of a certain copper ring, crafted in the shape of a serpent, from a house in Mayfair a month after that."

"That was a tricky one," Alessandra said, taking a cautious sip. Then a slightly longer one. "Took me two weeks to prepare. I had to get a job as a chambermaid."

Zamacona ignored her commentary. "We also know that a number of individuals, including the aforementioned Comte d'Erlette, have made it known that there is a reward for your apprehension, by means fair or foul."

She tensed. "Yes. I had heard rumors to that effect."

"More than rumors." Zamacona gave her a lazy smile. "As you can see, we know a great many things, countess. We even know about that night in the Rue d'Auseil, when your parents died..."

Beneath the table, Alessandra opened her clutch. "Did you bring me all this way to threaten me, Mr Zamacona? If so, I must say you are doing a poor job." Her fingers found the shape of her Webley, but she didn't retrieve it. Not yet. "I would expect any halfway competent underling in your line to be capable of compiling a semi-decent curriculum vitae."

A flicker of annoyance crossed his features. "I could tell you about it, if you like. We could call it part of your payment."

"No, the money will be more than satisfactory, thank you."

"You are a singularly incurious woman."

"In my experience, people who hire thieves prefer them to be incurious. Now, get to the point. You want me to steal something. What, where, when and who from."

Zamacona was silent for a few moments. Then he sighed and leaned forward. "The exhibition," he said. "You read the news clipping we sent?"

"I skimmed it."

"These men … found something. It does not belong to them."

"There's a saying Americans are fond of, about possession being the law or some such." She took a sip of her drink, paused and took another sip. It had been difficult to acquire proper alcohol since coming to the United States. This was the real thing, and she intended to savor it.

Zamacona gestured sharply. "Our claim supersedes theirs in all the ways that matter."

"Then why not try to acquire it through legal means?" she asked, genuinely curious.

"How do you know we have not?"

"If so, obviously you failed." She saw a flash of something in his eyes as she said it. Anger – real anger. It was clearly a sore spot for him. She filed the thought away for future reference. "Else why turn to me?"

"I am beginning to wonder if we made a mistake in that regard."

She smiled. "No. You didn't. You want me to steal a mummy, then." She paused. "Or perhaps just the mask? It looks valuable."

"No," he said, harshly, slamming a palm onto the table. "Do not, under any circumstances, attempt to remove the mask. It is sacred. Your hands are not fit for such a task." His eyes blazed with righteous fervor as he said it, and she knew he meant every word. Heads turned towards them, and then hastily away as they caught sight of Zamacona's face. Alessandra took another swallow of her drink, allowing him to compose himself.

When he'd recovered, she said, "Noted." She took a piece of hotel stationery from her clutch. "This is where I'm staying. Penthouse suite. You are paying for that, by the way."

Zamacona took the paper but didn't look at it. "We are aware of your choice of lodgings. When will you do it?"

"The opening gala for the exhibition is tomorrow, at the Miskatonic Museum. You will acquire tickets for me, so that I might take stock of what awaits me, and plan accordingly."

"When?" he repeated.

"A day, maybe two at the most." She finished her drink and set it down. "I am a thief, but not a stupid one. I do not throw myself into situations without first assessing them."

For a moment, Zamacona looked as if he wished to argue. Then he stood. "I must confer with my employers. You will wait here." He stalked over to the bar and spoke to the bartender. The latter brought out a telephone in a glass case.

"He must be a big shot, if they're bringing that out."

At the words, Alessandra blinked in surprise and looked down. Pepper grinned up at her, from where she crouched on the floor.

"What are you *doing*?" Alessandra hissed, equal parts startled and annoyed. She hadn't even noticed the younger woman approach.

"You told me to buy some spaghetti."

Alessandra stared at her. Pepper's grin faded. "Fine. Watching out for you. This is a rough joint." She peered over the table, eyes narrowed. "Lots of trouble in here tonight."

Alessandra took in the neat tables and well-heeled patrons. "Yes. Positively *barbaric*."

"You don't know who runs this place."

"I do, actually. A family called the O'Bannions."

Pepper goggled at her. "You know the O'Bannions?"

"Not intimately." She'd never had the bad luck to cross paths officially with the gang. But she made it a point to learn what she could about the local criminal element – it often saved time later. The O'Bannions were the largest of several bootlegging outfits with an interest in Arkham, and she intended to steer clear of them if at all possible. "Regardless, while I thank you for your concern, I hired you to drive me – not be my bodyguard."

"Look, you don't know Arkham, countess," Pepper said. She ducked down as a waitress glided past, heading for the bar. "Say, get me a drink, would you? All this crawling has made me thirsty."

Alessandra frowned. "Get your own. I'm paying you enough."

"I'm not even supposed to be in here. Not after last time."

Alessandra decided to let the comment pass. "How did you even get in here?"

"I know a guy. He let me in the back."

Alessandra waited for her to elaborate. Pepper didn't seem interested in doing so, however. Alessandra sighed. "I assure you, I am capable of taking care of myself. So, thank you for your concern, but – go."

"But–"

"He is coming back. Go. *Now.*"

Pepper muttered an obscenity and scrambled beneath a nearby table, vanishing under the tablecloth. Alessandra shook her head and looked up as Zamacona sat. "Well?"

"Your terms are agreeable. The ticket will be arranged and waiting for you by tomorrow morning."

"Excellent. And my fee?"

"As you requested, half is waiting for you at your hotel. The other half will be wired to your account when the task is completed to our satisfaction."

"Prompt as well. You might just be my new favorite client."

"If all goes well, we will never see one another again." Zamacona pushed himself to his feet. "We will contact you when the task is done."

"I am sure you will. Are you not staying for the rest of the show?"

"No." Zamacona smiled. "The music is not to my taste. But stay. I took the liberty of opening a tab." He sketched a bow and departed. Alessandra watched him go. He moved smoothly – like a dancer, or a swordsman. She'd had a fencing tutor as a girl who'd moved like that. Quick and graceful. Zamacona was a dangerous man, no two ways about it. The sooner this affair was concluded to everyone's satisfaction, the better.

But in the meantime, the music was good and the drinks were paid for. She waved to a passing waitress. "Another drink. And put it on Mr Zamacona's tab, please."

"Make it two," Pepper said, as she occupied Zamacona's seat. She peered in the direction he'd gone. "Brrr. That guy gives me the willies."

"What did you hear?"

"Only that he left his tab open. Think they serve food down here?"

Alessandra sat back and laughed.

"Let's find out, shall we?"

CHAPTER FIVE
Tickets

Milo was still on duty when Alessandra approached the front desk the next morning. "Do you not have a home to go to, Milo?" she asked. "Or were you on duty all evening?"

He shook his head ruefully. "Both, actually. I got a cot in the back, and two squares a day, plus tips. Lot of folks got less, these days." He rubbed his eyes and yawned. "Something I can help you with, miss?"

"I believe there is a set of tickets waiting for me."

Milo nodded. "Oh yeah. Guy left those earlier this morning. I would have called up to your room, but you said you didn't want to be disturbed." He grinned. "Late night at the Clover Club, huh?"

"A touch too familiar, Milo. But yes. It was quite an evening." She smiled, remembering the night before. Pepper had proved a most entertaining companion. The young woman was no stranger to alcohol, though her attempts to sing had been met with resistance by both the audience and the staff. They had been summarily ejected from the club sometime around one in the morning and returned to the hotel somewhat worse for drink.

Alessandra felt no ill-effects from her carousing. She often indulged on the evening before a job. It was a ritual, of sorts. A celebration of triumphs to come.

Milo retrieved the tickets and handed them over with a rueful grin. "Boy, that's going to be something. Wish I was going."

"Interested in mummies, Milo?" She studied the tickets, wondering how Zamacona had procured them so quickly. It was obvious that he – or more likely the people he worked for – had significant resources.

"When they're American, sure," he said. "That's got to be better than some old Egyptian bones, right?" He paused. "You had a visitor last night, while you were out."

"Oh? Did they leave a name, by chance?"

"A Mr Whitlock."

Her smile faded. "And what did he want?"

"Access to your room, mostly. Said he had something of yours he wanted to drop off." Milo caught her look and gestured quickly. "Don't worry, we got a strict policy against that sort of thing."

"Did he leave whatever it was here?" She wondered who Whitlock was really working for. If he was after the price on her head, he was going about it in an altogether strange way. She would need to warn Pepper as well, just in case.

"Nope." Milo frowned. "He wasn't carrying anything that I saw."

"Of course not." She held up the tickets. "What about these – who dropped them off? A tall man? Dark, well-dressed?"

Milo shook his head. "Not even close. Short guy. Black raincoat. Slouch hat." He paused. "I didn't… get a good look at him. Something told me I didn't want to either."

"Why?"

He shrugged. "You live in Arkham long enough you start to get a feeling about that sort of thing. Like maybe it's better you don't see something. You know how it is." He shrugged again, apologetically this time. Alessandra understood. Pepper had said much the same. Every town, every city, had its own unspoken rules, from Paris to the nameless hamlets of the Black Forest.

She slid a few coins across the desk. "Thank you, Milo. Keep an eye out for Mr Whitlock, would you? If he shows up again, do let me know."

Milo made the money vanish. "Sure thing, countess. You can count on me."

When she got back to her room, Pepper lay where Alessandra had left her. The young woman sprawled across the foot of the bed, fully clothed and snoring like a diesel motor. Alessandra nudged her but received no response. "Wake up," she said, patting the young woman's cheek.

Pepper made an inarticulate sound and attempted to roll over. Alessandra sighed, caught the young woman's ankle, and dragged her off the bed. Pepper yelped as she connected with the floor. "What? What is it?" she asked, looking around wildly.

"Go home. Take a bath."

Pepper sniffed her shirt. "I smell fine," she protested. "Wouldn't be the first late night I've had, you know. Besides, nobody cares if their cabbie looks like hell."

"I am sure. Very well. Make yourself useful and go buy me a newspaper."

"Which one?"

"All of them."

"Can I stop for breakfast first?"

Alessandra raised an eyebrow. "Considering how much spaghetti you ate last night I am surprised you can even think of food at the moment."

"I'm a growing girl," Pepper said with a grin.

Alessandra snorted and waved her towards the door. "Go. And be quick. The exhibition is in a few hours. I want to get there early, if possible." When preparing to commit a crime, it was always best to establish potential escape routes.

"Scope out the joint, you mean?"

"Something like that, yes. Go. I must shower."

As Alessandra showered, she made a mental list of things she might need. She knew that a visit to the local records office might be in order later. Blueprints were a vital resource in her line, and she took advantage of the hard work of others whenever possible.

Today was just about information-gathering, about calculating the difficulties involved in making off with an intact mummy. It was a first, she had to admit. Mostly, the objects she stole tended to be small or easily portable. Books, statuettes, amulets, the sort of bric-a-brac that could easily be stuffed into a handy pocket or beneath her blouse, into a specially sewn pouch.

This would be more difficult. Not impossible, though. More to the point, it was exciting. A challenge. Something she hadn't had in a long time. Not since Vyones. Then, stealing a gargoyle had been much easier than she'd thought. Some falsified paperwork, a few hired workmen and a pleasant brandy with the bishop was all it had taken to get the thing onto the back of a hired truck and out of the city.

She doubted that was going to work this time. She needed an in – a gap in security to slip through. It didn't have to be large. Hopefully she'd be able to identify it at the exhibition this afternoon. When she got out of the shower, she pulled on a dressing gown and sat on the bed, still mulling over her options.

She looked down at the floor where several newspapers from the previous day were scattered, including editions of the *Arkham Advertiser* and the *Arkham Gazette*. Each had a story on the exhibition – some were only a few paragraphs, but the two local rags had double page spreads. She'd spent the morning taking notes on the names of the known attendees; besides the usual local aristocracy, there were plenty of out-of-towners.

She recognized some of the names as former clients – or targets. Men and women who haunted the edges of the demimonde. They collected scraps of esotericism: rare books and the like. A find like this would be irresistible to them. Both for what it meant, and what they might be able to get out of it. That was a possible angle.

Alessandra paused, considering the pistol on her bed. She didn't think she'd need it. As she made to put it away, however, she heard a creak from the hallway. The hotel was full of noises, and she didn't think anything of it at first. When it came again, however, she stopped and listened. Straining against the background noise of the day.

Someone was outside her door. Quietly, she rounded the bed and crept towards it, the Webley in hand. She could hear them clearly now – their breathing was labored. Raspy. It was suddenly stifled as she reached the door. As if they'd heard her coming.

She paused, hand on the knob, thumb on the Webley's hammer. Waiting. Her patience was rewarded by a creak. And then another. As if whoever it was, was moving off down the hall. She cracked the door but saw nothing. No one. But there was a curious smell on the air – one that was at once familiar and unsettling.

Whitlock again, maybe. Or perhaps someone just confused about their room. She took a deep breath and looked at her hands.

They were trembling. She felt as if she'd narrowly avoided some unforeseen disaster.

Someone pounded on the door. She whipped it open without thinking, and Pepper jumped back, eyes wide, spilling newspapers onto the floor. "Jesus!"

Alessandra lowered the Webley. "My apologies. You startled me."

"Startled you?" Pepper gasped, clutching her chest. "Why do you have a gun?" She stooped to pick up the fallen papers.

"Everyone in America has a gun. I am trying to fit in. Come in." Alessandra stepped back and Pepper bustled in, throwing her a wary glance. "Did you see anyone out there when you came up?"

"No. Why?"

"No reason." Alessandra uncocked the Webley and set it aside. "You brought the papers. Good. See if they say anything about the exhibition." As she spoke, Alessandra shed her dressing gown. Pepper turned away with a strangled yelp, trying desperately to look anywhere else as Alessandra got dressed.

"You – ah – you got a lot of scars, huh?" the cabbie said, after a moment.

"I have lived an interesting life. I am finished. You may turn around now."

Pepper turned, a frown on her face. "You ought to warn people when you're going to shuck off. It ain't polite."

Alessandra laughed. "I do not have anything you haven't seen before." She smoothed her dress and paused. "Maybe the proportions are somewhat different, but…"

"Yeah, yeah. Nice dress, by the way. Bet it cost a bundle."

"It was practically a steal," Alessandra said, with a straight face. "What do the papers say? Anything of interest?"

"Depends on what you mean by interesting," Pepper said, sitting on the bed. She tossed a copy of the *Advertiser* aside and looked at Alessandra. "You sure you want to pay me to sit and wait outside this thing for you?"

"Yes. I might wish to leave quickly. I trust you can occupy yourself for a few hours."

"I could occupy myself better if I were going to this party of yours. What's the big deal about some stiff anyway?"

Alessandra sat back. "Someone found a mummy in Oklahoma. A place where mummies are not commonly found." It was something of an understatement. While Alessandra was no archaeologist, she knew enough to know how unexpected such a discovery must have been.

"Might be a hoax."

"According to experts, it is not."

Pepper snorted. "Experts. What do they know?"

"Yes, well, hoax or no it will be worth seeing, I think."

"Only if it comes to life, like in the magazines."

Alessandra frowned. "Magazines?"

"Yeah, you know... *Weird Tales, Unknown, Startling Stories, Unspeakable*... that kind of thing. High quality literature." Pepper grinned. "Got a stack of them this morning. Figure it'll keep me going while you're inside."

"You... enjoy these magazines?"

"Why not?" Pepper said, defensively. "Got all the good stuff in them. Monsters, guns, romance – what more could a girl want?"

"Yes, what more indeed?" Alessandra looked at herself in the room's full length mirror. Her clothes were as much a disguise as what Pepper was wearing. In Paris or Milan, she would have been indistinguishable from other women. Here she would stand out, but that could be to her advantage. People would remember what she wore, but not her face. "I myself quite enjoyed the works of Marcel Allain and Pierre Souvestre when I was younger. Bodies substituted for church bell-clappers, plagues of rats, that sort of thing."

"Sounds swell." Pepper watched her preen. "Where are you going to hide the gun?"

"I will not be taking the gun, I think."

"Probably a good idea. I hear they got cops all over."

Alessandra paused. "Oh? And where did you hear that?"

Pepper shrugged. "I know a guy."

"You seem to know a lot of guys. How many police?"

"No clue. Why do you care?"

Alessandra paused. She trusted Pepper, but not that far. Not yet. And whatever the young woman's suspicions, she was keeping them to herself. "Curiosity," she said, finally. "It seems that they are taking no chances."

"God knows why. Ain't like nobody would want to steal a mummy, right?"

Alessandra hid a smile. "No. I cannot imagine anyone doing so." She retrieved her hat and coat, glancing out the window as she did so. She paused, frowning.

For a moment, she thought she'd seen someone by the entrance to the park. A small man, hunched, in a black coat and slouch hat. But he wasn't there now, if he had ever been there at all. She shook her head and turned back to Pepper. "If you are ready, we can depart."

"It's your nickel." Pepper rose. "Say – something going on I ought to know about?"

"What do you mean?"

"Well, you seemed pretty uneasy earlier. The thing with the gun and all." Pepper peered at her. "Does this have something to do with last night?"

"No, not at all," Alessandra said, forcing a smile. "I am merely cautious. Now, let us go see this great discovery. I am eager to see if it lives up to the excitement."

CHAPTER SIX
Miskatonic Museum

Pepper smacked the horn. "Get outta the way!"

A produce truck honked in reply as it lurched past, heading the opposite way along the bridge at uncertain speed. Pepper thrust her hand out the window and tossed off an obscene gesture. The truck driver slowed and shouted something, but Pepper gunned the engine and sped off.

She blinked against the sharp light of day. Her head hurt and her stomach was making unfriendly noises. She wished she'd stopped for breakfast. Even just a piece of pie from Velma's. Pie and coffee. The thought of food made the headache worse.

As they passed over the bridge, she glimpsed the oblong island in the river. It was covered in gnarled trees and thick underbrush and even at a distance she thought she could make out what looked like stone pillars rising above the treetops. She shivered slightly and concentrated on the traffic. It never failed. Something about the island always put her ill at ease. That was why she tried to stick to downtown, and away from the river when possible. But money had a way of making her break old habits.

Behind her, Alessandra cleared her throat. "Your employer had no objections to you acting as my chauffeur, I trust?" Of course, she didn't look any the worse for wear. Pepper frowned. They'd had fun, the night before. It had been a long time since she'd had fun, let alone hung out with someone who knew she wasn't packing the right equipment.

"Not so as you'd notice. Mostly because I haven't told him yet." Nor did she intend to do so. De Palma was a tiny tyrant. The head dispatcher of the Miskatonic Cab Company hid in his office at the fleet garage until it was time to bully someone – usually one of the new drivers. He was short, fat and unpleasant. Pepper avoided him as much as possible.

"Won't he get suspicious?"

"Nah. So long as the logbook looks straight he don't care." The only good thing about De Palma was his utter lack of scruples. He ran booze for the local outfits, using the cabs to carry it to the buyers. Pepper had made those runs once or twice herself. De Palma didn't pay his drivers any extra for the risk. It was that or lose their jobs.

Pepper honked the horn again, in a more amiable manner this time. She waved at the driver of another cab, heading in the opposite direction, back across the bridge.

"Friend of yours?" Alessandra asked.

"One of the guys."

"Does he know? That you are not one of the guys, I mean."

"No," Pepper said, flatly. None of them knew, especially De Palma. God only knew how he'd treat her then.

Alessandra was quiet for a moment. Any hope Pepper had of her dropping the matter, however, proved in vain. "Why pretend to be a man at all?" the other woman asked.

"What?"

"Your disguise. Why bother? It is not illegal for a woman to drive, after all. And you seem competent enough."

Pepper was silent for a moment. "It's easier, is all." She hunched forward, over the steering wheel. "Safer too. Not all of us got guns, you know."

"Maybe you should get one."

"And maybe I should get a rich husband while I'm at it," Pepper said and looked out the window. Decaying row houses rose along the riverside. Overgrown green spaces, covered in thorny weeds and rubbish, broke up their crumbling grandeur. Even through the glass, she could detect a miasma of fish and industrial waste. She hated this part of Arkham. It seemed worse every time she passed through it.

Alessandra was silent for a moment. Then, "Do you want one?"

"What?"

"A husband."

"No!"

Alessandra laughed. "A sensible reaction."

Pepper glanced at her. "I can't figure you out, lady. You ain't like nobody I ever met."

"I will take that as a compliment."

"Take it however you want. No skin off my nose." Pepper fell silent. She wondered if she'd made the right decision. Last night seemed like a different country in the light of day. Whatever Alessandra Zorzi was up to, it wasn't kosher. Whatever it was, Pepper hoped it wasn't going to wind up costing her more than it brought in.

Gabled rooftops and red brick became more prominent, the farther from the river they drew. The houses were older here, and larger. She could almost smell the money on the air. Not much call for cabs up here. Everyone had their own cars – and their own drivers.

The closer they got to the university, the nicer the surroundings became. She'd always wondered what it was like to go to college, but doubted she'd ever have the chance to find out. Still, it was pretty enough.

"Here we are," Pepper said, as she brought the cab to a rolling halt. "The Miskatonic Museum."

Alessandra looked up. The museum was an opulent, stately building on the edge of campus, with wide steps leading to the main doors. People milled about in front, and on the lawn, as if waiting to go in. "Drive around the block."

"Why?" Pepper asked.

"If you insist on asking me to explain every little thing, we will never get anywhere."

"I'm the one driving, remember?"

Alessandra sighed. "Someone might be watching. I do not wish them to associate us."

"You ashamed of being in a cab, is that it?"

"No. Do as I ask, please."

Pepper sighed noisily and took the cab away from the campus. She circled the block and parked one street over, underneath a tree. "I'll be here when you're ready, countess," she said, somewhat petulantly.

Alessandra got out without replying. She looked around as she closed the door, her eyes coming to rest on a car across the street. Four men sat inside, smoking like chimneys. They did not look like students. Something about them made her uneasy, and she considered getting back in the cab and having Pepper return her to the hotel. But only for a moment.

Waiters navigated the small crowd in front of the museum, bearing trays of drinks and canapes. Alessandra pilfered a flute of what the waiter insisted was grape juice but looked and tasted very much like champagne as she made her way up the walk. Prohibition was less an obstacle to the rich than the poor. The doors were propped open by a pair of decorative grotesques, and she wondered how much they were worth as she stepped inside.

A large entry hall stretched before her, with a wide doorway at the other end and exhibits lining the walls. There was a set of stairs to either side of the hall, curving up and away, as well as several open doors, leading to smaller rooms, full of glass cabinets, exotic statuary and other bric-a-brac. Soft music emerged from one of the rooms, riding the tide of conversation.

There was already a crowd gathered in the central hall. Well-wishers, society boors and envious academics. One or two familiar faces nodded in wary greeting, others frowned or looked away. Alessandra smiled and wondered how many of them were staying at her hotel. It might be worth finding out. She filed the thought away.

"Alessandra?"

She turned. The voice was familiar – the flat, sharp face even more so. "Tad," she said, warmly. She looked him up and down. He was taller than her, and older if only by a few years, with a lean frame and slicked back blond hair, parted in the center. "How are you?"

"Better for having seen you," he said, grinning. Thaddeus Visser was from a fine old Knickerbocker family. To hear him tell it, they'd lived in Marble Hill since 1646. He was a client, as well. One of the better ones. He paid on time, and his requests weren't too onerous. "How long has it been? Feels like years."

"Two years. Rome, I believe."

"Oh yes. You got me that saint's bone I was after."

"Keep it down to a dull roar if you would, Tad." She made a show of looking around. "Never know who might be listening."

Visser's grin turned sly. "Are you here with glorious purpose, then?" he whispered. "Come to snatch an ancient Wampanoag treasure from the museym? Or maybe some of that Innsmouth gold I've heard tell of…"

"No, and no. I'm here to see the mummy, actually."

"Really? Where are you staying? Not the Hotel Miskatonic, I hope."

"No, the Independence."

"How fortuitous! That's where I'm staying. Not the penthouse, mind. Got to watch the pennies these days. The markets are a trifle skittish."

"A shame. The penthouse suite is quite nice."

Visser laughed. "I should have known. Only the best for royalty, eh?"

"More like the only room left. The hotel was rammed and I suspect the exhibition is to blame." Alessandra looked at him. "A bit unexpected, seeing you here."

"Sort of mandatory, in my case. I was actually one of the backers for the expedition. It was privately funded, no matter what the university claims." He leaned close. "Between you, me and the bees' knees, we were looking for Spanish gold."

"Find any?"

"Not a dime."

"Some might say a mummy is worth more than gold."

"Not me." Visser produced a battered cigarette case and opened it. "Coffin nail?"

"Thank you." Alessandra bent so that Visser could light her cigarette. "Not worth anything then? What about publicity?"

"Not so as you'd notice." Visser lit his own cigarette. "A few lines in the local rag, maybe a write up in a journal or three. Nothing serious."

Behind them, someone cleared their throat. "There are other forms of value than monetary, Mr Visser." Alessandra turned to see a stooped, older man, with thick gray hair and muttonchop whiskers studying them. He was dressed well, but in somewhat haphazard fashion. She pegged him for an academic, and was proven right when Visser introduced him.

"Alessandra, allow me to introduce Professor Harvey Walters," Visser said, brightly. "Professor Walters, this is Countess Alessandra Zorzi."

She extended her hand and Walters took it with old world courtesy. "Countess," he said, in greeting. He studied her face. "Zorzi – Venetian?"

"Yes," she said, somewhat surprised.

"I thought so." He smiled warmly. "I fear Arkham must seem bucolic, in contrast. We are hardly a cosmopolitan metropolis."

"Neither is Venice, these days."

"Have you come to see the… mummy then?" There was something in his voice as he said it. A hesitation before the word. Curious.

"Indeed I have. I assume you have as well."

"I wouldn't miss it. When young Visser here invited me here, I immediately canceled my classes." Walters glanced at Visser. "Though why he invited me, I have yet to understand. Especially given that I turned down his offer to accompany the exhibition on tour."

"No reason but spite, I assure you, professor," Visser said, grinning. "I wanted you to get a good look at what you missed." He looked at Alessandra. "The professor here is one of the country's leading lights when it comes to archaeology. At least to hear the stuffed shirts at Miskatonic University tell it."

Walters looked uncomfortable with such backhanded praise. He coughed discreetly. "Yes, well, a pleasure to meet you, countess. Perhaps we will have time to speak again, after the exhibition." With that, he turned away and shuffled into the crowd. Alessandra slapped Visser's arm.

"That was uncalled for."

"What? The old goat had it coming." Visser blew a plume of smoke into the air. "I offered him a great opportunity, and what did he do? Threw me out of his office."

"To be fair, you just got done saying you didn't find anything of value."

"Not to me, obviously. But to science?" Visser scratched his cheek. "I mean, look at this crowd. Bigwigs from Miskatonic, Harvard, Yale… even my alma mater Empire State sent a few representatives. I recognize faces from half a dozen amateur archaeological societies." He turned, using his cigarette as a pointer. "The state folklorist, a congressman, and – yes – that's one of JD Rockefeller's representatives. And look there, the fellow in the monocle, that's Walsted, the curator."

"Quite the crowd," Alessandra said.

"Truth to tell, I'm a bit out to sea with all of this. Not my sort of thing."

"Then why come?"

"Same reason as you, I imagine – curiosity." He gestured towards the far doors. "Looks like we're about to begin. Finally. I was getting tired of necking cheap champagne."

A tall man, with iron-gray hair, and a tailored suit, stepped out of the room and tapped a champagne glass with a spoon, signaling for silence. The crowd quieted down in stages. The man smiled and cleared his throat.

"Ladies and gentlemen, I am Matthew Orne and it is my greatest pleasure to welcome you to the Miskatonic Museum."

CHAPTER SEVEN
Exhibition

"Thank you all for coming." Orne had a strong voice, clarion clear in the great hall. "I'm pleased to see so many familiar faces, and new ones as well. Professors Ashley and Freeborn, the men responsible for this momentous discovery, are just making some final adjustments to the exhibit. As you all know, our... friend will only be here for a short time, before beginning a tour of the States, and possibly Europe."

Alessandra raised an eyebrow. Mummies, it seemed, were as popular now as they had been during the previous century. Then again, it had only been a few years since Howard Carter had pulled poor Tutankhamen from his centuried sleep. She was surprised there weren't more reporters here. Photographers clustered at the doors like crows, flashbulbs popping.

Orne raised his glass. "And I'd like to take a moment to thank Harold Walsted, the curator for this fine museum. Take a bow, Harry!" Walsted, beaming in delight, waved a hand, and the crowd applauded.

Orne, Alessandra thought. "Why does that name sound

familiar?" She watched him continue to speak, thanking various people. He really was very good. A nice smile went a long way here.

Visser snorted. "Probably because it's on a good many buildings hereabouts. The Orne family has deep roots in Arkham and many branches." He paused. "He was another of the expedition's financial backers. The main one, in fact." He had the good grace to look embarrassed.

"Did he bring you in, or did you bring him?" she asked, somewhat archly. Tad had a habit of spending other people's money. It made him a good client, but a terrible friend.

"He brought me in. As well as a few others."

"If he's as rich as you say, why would he need you?"

"A smart investor spreads the risk." Visser shrugged. "Truth is, I've been hoping for something like this for months. Orne's a popular fellow, if you pay attention to that sort of thing. Knows all the right sort of people. And the right sort of wrong people as well." He leaned close. "Word has it he's in bed with the local bootleggers."

"What rich American isn't, these days?"

"I'm not," Visser said, a trifle defensively. Alessandra gave him a steady look. Visser's smile was weak. "All right, I would be, if the opportunity arose..."

She almost laughed, but restrained herself. Her eyes narrowed as she spied a uniformed police officer standing near the inner doors, conversing quietly with a security guard. Young, good-looking in a rough sort of way. The sort of young man who looked born to wear a uniform. "A policeman," she murmured. Visser followed her gaze.

"Yes, Orne is on a first name basis with both Chief Nichols and Sheriff Engle, I understand. He gets a good rate for security."

"And they look the other way while he serves alcohol at his party?"

"That too."

"The officer doesn't look happy."

"I assume he'd rather be out catching criminals." Visser nudged. "Come on. Looks like they're letting us in. Stick close."

"Worried I might embarrass you?"

"Worried you might try to pick a pocket or three." He smiled as he said it, so she didn't hold it against him. She hooked his arm and allowed him to escort her into the exhibition room. Visser made for excellent cover, whatever else. A woman alone was easily noticed. One on the arm of a man – merely part of the background, as far as many people were concerned.

The room was large and square. Glass-topped cases lined the walls, between ornamental pillars and decorative statuary. Every effort had been made to make the space seem larger than it was, and it was plenty large already. Alessandra noted a large door at the back of the room, and a smaller one to the left, partially hidden behind some form of native blanket.

A set of calculations began. She'd always had a head for geometry and a talent for off-the-cuff measurements. They'd served her well so far and looked to do so now. There were at least two floors above, which meant access by the roof would be tricky. A lot could go wrong in two floors. But the rear door held potential. If it led to the kitchens or a loading dock, that meant there would be access to the backyard, and the street behind.

She'd seen no sign of guard dogs. At least nothing obvious. A human guard was more likely – a night watchman. Low paid, likely little in the way of skill. A policeman being paid under the table, perhaps. Someone to make a thief think twice. A common thief, rather. But she was anything but common.

If she could identify them, there was the possibility of

exploitation. It was a trick she'd used before to great effect, but required time – unless they were a drunk, or excessively gullible. She glanced at the policeman on duty. He was young but didn't look particularly gullible. Quite the opposite in fact. His gaze was sharp, hawk-like. The way he scanned the crowd was somewhat unnerving. If he was the one on duty at night, she'd have to find another avenue of approach. The usual tricks weren't going to be good enough.

As she was observing him, a familiar face surfaced from the crowd – Whitlock. The insurance man said something to the policeman and glanced around. Alessandra quickly ducked her head, and interposed Visser between herself and Whitlock.

"Problem, Alessandra?" Visser murmured, without looking at her.

"An unwelcome suitor."

"Really? Who?"

"Over by the policeman. The man in the gray suit. Do you know him?"

"Can't say that I do. Not your sort of fellow at all, though. Slumming it, are we?"

Alessandra frowned. "No. He's an insurance man."

"Ah. That explains it – Orne's taking no chances at all. He slapped a fat policy on that shriveled up thing. Just in case, he said. Just in case of what, I want to know." He looked at Alessandra. "Though, knowing you, I'm starting to get the picture."

"I am not here for any reason besides curiosity, Tad."

"So you say. Would you tell me if you were?"

Alessandra paused. He had her there. Before she could reply, Visser caught her arm. "There's Carl Sanford," he said. Alessandra saw an older man, with a slight build and an air of refinement, talking animatedly with Orne.

"And he is…?"

"Head of the Silver Twilight Lodge." Visser took her empty glass from her and set it down on a passing tray.

Alessandra looked at him blankly. Visser frowned. "Closest thing this town has to the Masons, though they've got branches in Boston and New York; the usual stuff… charity work, bake sales, and a big holiday supper every year."

"I see."

Visser looked at her. "I don't think you do. The members list is like a who's who of the wealthiest and most influential people in town."

"Is Orne a member?"

Visser paused. "Well… no."

"Is that why Sanford looks upset?"

Visser grimaced. "I gather Sanford is a bit hot under the collar because Orne didn't invite him to invest in the expedition."

"Is that so?" Alessandra murmured, filing the information away. "And why not?"

"Not a clue." Visser snagged two glasses of champagne from a waiter and handed one off to her. She sipped at it appreciatively. "He didn't include any Lodge members that I know of, though heaven knows you can't throw a rock in this town without hitting one."

"Perhaps not the wisest course," a new voice interjected. A young man, dressed to the nines, with a pencil thin moustache, had joined them unobtrusively. Visser smiled.

"Hallo, Preston, how's tricks?"

"Poorly as ever, Tad." The newcomer turned his smile on Alessandra. "Introduce me to your companion, would you?"

Visser laughed. "Preston Fairmont, may I introduce Countess Alessandra Zorzi?" He leaned close. "Preston's well-heeled, as they say. Rich as Croesus."

"Not quite." Fairmont shook his head. "And a countess? In Arkham?"

"By way of Venice," she said, smoothly. She extended her hand and Fairmont took it, brushing his lips across her knuckles.

"A pleasure to meet you. Though I must question your taste in friends."

"Hey now," Visser began. Fairmont slapped him on the shoulder.

"Easy, old man, just playing." Fairmont looked around. "I'm starting to regret turning down Orne's invitation. This may well be the find of the century."

"Or so the newspapers say," Alessandra murmured. Fairmont grinned boyishly.

"They do like to bandy that phrase about an awful lot, don't they?" He smoothed his moustache. "Still, it is quite the show. Matthew has gone all out. Speaking of which…" He looked at Visser. "I need to borrow Tad for a moment, countess. If you don't mind?"

"Take him, with my compliments."

Visser threw up his hands. "See how I'm treated."

Now on her own, Alessandra wandered among the cases, studying their contents with an appreciative eye, even as she made sure she stayed away from Whitlock. Most of it was the sort of thing that any local museum might see fit to commemorate. Bits of pottery and arrowheads; beaded necklaces and rotting moccasins; pistol balls and old Bibles. Amazonian relics and animal bones. The ephemera of history.

There were more interesting oddments as well. Pieces of more recent manufacture, with obvious importance. But strange, unlike anything she'd ever seen – they reminded her of the sort of thing she usually purloined.

She looked up and saw Orne standing nearby, frowning down into a case, as if its contents had personally offended him. He was a good-looking man, despite his age. Acting on impulse, she sidled up to him. "Strange to see such things in a museum," she said.

Orne started. He'd obviously been lost in thought. He gave her a wan smile. "The influence of one Carl Sandford. A new exhibit. These objects relate to the history of the Silver Twilight Lodge, in Arkham. Or so he insists."

"You don't believe him?"

"I'm a skeptic by nature, Miss…?"

"Countess, actually. Countess Alessandra Zorzi." As she'd done for Fairmont, she held out her hand. Orne took it, but did not kiss it. His grip was warm and strong. The handshake of an honest man. She wondered if he practiced it.

"Well, countess, I am Matthew Orne. I am pleased to make your acquaintance." He peered at her. "Forgive me, but… you seem familiar. Have we met before?"

"I am sure I would remember if we had."

Orne smiled, pleased by the implied compliment. "Ah well. I'm getting older. Memory isn't what it used to be." He paused. "I noticed you came in with young Tad. A friend of his?"

"Something like that." She turned. "Really, I came to see the great discovery. Find of the century, you know."

Orne chuckled. "So I'm told. Would you care to see it up close?"

Alessandra smiled. "I would love nothing more."

• • •

Abner Whitlock watched the crowd, taking in the faces and matching them up to the names in his mental filing cabinet. He was looking for one in particular, but all of them bore watching, in his opinion. He'd never yet met a rich man who didn't have at least one skeleton in the closet. Matthew Orne was no exception.

His eyes strayed, searching for the client. The hall was crowded, but he spotted Orne over near the doors, talking with someone. He craned his neck, trying to get a better look, but saw only a flash of a shapely shoulder. He grunted. Orne was a ladies' man. He liked women, and liked to show off for them. That was a problem.

He'd met Orne for dinner the previous night, and his first impression hadn't been all that favorable. Orne had too much money and not enough sense, in Whitlock's professional opinion. He'd talked a lot but said little. Orne had other problems than the ladies, too.

Still, he was a client of Argus Insurance and Whitlock had a responsibility to make sure their investment remained safe and sound. The thought made him turn his mind back again to the previous night. After dinner, he'd scoped out the Independence Hotel, hoping to get a look at Zorzi. He'd imagined confronting her – convincing her to get the next train to Boston.

Part of him was glad she'd been out. He realized that he wanted her to try something. He'd catch her this time. He was sure of it.

"Lot of swells here today," Muldoon said, from beside him. Whitlock looked at the uniformed officer and frowned. Officer Muldoon was a good kid, but he was still just a rookie. Not the sort of backup Whitlock preferred.

"Kind of the point," he said, tersely. "You talk to Lynch?" Lynch was the head of museum security, such as it was. Four guys, one of whom was out sick and one of whom was Lynch.

"I talked to him."

"And?"

Muldoon grunted. "He's a security guard."

Whitlock nodded. "So, did he see anyone who shouldn't be here?"

"Yeah, me."

"Funny," Whitlock said, without a trace of a smile. "You're not here to make jokes."

"Still not sure why I'm here at all."

"Because my company's client wants protection, and your boss was only too happy to provide it." Whitlock turned away. "Cheer up. Could be worse."

"How?"

Whitlock considered this. "I'll let you know when I figure it out," he said, finally. "Now keep your eyes open and your hands off the canapes." Muldoon might be young, but he had that hungry look in his eye – he wanted to make a name for himself. Whitlock sympathized. But that didn't mean he was going to take any guff from a rookie cop.

"I don't even know what a canape is," Muldoon protested.

"They're tasty, is what they are," a voice said, from behind them. Whitlock and Muldoon turned. Professor Ferdinand Ashley smiled thinly and wiped a few errant crumbs from his mouth. He was a tubby sort, with slicked back hair and round, open features. "How are the defenses looking, gentlemen?"

"Defenses?" Muldoon said, in obvious confusion.

"As tight as can be expected," Whitlock interjected. He didn't like Ashley, though they'd only just met this morning. The professor was the twitchy sort. Whitlock wondered what had him so nervous. Maybe it was just the exhibition. From what he knew,

Ashley's continued career with the local university hinged on this shindig going well. "Shouldn't you be with the mummy?"

"I was hungry," Ashley said, somewhat petulantly. "And anyway, Tyler – Professor Freeborn that is – is handling things on that end well enough." He gestured to a nearby waiter and took a glass of champagne. Muldoon frowned, but pretended not to notice. "Surely you're not against a bit of bubbly, officer?"

"Prohibition is the law of the land," Muldoon said, not looking at him. Ashley turned to Whitlock, as if seeking support. Whitlock shrugged.

"I don't drink."

Ashley sniffed and knocked back the champagne. He was already a bit flushed and from the way he wobbled on his pins, Whitlock suspected that it wasn't his first drink of the day. Ashley smacked his lips and turned, as if looking for someone. Absently, he dabbed at his face with a handkerchief. He was sweating bullets.

"You worried about something, professor?" Muldoon asked. He'd noticed as well.

Ashley started. "No, no. Just… just a touch of nerves. I always get this way at these things, you know. Not one for parties, really."

"Just party food, huh?" Whitlock said. Ashley looked at him in momentary incomprehension. Then he laughed. The sound was brittle. Uncertain.

"Ha, yes. Yes indeed. Forgive me, gentlemen. I'll leave you to it. Excuse me." He turned and headed back into the main exhibit hall. Whitlock watched him go.

"That strike you as odd?" he said, softly.

"Yeah. Just a bit." Muldoon straightened his coat and his hand drifted across the service revolver holstered on his hip. He looked around. "He's a squirrelly one."

"I wonder why," Whitlock said. He looked around. "Something feels off."

Muldoon nodded. "It's that damn ugly thing in there, is what it is," he said.

"The mummy, you mean?"

"Have you seen it?"

"Not up close," Whitlock said. He frowned. Orne was still in the same spot, but Whitlock had a better line of sight to his companion now. And he didn't much like what he saw. Countess Alessandra Zorzi, bold as brass. "Why?" he added, absently.

"No reason. Gave me the creeps, is all." Something about the way Muldoon said it made Whitlock look at him. Muldoon was pale, his gaze turned inwards. Like his mind was elsewhere. Annoyed, Whitlock prodded him.

"Then don't look at it. Look at the crowd." Whitlock spied a knot of men entering through the main doors. They were dressed well, but something set his alarm bells off. He frowned. "Like them, for instance."

Muldoon followed his gaze, and his face hardened. He'd picked up the same vibe Whitlock had. The newcomers telegraphed trouble. "Maybe I should go take a closer look."

"You do that." Whitlock turned away. "I'm going to stick close to Orne, just in case."

CHAPTER EIGHT
Whitlock

The crowd flowed around the large, central case in knots and tangles. The photographers had already been and gone, but there were still a number of journalists scribbling away in notebooks as they hobnobbed with the guests.

"What do you think of our fine town, then?" Orne asked. "Does it compare favorably with… the European vintage?" He gave her an expectant look.

"I have seen worse towns, certainly."

Orne's smile went brittle. "Damning us with faint praise."

She patted his arm. "That was not my intention, I assure you."

The crowd parted for them without so much as a murmur. A tall, thin man stood attentively nearby. Obviously an academic. A perfect example of the species, Alessandra thought.

"Professor Freeborn," Orne murmured into her ear. "I am burdened with he and Professor Ashley for my sins." He laughed and she laughed with him, touching his arm as she did so. Orne was charming, despite being at least two decades her senior. Or at least, he thought of himself as such. That could be useful.

Alessandra did not favor breaking and entering. She'd done it often enough, but it was so much easier when the mark invited you inside and showed you their valuables. The problem was, it took time to win someone's trust, and Zamacona struck her as the impatient sort. He might well make a move himself if he thought she was taking too long.

The professor hovered like a mother hen, ensuring no one got too close to the thing. He looked up as they drew near. "Where's Professor Ashley gotten to then?" Orne asked, loudly. "Raiding the refreshments again?"

"You know how he is," Freeborn said. "He should have been back by now, though."

"Go find him," Orne said, a note of command in his voice. Here was a man used to being obeyed. Freeborn frowned, but did as he was told. Orne turned back to her. "Beautiful, isn't it?" he said.

Alessandra looked down at the ancient thing. It was beautiful, but in the way of Goya's so-called "Black Paintings", abstract and unpleasant. She had never found the dead inherently terrifying. The living were more than frightening enough, when they put their minds to it.

It lay on its side in the case, curled into a fetal ball. It was smaller than she had thought. From a cursory glance, it seemed brittle. She'd seen bodies like that before, curled up in the mud of a trench wall, forgotten by God and man, with only the rats for company. Too many of them.

"Are you all right?" Orne asked, startling her.

She blinked. "Yes. Just… it is quite amazing." The mask was as ugly as she recalled from the photo. It reminded her of a toad, or maybe a bat – or perhaps a sloth. She had enough experience with such things to know that it had taken real skill to carve it. To make what she thought was some form of onyx look almost... organic. The flat panes of its cheeks and brow were covered in strange marks that reminded her somewhat of cuneiform.

The right people would pay well for it, she thought. But she remembered Zamacona's insistence that it not be touched and felt a sudden vague, unpleasant sensation in the pit of her stomach. "A most curious thing," Orne said. Grateful for the distraction, she looked at him.

"Curious how?"

"Mummies, at least the Egyptian ones, are normally wrapped in a... standard way. Resin is slopped onto the cadaver, and then several long sheets are wound about them vertically, before being folded over the head in order to cover the face. Then the rest of the body, starting with the neck, is wrapped in horizontal fashion, with whatever scrap linen is to hand. Sometimes they even used old clothes."

"Hardly the ornate ceremony of popular fiction," Alessandra said. "How is this one different?"

"No linen, for one thing. No wrappings at all, beyond those curious bindings about his limbs. Instead, he was placed into an airless environment, with low humidity and his tissues contracted until they resembled something very much like jerky." Orne looked at her. "An all-natural mummification."

"How splendid. You sound as if you know something about it?"

"I consider myself a student of the dead," he said, without a trace of modesty. "They have much to teach us, if we but listen."

"And what about the markings on his flesh?" She indicated the shallow, groovelike scars. "What do they say?"

"Battle scars, perhaps."

"I fancied them to be ritual in nature."

He smiled in a somewhat condescending fashion. "Did you now?"

She ignored his tone. "Yes. Tad mentioned you found it in Oklahoma?"

"Not me," Orne said. "But I helped fund the expedition. Professor Ashley came to me with an outrageous tale. Something to do with an old manuscript that had been donated to the university library. He needed funding, and I was intrigued, honestly."

"Tad mentioned Spanish gold."

Orne laughed. "Well, there was that as well."

"No gold then?"

"Only on the mask."

She looked at the mask. "I'm surprised you didn't take it off."

Orne frowned. "I wanted to but I was informed that it might lead to the dissolution of our prize. The risk was too great, so I left it where it was. Bit grotesque, but it does lend the old gentleman a certain panache, don't you think?"

"It does give it a certain something, yes." She stared at the ancient thing. As Orne said, it resembled jerky – thin and brown and leathery. Alive, he – or she, she admitted – might have been tall, but not broad. Thin, not heavy. There had not been much substance there to lose. It wore nothing besides the mask save the brown, crumpled remnants of a loincloth or shift.

She was certain that it would crumble if she attempted to remove it from its case. Getting to it wasn't an issue. Locks could be picked and glass cut. But she would need some method of keeping her prize intact. Just tossing it in a sack wasn't the answer.

That presented a problem. Not an insurmountable one, but a definite obstacle to a quick exit and entry. It called for thought. More and more it was looking as if this job was going to be neither swift nor easy. She touched Orne's arm again. "I am surprised you were able to... hijack – is that the right word? – hijack this place to show off your discovery."

"My family have lived in Arkham a long time. The Orne Library is named after us, and we endowed the university with quite a bit of lucre over the years." Orne smiled genially. "We take care of Arkham, and Arkham takes care of us."

"*Noblesse oblige*," Alessandra said.

Orne nodded. "If you like. I prefer to think of it as *quid pro quo.*" He studied her. "You, however, are not from here. Italy, I think. Milan?"

"Venice."

"Ah, *la Serenissima.* A fine city. There is a wisdom in those stones."

"You've been?"

"Once or twice. In my youth. What do you think of our tiny town?"

"Not so tiny as all that."

Orne frowned. "No, I suppose not. Things change, and not always for the better." He cracked his knuckles. An ugly habit, one many Americans – and many big men – had. "Did you come purely for the exhibition, then?"

"I was in Boston on business when I read about it. I thought it sounded like a lark, so I changed my plans."

Orne chuckled. "A lark. I suppose it is." Despite his smile, she could tell he was somewhat insulted. "I suspect you are not the only one here to think so. The greatest archaeological find of the century, reduced to a carnival display."

"I would not go that far."

"Perhaps not. Even so, I have ensured that it is well-protected from the hoi polloi." He gestured to the police officer standing near the doors. "Chief Nichols has been very accommodating. One of his best is on duty. And of course, my insurance company sent one of their own investigators to oversee things... isn't that right, Mr Whitlock?"

Alessandra turned.

Abner Whitlock gave her a thin smile.

"Countess," Whitlock said. He allowed himself a moment to relish the brief look of consternation on Zorzi's face. She recovered quickly though.

"Mr Whitlock." She looked him up and down. "Is that a new suit?"

He frowned. The suit was indeed new, but he saw no reason to admit it. "I'm here representing my employers. I thought it best to dress for the occasion."

Orne raised an eyebrow. "You two have met?" Whitlock heard something in his voice – a touch of jealousy, perhaps? She worked fast. He'd interrupted just in time.

"We shared a train," Zorzi said.

"A Mrs Peterson was looking for you, Mr Orne," Whitlock said, smoothly. "She's just over there, near the collection of Narragansett arrowheads." It was an utter fabrication, but it served its purpose. He needed to extricate Orne from the line of fire.

"Ah, thank you. Countess, I'm having a private soiree later this week, to... celebrate, you might say." Orne smiled. "If you're interested in attending, find me before you leave. We'd love to have you. Now, if you'll excuse me..." He turned away. Whitlock waited until he was out of earshot and then turned to Zorzi.

"You move quick."

"Forgive me, but I am unfamiliar with your American idioms," she said, with studied mildness. "What do you mean?"

Whitlock let her stew for a moment before speaking. "I saw you casing the joint. Checking for weak points. You think Orne is your way in, don't you?"

She looked around, as if bewildered. "I thought I was already in."

"Yuck it up, but I'm not falling for that wide-eyed ingénue act. It might play for a guy like Orne, but I'm fairly hardboiled."

"You … are an egg?"

Whitlock flushed slightly, annoyed despite himself. If she wanted to play it that way, fine. He was more than happy to go hard. "Stop playing stupid. You speak perfect English." He looked down at the mummy. "Ugly goddamn thing."

"Beauty is in the eye of the beholder, or so I hear."

"And what do you behold?"

She smiled. "An ugly goddamn thing."

Whitlock grunted. "You don't seem surprised that I know you're a countess." He'd been hoping she'd be more worried – on the back foot. Instead, she was playing it cool.

"Why would I be?"

"Given that you've avoided giving me your name at every opportunity, I thought you might be a bit put out."

"I am more put out that you tried to break into my hotel room last night." She studied the case, and he knew she was watching his reflection in the glass. He was careful to show no sign of surprise. "Why did you visit, by the way? And how did you know where I was staying?" She looked at him. "Have you been following me, Mr Whitlock?"

"And if I have?"

"I shall have to report you to the police for harassment." She turned. "Where is that officer I saw you talking with?"

"Who? Officer Muldoon? Yeah, I'm sure he'd be real pleased to hear from you. We could go talk to him together, if you like." He gave her a hard smile.

"Perhaps we should. I am certain that he would be very interested to know about these tendencies of yours ..." she said lightly. Almost laughing at him.

Angry, Whitlock caught her wrist and pulled her around to face him. "I know who you are," he hissed. "Who you really are. And I know why you're here."

She glanced at his hand, and then at him. "Let go of me."

"Not until you answer a few questions, *countess*."

She jerked her wrist free of his grasp and stepped back. "You're causing a scene, Mr Whitlock. I do not think that is what your employers had in mind, do you?" She looked around pointedly, and Whitlock followed her gaze. Eyes swiveled, avoiding them. But his outburst had been witnessed and would be the subject of whispers. Whitlock's frown deepened. He jerked his head towards the wall.

"Over there."

She followed him, clearly bemused. "What do you want, Mr Whitlock?"

He didn't look at her. "My employers want me to ensure that this exhibit stays where it's at, and in one piece. That means I have to identify potential threats." He fixed her with a meaningful glare. Now that she knew the jig was up, it was only a matter of time until she made a break for it. He wondered which way she'd go – out the front, or the back?

"And I am a potential threat?" she asked, with a smile.

"Biggest one in the room. It's all very textbook." He made a show of looking around again. Giving her time to consider her options. "You got some swell to guide you in, then made a circuit of the room. You checked out the doors, looked for windows. I watched you do it. Then you caught Orne, started chatting him up. I wonder why?"

"He's very handsome."

"He's very rich. And he thinks you're attractive."

"Does he?"

"I thought I said not to play stupid."

Zorzi frowned. "You do not know anything about me, Mr Whitlock. We are strangers, you and I – and I would ask that you not talk to me as if we are … familiar."

"Oh, but we're practically on a first name basis," he said, pitching his voice low, so that she could hear. "I recognized you on the train, countess. Soon as I saw you, I knew you were trouble. And as soon as I remembered where I'd last seen you, I knew why you were here. And I promise you, you're not getting your hands on this mummy."

Before she could reply, the sharp, unmistakable crack of a gunshot split the air. They both spun, following the sound. For a moment, the crowd looked confused as the music screeched to a halt. Then a murmur of concern swept through the hall. The screams began a moment later as the echoes of the shot faded and a trio of masked gunmen shoved their way into the exhibition room.

"Everyone on the floor," one of them bellowed. "This is a robbery!"

CHAPTER NINE
The Robbery

Whitlock caught Alessandra and shoved her back against the wall, behind a pillar, out of sight of the newcomers. "What are you–" she began, but he held a finger up to his lips. Understanding him, she fell silent.

The crowd collapsed in disorder. Some screamed, some knelt. Others ran for the doors, only to find them locked.

"Stop yelling," a second gunman bellowed. He was shorter than the other two, but built like a fireplug. He hefted the distinctive shape of a Thompson submachine gun in one hand as he strode into the room. "Jodorowsky – watch the crowd in the hall. Make sure that damn cop doesn't do anything stupid. Phipps, with me."

"You ain't supposed to use our names, Gomes," the one called Phipps barked.

"Shaddup. Nobody cares." Gomes looked around. "Heads down, I said!" He let off a burst from the Thompson, carving chunks from the ceiling plaster. "Think I won't shoot you? Think again. I got no problem filling you with enough lead to make you rattle." He stopped as he noticed Alessandra and Whitlock. "Down on the goddamn floor," he snarled, swinging his weapon towards them.

"Hold on, hold on," Whitlock began, hands raised. "What are you after? Maybe I can help." He took a step towards the gunman, and Alessandra wondered what his game was.

"I said, get on the floor!"

Whitlock took another step. "This is a new suit, pal. Rather not get it dirty."

Alessandra stepped back. She was annoyed with herself for leaving her own weapon behind.

"Hey, you think I don't see you, lady?" the gunman barked. "On the floor."

"Leave her out of this," Whitlock said.

"Shaddap." The gunman made to ram the stock of his Thompson into Whitlock's midsection, but the insurance investigator caught it at the last second.

"Hey – let go!" the gunman yelped, as Whitlock struggled with him for control.

Suddenly, Alessandra understood – Whitlock was an idiot.

They staggered back and forth, the Thompson caught between them. As they grappled, the gunman's finger tightened on the trigger and the weapon spat fire. The fusillade chewed the walls and shattered cases. Priceless artifacts were rendered worthless in moments, reduced to brightly colored splinters by the spray of lead. People screamed.

Alarms were ringing now, nearly drowning out the cries of the guests and the curses of the thieves. Alessandra saw the Thompson clatter to the floor and Whitlock stumble back. The gunman staggered off-balance, his hand clawing for something – another weapon? – beneath his coat. In another moment, Whitlock was no longer going to be a problem. The thought should have cheered her.

And yet, before she realized it, she was diving for the Thompson. She slid across the floor and snatched it up. The gunman stared at her in shock as she rose and pulled the trigger. The gunman spun, crying out in pain. It wasn't the first time she'd fired one, but even so her aim was off. She was a fine shot with a pistol, but less so with anything larger.

One of the other thieves appeared in the doorway, shotgun in hand. She ducked behind a nearby case as he returned fire, dropping the Thompson in the process. Shards of broken glass rained down over her as she huddled on the floor. She hoped Whitlock was smart enough to find cover. The shotgun boomed twice more, and a nearby display case exploded. She heard the clack of spent shells being ejected, and risked a look.

It was a mistake. Something – a pistol, perhaps – connected with the back of her head and she fell. The room was spinning, and it felt as if every bell in the world were ringing inside her cranium. She was amazed her skull hadn't been cracked by the blow.

"Get the goddamn case over here, quick," Gomes snarled. He stood over her, the revolver he'd hit her with held in his good hand. Blood stained his other sleeve. "And somebody keep an eye on that damn cop."

"Pulanski's got the front covered," Phipps said. From beneath the case, she could see him lugging what looked like a sea chest into the room. "Jodorowsky, help me with this." The wielder of the shotgun turned and caught the other side of the chest. They moved quickly towards her. Groggily, she looked up and into a pair of black eyes – wet and staring.

The mummy was where it had been before, but now its head was tilted, looking down at her. When had it moved? How had it moved? She tried to shake her head, to look away, but couldn't. All she could do was meet that empty gaze.

Only, now it wasn't so empty. The world seemed to stutter and dim. Like a film coming to the end of its reel. She felt flushed and freezing, all at once, as if she were being consumed by cold fire. The black gaze seemed to expand, filling her perceptions.

Something moved, in the darkness. A squirming, twisting sort of motion that reminded her of maggots eating away at the belly of a dead animal. Her breath caught in her throat. Glass crunched like thunder.

The motion grew more frenzied. Her heart spasmed. Something stretched towards her. She tried to blink, to look away, but the blackness held her. A line of shadow stretched... stretched... *stretched.*

She felt something like a spider's web or a moth's wing brush across her. She blinked and fell back, clawing at her face. It was as if someone had blown chili powder into her eyes. She thought she cried out. She heard a growling voice, and through a veil of tears she saw the cold barrel of a pistol pointing down at her.

"Get her up," Gomes said. "What the hell was she doing?"

"How should I know?" Jodorowsky snapped. "You're the one who hit her. Maybe you rattled her brains. Phipps, help me get this damn thing in the crate, would you? And be careful – if it's damaged, we don't get paid!"

Alessandra shook her head in an effort to clear it. She blinked as something swam across her vision. When her eyes cleared, she saw the two men carefully lowering the fragile shape of the mummy into a wooden chest. Gomes stood nearby, glaring at her. He'd retrieved his Thompson. "What about her?" he growled, as his partners sealed the chest.

"Leave her," Phipps said. "We got what we need."

"She shot me!" One of Alessandra's fumbling hands found a shard of glass and she snatched it up. It wasn't much, but it would serve, if he decided to settle the score.

"She grazed you and you gave her a thump. That settles it in my book. Now come on – help us get this damn thing up."

"My arm hurts and you two can manage. I'll cover you."

There was a yell from the entry hall, and a shot sounded moments later, followed by the screams of frightened attendees. "Pulanski?" Gomes bellowed. "What happened?" He started towards the door, but stopped as a uniformed figure appeared, revolver levelled.

"Hands up, boyos!" the policeman, Muldoon, called out. The other two men turned at this, and Alessandra took the opportunity to scramble away.

Gomes sprayed the doorway, forcing Muldoon to duck out of sight. "Get the thing, Tony," Gomes shouted. "Head for the back!" Phipps and Jodorowsky did just that. They hurried towards the far door, while Gomes steadily emptied the drum of his weapon. When the air was full of dust and splinters, he turned and galloped after the others.

Alessandra, crouched behind a piece of toad-like statuary, watched them go. She considered pursuing them, but only for a moment. She spied Muldoon huddled against a doorway as he reloaded his service revolver. "Looks like they skedaddled," he called out, to no one in particular. He had a cut on his chin, and his uniform was mussed. "I got one of them, though. Plugged the bastard through."

Confusion reigned in the exhibition room. People were shouting questions, or crying, or hurrying for the doors. She could hear sirens in the distance. And she could see Whitlock, staring in her direction. As he started pushing through the crowd towards her, she got to her feet and hurried towards the doors.

She felt a twinge of guilt for not saying goodbye to Visser, but he'd understand. She had no wish to become involved with the police. And certainly no wish to speak to Whitlock. No doubt he was already attempting to figure out how to blame this on her.

She spotted the dead robber – Pulanski – laying in the middle of the floor, crumpled into a ball. Muldoon had indeed plugged him through, as he said. The crowd was giving him a wide berth, flowing around him like a rock in a stream.

She was out the door and moving towards the street, one more face in the crowd. Police cars pulled up, sirens wailing, lights flashing. Alessandra didn't wait to see what happened next.

Pepper was standing on top of her cab when Alessandra reached it. She was craning her neck, trying to see. "What happened?" she called out as she hopped to the ground.

"A robbery," Alessandra said. "We need to go. Now." She slid into the back.

Pepper clambered behind the wheel. "A robbery? That explains the cops. Sure you don't want to stay?"

"Definitely not."

"Because they might ask questions?"

"Yes. Among other reasons."

"Fair enough. Weird time of day for a robbery." Pepper sniffed. "Right in the middle of everything like that? Seems like they were asking for trouble."

"No. It was smart, if crude. The more confusion, the better. Every eyewitness will have a different story." Alessandra shook her head. "I knew I should have brought my pistol."

"Why didn't you?"

"I did not want to explain why I had it, if someone saw it."

Alessandra pulled her cigarettes out and selected one. A mote of blackness passed across her eye and she blinked rapidly, trying to clear it. She hoped it wasn't glass. That was the last thing she needed.

"Why *do* you have it?" Pepper asked. "The real reason, I mean. 'Cause, it ain't every day I get a gun aimed at me when I knock on a door."

"I did say I was sorry about that."

"You didn't, actually."

"No?"

"No."

"My apologies, then." She extended the pack of cigarettes to Pepper. She thought about not answering, but almost being shot had a way of making her talkative. "I have carried it since the war. I feel… unclothed without it."

Pepper took the pack and extricated a cigarette with her lips, one hand on the wheel. "You were in the war?" She asked the question softly, carefully. The way one might probe an old hurt, to see if it had healed yet.

Alessandra paused as the memories rose to the surface, even as they had when she'd seen the mummy. Her mouth was suddenly dry and she licked her lips, trying to work some moisture into them. "I was an ambulance driver. Not for long. A few months. Long enough. War is an ugly thing, and much of what comes after is worse."

"Why'd you do it?"

"I wanted to help." Alessandra paused. "No, I tell a lie. I thought it would be exciting. And it was, briefly." She frowned, trying not to think about it and failing. The crack of gunfire, like rain. Fire from the sky. The way the mud caught at your ankles and shins. It was always muddy, even when it hadn't rained for days.

The smell was the worst of it. It never went away. Even now, it was with her. "My ambulance broke down once. I'd gone too far, run over a crater." Her voice grew distant as she recalled that moment of blind panic. She swallowed. "Men came hurrying towards me out of the chemical fog. They looked like monsters in their masks. And maybe they were."

"Germans?"

Alessandra shook her head. "They weren't on anyone's side. They were detritus. No better than rats, scavenging from the dead and dying." She puffed on her cigarette for a moment, remembering. "War makes animals of some men." She patted her Webley. "That's when I learned to shoot. We all had guns, just in case. I used mine that day."

Pepper stared at her. "You shot 'em?"

"Some of them. The others ran." Alessandra looked at her. "It was luck. Nothing more. If they'd had a bit more courage, or my aim had been a bit worse, we might not be having this conversation." She was talking too much. Too freely. She knew it and bit back any further elaboration.

Pepper shook her head. "I don't know that I could shoot somebody."

"Hopefully, you'll never have to." Alessandra flicked her cigarette out the window. She took a long, shuddering breath. She felt as if she wanted to be sick.

"Take me back to the hotel."

CHAPTER TEN
The Getaway

As Alessandra climbed out of the cab, Pepper said, "You sure about this?"

"What? Getting out of town before the police come calling? Yes, I rather think I am." Alessandra looked around. The train station looked no less grim than before, though it was somewhat busier as late afternoon trains arrived and departed.

She'd packed quickly when she returned to the hotel, grabbing only the necessities. She'd made the hard choice to leave most of her luggage behind. Travel light, travel quick, as her father had said. All in all, it had only taken a few minutes.

Pepper frowned. "And here I was getting used to playing chauffeur."

"If you wish, you may accompany me to Boston and continue to do so," Alessandra said. She paused, startled by her own offer. "I could buy you a ticket."

Pepper looked at her incredulously. "You serious?"

"I would not have offered, were I not."

Pepper shook her head. "No, I- I got things to do here. I got a job."

"We could find you a better one." Even as she said it, Alessandra wondered why she was so intent on keeping the young woman close. Better for Pepper – better for her – if they parted ways now, before anyone connected them.

"Not likely."

"I suspected as much." Alessandra smiled, somewhat relieved. "It was a pleasure to meet you, Pepper. I trust you will stay out of trouble from here on out?"

"In this town? Not likely, lady." Still, Pepper hesitated. "I'll wait. Just in case you change your mind or something, OK?"

"I will not, but thank you."

She entered the station and was immediately struck by the noise. The stone walls muffled the clattering roar of the trains and the shriek of steam engines. Voices spun about her as men and women hurried towards their platforms, or moved more sedately for the exit. The afternoon crowd wasn't so large as it might have been in Kingsport or Providence, but it was substantial. She hoped there would be seats left on the next train to Boston.

She stopped, suddenly aware of a faint, familiar odor. Like rotting meat. It was the same odor she'd smelled in the hotel hallway earlier in the day. She found her eyes drawn to a hunched form sitting on a bench near the cab rank. A man clad in a dark coat, and a slouch hat. He sat hunched forward in a curious fashion, as if he were afflicted with some congenital deformity or spinal injury.

As if aware of her gaze, his head tilted up. There was something… wrong with the face. A vague sense of abnormality. Then, he rose with a peculiar lurching motion and crept away, vanishing into the crowd of new arrivals.

Bemused, Alessandra turned as a whistle sounded, and steam washed across the platforms. She put the strange man from her mind and hurried towards the ticket office, hoping that someone was on duty. Thankfully, a sleepy-eyed clerk was at the window. As she bought a ticket for the next train to Boston, she kept an eye out for railroad bulls.

It was time to leave. A good thief knew when to go. The artifact was gone, and the police were involved. There was no profit in staying, and a risk that she might be caught. Whitlock knew who she was, and seemed the type to hold a grudge.

She remembered him now: they'd crossed paths once before, but never been formally introduced. His employers had insured a certain collection of antiquities she had plundered on behalf of a gentleman in Vienna.

Best to get out now, before he came knocking. It wouldn't be long. They'd be questioning everyone who'd been present, comparing their statements. By now, the police might even be knocking on her door, looking to clap her in irons.

The thought of being confined to a cell sent a shiver through her. She had been arrested only a handful of times in her life, and never anywhere that kept records. But it had left a mark nonetheless. To be caught in so small a space, with no way out, was unthinkable. Better to run away, and live to steal another day.

The station wasn't large, and she chose a bench from which she could observe the entrance. There were a few other people waiting for the same train. A newspaper stand was opening up at the far end of the platform, the vendor unleashing a salvo of great, racking coughs.

She checked the great clock mounted above the platform. Five minutes until the train to Boston arrived. Five minutes to freedom. From Boston, she would go to New York. Perhaps catch a ship for Canada. She knew several people in Canada who were always in need of services of the sort she provided. From there, perhaps back to England, or maybe even Australia. Or maybe she would stay in America, but head west, to California perhaps.

Though she tried not to think about it, her mind kept returning to the robbery. Analyzing it from every angle. She was a thief, and thieves analyzed robberies the way statisticians looked at census data. It had been organized, but sloppy. Four men, enough to cover the crowd and see to the merchandise. Not enough to fully control the situation, however, given that one of them had wound up dead. But a four-way split was easier on the payoff than a five-way or six-way. And four men could work as well as five, if they were willing to use violence.

She had always drawn the line at violence. Not out of any inherent pacifism, but rather because once that line was crossed there was no telling what would happen. She carried a pistol for protection – and had fired it more than once. But never out of malice or intent to harm. Once you saw a gun as a solution, every obstacle became a problem.

She knew of others in her profession who were like that. Violent and lacking in restraint. The Turk, Bayezid, for instance. Or that charlatan, Lampini. They were thieves and worse than thieves. She fancied herself a cut above them, at least. But sometimes... she wondered. It rarely kept her up at night, but she thought about it all the same.

The robbery had been a smash and grab, but the only thing taken was something with no apparent monetary value. Something they'd come prepared to transport. Someone had hired them. That was the only explanation. She had names as well. Gomes. Jodorowsky. Phipps. Pulanski. She wondered if the police had those, yet.

If not, it might be worth it to call in an anonymous tip, when she was a safe distance away. Not out of any sense of civic duty, but rather to ensure that someone like, say, Whitlock, didn't get it into his head to come after her. America would be no fun at all if she had to spend the entire time looking over her shoulder. She'd had enough of that in Europe.

The bench squeaked. She glanced sideways, and saw a small figure, wrapped in an outsized black coat and battered slouch hat, sitting at the far end. Her heart stuttered slightly as the too-pale face turned towards her and milky, sightless eyes fixed on her for an instant, before a gout of steam from an arriving train momentarily obscured them. She heard the rustle of the coat as its wearer rose. She leapt to her feet and backed away.

She heard the sound of awkward shuffling, and saw the black splotch of a shape moving closer through the thinning curtain of steam. She thought about the pistol in her clutch, but she couldn't risk it, not here, out in the open. Instead, she looked around for help, but true to the old adage there was never a policeman around when you needed one.

The shape stopped. Alessandra watched it warily, ready to run at the first sign of renewed intent. She heard a low, querulous grunt. Then, a hurried shuffling as the strange figure headed off down the platform. The steam faded, and she saw why he'd been in such a hurry. Several police officers were approaching her bench.

Quickly, she made her way across the platform, towards the edge of the station where she sought cover behind one of the brick crenulations that lined the walls. The jutting brickwork was decorated with carvings – historical scenes, perhaps. It wasn't quite large enough to hide behind, but it would serve well enough. She was still close enough to make a run for the train when it arrived.

More police appeared. There were five of them now, milling

about the platform, observing the waiting passengers, even questioning some of them. She felt a cold knot in the pit of her stomach. Perhaps they were looking for the robbers. Then she saw Whitlock questioning the newspaper vendor, and knew she was out of luck.

She cursed softly and turned, looking for an unobtrusive way out. If she could make it outside, Pepper might still be waiting. She weighed the odds and stepped out into the open. No shouts, no whistles. A train was pulling in, not hers. She could board it anyway, and plead confusion when the porter came by to check tickets. Decided not to risk it. Too much open space to cross, and Whitlock was already turning around.

She hurried towards the far entrance, trusting in the momentary chaos of the train's arrival to mask her exodus. Passengers disembarked, adding to the noise. She joined the trickle of early morning arrivals, head down.

And bumped into Officer Muldoon. He reached automatically to steady her, an apology on his lips. His eyes widened. She stomped on his foot and slammed her valise into the side of his head, sending him stumbling.

He cried out as she darted past. Running in heels was a chore, but better that than slowing down to take them off. She wished she'd changed into her working clothes before attempting to leave, but a woman dressed like a bricklayer would have attracted more attention than she was comfortable with.

Muldoon was on his feet, shaking his head. The other policemen were converging on her. She didn't see Whitlock, thankfully. She needed to get out of the station, put some distance between her and her pursuers.

As she wove through the crowd, she spotted a black figure,

hunched and moving towards one of the platforms with spider-like quickness. "Where do you think *you're* going?" she murmured, following him. Whoever he was, if he knew of a way out, she intended to make use of it – unsettling as he was, the police worried her more.

He led her to the edge of the outer platform, where he vanished over the side. He was escaping across the tracks. She glanced back. They hadn't spotted her yet. She'd rung Muldoon's bells hard enough that he hadn't seen which way she'd gone.

She climbed carefully down on to the tracks, and followed the black-clad figure towards the flatcars in the distance. Then on past them, to the coach yard. His intentions were obvious, now. There would be places to hide there, among the empty passenger cars. At least for an hour or two. Every so often, he glanced back. Did he know she was following him? Is that what he'd intended?

She heard a shout behind her and turned. She spied a flash of blue and bit back a curse. Muldoon. He'd recovered more quickly than she'd thought. Her eyes flicked down to her valise. She'd stowed her clutch in it. A few moments, and she could have her pistol in hand. But what then? A shoot-out with the police wasn't the sort of thing a smart thief engaged in. She kept moving, trying to keep her unwitting guide in sight. He was moving fast, for so crooked a figure, and she lost sight of him more than once. The switchyard was an industrial labyrinth. Great boles of fiber bound for textile mills rested under waterproof tarpaulins. Refrigerated cars, mercifully empty of fish, sat waiting to be pressed into service. It was no wonder her black-coated friend had sought refuge here. It would take the police hours to search it.

The sun slipped behind a gray pall, and a chill drizzle began to patter down, stinging her cheeks and the back of her neck. She pulled up the collar of her coat and concentrated on not slipping in the gravel and mud. Workmen ambled past at a distance, paying her no mind.

The coach yard was claustrophobic, with walls of iron rising high above her. Lines of filthy windows glared down at her as she followed the tracks. She considered boarding one, but something about the shadowed confines of the cars made her hesitate.

A whistle pierced the air. Gravel crunched beneath running feet. That decided the matter for her. She steeled herself and climbed aboard one of the cars. Needs must, when the Devil drives.

She sank down, hiding among the seats and waited.

CHAPTER ELEVEN
Teeth

Alessandra sat on the floor of the train car in silence, wishing again that she'd chosen to wear her work clothes. Her dress wasn't the most comfortable attire for the current situation. She shifted, trying to ease the ache growing in her limbs and back.

If she waited long enough, she might be able to make it across the street and to the river. From there – Rivertown, perhaps. She might be able to find a boat heading downriver to Kingsport or Martin's Beach. It wasn't the train, but beggars couldn't be choosers. Getting out of Arkham was the important thing.

Whitlock had obviously convinced the police that she was connected to the robbery in some way. Otherwise, why would they have come looking for her? That they might not be on her trail never entered her mind. Coincidence was a fine thing, but this wasn't it. She might have thought it an omen, if she believed in such things.

Despite what some of her clients insisted, omens and mysticism were nothing but hokum. And yet there had been things she was at a loss to explain. The way the stone of the gargoyle at Vyones had felt like living flesh for a moment. The sounds she'd heard in

the Comte d'Erlette's home. And of course, that night in the Rue
d'Auseil.

Her mind shied away from the memory, tattered as it was.
Even now, nearly a decade on, she could barely remember what
had happened. Or what she thought had happened. The way the
shadows had gathered like a flock of hungry birds – the sound of
her father, arguing – her mother, screaming – lights, not electric
ones, but something else, something almost… unearthly – and
then, the silence. That awful, heavy silence.

She'd felt something similar in the museum. When she'd met
the mummy's empty gaze, it had not seemed so empty at all. She
pushed the thought aside. Her head still ached from the knock to
it she'd taken. Whatever she thought she might have seen or felt, it
wasn't real. Just like that night on Rue d'Auseil.

The sound of running feet interrupted her dark reverie. She
tensed, straining to hear. The echo of bootsteps grew louder… and
then passed by, following the tracks. She risked a look through the
windows, and saw two officers headed towards the other end of the
yard. A flurry of voices made her turn. More of them were making
their way down the opposite side of the car, Muldoon among them.
She crouched, waiting for them to go past, her eyes on her valise. If
they decided to check the car, she might have no choice.

Metal creaked, and she glanced over her shoulder. Milky eyes
stared into her own. A wash of fetid breath rolled over her as rotten
teeth gnashed behind frayed lips. Then, the man in the black coat
was scuttling towards her in a way that sent a shiver of repulsion
through her. She reacted on instinct, much as she had with
Muldoon. Her valise came up and the slouch hat went flying.

Pale hands darted for her throat. She saw a mottled scalp, and
wisps of patchy hair the color of grave moss. Then she was falling

back, driving her heels up into the chest of her attacker. He fumbled backwards with a peculiar groan, as if he were unable to draw enough air into his lungs. She scrambled to her feet, valise held protectively before her.

"What do you want?" she hissed, in a low voice.

"Not… leave…" he gurgled. In the shadows of the car, it was hard to make him out. Despite that, her skin crawled as he took a herky-jerky step towards her. "You… not… leave."

"That is not your decision to make, I fear," she said, glancing at the nearest window. She heard shouts and gravel rattling against the track. Her attacker had alerted the police to her presence. Maybe that had been his aim the entire time. "Who do you work for?"

"Work… for…" he rasped as he clawed at the backs of the seats, hauling himself towards her. Bands of gray light fell across him through the grimy windows. His coat was caked in filth and his face had a peculiar, sagging quality. As if he suffered some nervous ailment.

She backed away. "I am armed. If you come any closer, I will have no choice but to shoot you, whoever you are."

"Shoot… me…" he groaned. At first, she took it for mockery. But it sounded almost like a plea. Another swaying step. "Shoot… me… shoot…" His eyes rolled and met hers, and she saw nothing in them. Nothing save shadows.

The moment stretched. It unfurled and enveloped her, even as it had in the museum. In that instant, she was somewhere else, surrounded by wet rock and shadows. A harsh, blue radiance pierced the dark, and she convulsed away from it. She heard screams, babbling in a language she could not possibly understand, but did nonetheless.

Tsathoggua en y'n an ya phtaggn N'kai!

The bizarre words punched through the dark. Figures moved quickly, running now, running away from the dark. Away from her. She – was it her, or someone else – pursued, eager to catch them, eager to enfold them in her arms; only they didn't feel like arms, or move like them. Nonetheless, she would take them to see the one who had created them all. That was why they had come, after all. It seemed only fitting that they should be given this last gift, before they, too, were consumed.

She blinked. *Consumed*? The word echoed in her head, and the moment shattered. Her vision swam and she stumbled back, shaking all over, clutching at her head. She felt sick, her stomach twisting itself into knots. Her throat felt raw, as if she'd swallowed broken glass, and her skull pounded with an ugly rhythm.

The man in the black coat stared at her, a curious expression on his sagging face. He grunted something that she didn't catch, and took a final, fumbling step. When he lunged, she was already moving, back towards the far end of the car.

She heard him stumble after her, but didn't look back. She knew only that she wished to be as far away from him as possible. She moved from car to car as quickly as she could, staying low so as not to catch the eye of anyone watching from outside.

From behind her, she heard the harsh grunts of her pursuer. When she reached the final car in the line, she stopped. Someone was waiting for her at the other end.

Zamacona was sitting at the rear of the car. He had no weapon that she could see, and his expression was as mild as ever, but something about him stiffened her hackles. She didn't know how he'd known where she'd be, but it was now clear that she'd been led to him. From behind her came a querulous moan.

"Quiet," Zamacona murmured. "Keep watch."

Alessandra didn't turn. She grimaced as the mephitic stink of the man in black washed over her. Zamacona motioned to the seat beside him. "Come. Sit."

She drew her revolver and pointed it at him. She didn't know why he was here, but she doubted it was for her benefit. "I'm afraid I have no time for pleasantries at the moment. I really must be going."

Zamacona stood, and the shadows of the car seemed to gather around him. She took an involuntary step back, nearly colliding with the hunched form of the man in black. "You failed," he said. If he noticed the revolver, he gave no sign.

Stung, Alessandra frowned. "I did not fail. I was not given a chance to succeed. Someone beat me to it."

"Who?"

"How should I know? You must have heard about the set-to? Armed hoodlums, gun battle, does that ring any bells for you?"

"I am aware. That does not exculpate you."

"Seems rather unfair."

Zamacona's smile was cold. "Fair does not come into it. You attempted to leave without fulfilling your end of the bargain. That implies you are guilty."

"It implies nothing save that I was planning to leave. As I assumed you would be doing. The merchandise is gone. No reason to stay."

"You are afraid."

"I am pragmatic."

"As am I. I seek the simplest explanation in all things." Zamacona studied her the way a snake studied a mouse. As if trying to decide whether to eat her now or save her for later. "Our bargain still holds, if you wish it to," he said, finally.

"You still want me to steal the mummy?" she asked, somewhat taken aback.

"We still wish to acquire it, yes. As before, how you do so is up to you."

"But it has already been stolen."

"Yes. You will acquire it for us. That is what we hired you to do." He held up a finger. "But you will also bring us the name of the one who stole it. As recompense for your cowardice. I have utmost faith in your ability to accomplish both."

Alessandra thought for a moment. A good bargain. "Double."

Zamacona frowned. "Double?"

"Double what you are paying me. For the added difficulty."

Zamacona was silent for a moment. "And if I say no?"

"Then I may as well cut my losses and get on the next train to Boston."

"Then I will kill you here and now."

The way he said it brought her up short. "Given that I am the one with the gun, you might find that difficult to accomplish." She tapped the trigger, considering. "Perhaps I should shoot you now and claim self-defense. It might save me trouble later."

"You won't."

"How do you know?"

"As I said before, I know a good deal about you. You are a thief – not a killer. After all, you did not shoot poor Yabuatl when you had the chance." He gestured to the man in black. She glanced back at the hunched figure. When she turned back, Zamacona was almost on top of her. He'd moved so swiftly it had barely registered.

For a moment, he seemed… larger. As if he somehow filled the space around him. In that instant, he was a giant – towering, black-eyed, with teeth like diamonds. His fingers flexed, as if in anticipation of wrapping themselves about something and *squeezing.* "You will not be allowed to leave until we are satisfied in this matter. So far, however, I am disappointed with your service."

She took another step back, pressing up against the wall of the car. Zamacona approached. "If it were up to me, I would take you in my jaws and grind your bones to powder." Before she knew it, his hands had thumped against the wall to either side of her head. Her pistol was pressed against his chest, but something prevented her from pulling the trigger. She could smell him now. Not just his cologne, but something else – a whiff of rot beneath the flowery scent, like the rank stink of his servant.

His eyes seemed to swell, filling her vision so that she could not look away from them – away from what was within them... stars and things that were not stars. The irises grew and split; one became two, two became four, and four – an infinity. She felt cold, as if she'd been doused in an icy river. His mouth opened, jaws distending. His teeth – God, *his teeth...*

"To... powder," he said again.

And then, he was standing across the car, his coat across his arm and his hat in his hand. He smiled politely. She found herself trembling, her pistol shaking in her hand. Her stomach twisted in on itself. "What...?" she began.

"Your terms are acceptable. We will be in touch. I wish you luck."

He departed, with barely a sound. One moment there, gone the next. The man in black was gone as well. Alessandra slid down the wall to the floor. The pistol slipped from her fingers. It was only luck that prevented it from going off. She stared at the far end of the car, trying to process what had just happened.

"Mesmerism," she murmured. The word was a comfort, if only a small one. Zamacona was a Svengali of some sort. That was the obvious answer. She'd met men like that before. Tricksters and fakirs, plying the gullible with sleight of hand.

He'd caught her off-guard. That was all. Shaken, she picked up the pistol and cracked it open. She checked the cylinder and snapped it back together. Next time, she would shoot first. And damn the consequences.

But until then – double her usual fee. The thought was tempting. Too tempting to resist. She needed money, and here was a lot of it. All she had to do was steal something that had already been stolen. "Easy enough," she murmured. But first things first. She had to avoid the police. She eased open the doors and peered out. There was no sign of her pursuers. She slid her pistol back into her valise and dropped to the ground.

As she did so, she heard the distinctive cock of a .45 automatic. She froze.

"Going somewhere, countess?" Whitlock said. She turned and looked into the barrel of the pistol he held aimed at her. He had a look on his face that said he wouldn't hesitate to shoot. "I'd hate to think that I might've scared you off."

"Somehow, I doubt that." She raised her hands slowly, so that there could be no mistaking her surrender for anything else. "You seem the sort of man who enjoys frightening women. At least from our few encounters to date."

He frowned. "Now, now… no need for rudeness. Drop your bag." He turned towards the car. "Who else was in there with you? An accomplice?"

"Decidedly not."

"We'll see about that. In the meantime, get your hands up."

"They are up."

"Higher, then." He glanced back the way he'd come. "Muldoon – I've got her," he called out. "Over here!" He turned back quickly. "Don't get any funny ideas."

"I would not dream of it."

He drew closer, grinning slightly. "I bet you thought you were clever, leaving your bags in the room like that. Oldest trick in the book."

"And yet, I almost made it."

His grin faded. "Yeah. Maybe you're luckier than you seem."

"Obviously not." She looked around as blue uniforms spilled into sight, including Muldoon. He looked at her, and then at Whitlock.

"What about the other one?" Whitlock asked. "Anyone see him?"

"What other one?" Muldoon asked.

"The little guy, in the black coat. Where'd he go?"

"I was only looking for her," Muldoon said.

"Who can blame you?" one of the cops murmured, eliciting laughter from his fellows.

Muldoon ignored his fellow officers. He had a pair of handcuffs in his hand as he approached Alessandra. "You'll be coming along peacefully, I hope, miss."

"Countess," Alessandra corrected, gently.

"Countess, then." Muldoon was the perfect gentleman, as he searched her and then handcuffed her. Whitlock looked as if he wished her arrest was a bit rougher, but he said nothing as he holstered his weapon. "All right, boys, it's done," Muldoon went on. He looked at Whitlock. "I hope you got a permit for that cannon."

Whitlock, looking through her valise, grunted. "She's got a gun in here," he said, a moment later. He looked up at her, grinning sharply. "What about you, countess? You got a permit for this pea-shooter?"

"Of course. I am a law-abiding citizen."

Whitlock laughed sharply. "I bet." He looked at Muldoon

expectantly. "I told you she was running," he said, with evident satisfaction.

Muldoon nodded. "So you did." He looked at Alessandra. "Why did you run?"

"I was not running. I was merely going on a daytrip to Kingsport."

"Via Boston?" Whitlock said.

"A mistake by the ticket office," she said, blandly. The lie was frivolous, and easy to disprove. But it clearly annoyed Whitlock, and that made it worth doing. "I shall take it up with the railway, upon my release."

"You aren't getting released, not if I have anything to say about it."

"Thankfully, you do not." She looked at Muldoon and held up her hands. "There is no need for these. I will come peacefully."

"Didn't seem so peaceful when you were clocking me with that bag of yours."

"You startled me. Under normal circumstances, I am always happy to help the police in their inquiries."

Muldoon studied her for long moments. Then, ignoring Whitlock's protests, he removed the handcuffs. "Don't make me regret this," he said.

"I would not dream of it," she lied.

CHAPTER TWELVE
Interrogation

Officer Muldoon showed her into the interrogation room and closed the door behind them. He took up a spot in the corner, leaning against the wall. "Sit," he said. Alessandra did.

Abner Whitlock sat across from her, looking vaguely out of place in the grey concrete square. Perhaps it was the telltale stains on the walls and the marks on the wooden chairs and table, contrasted with his clean suit and open face.

They'd left her in a holding cell most of the day. Outside, the afternoon was giving way to dusk. Her valise had been confiscated, as well as its contents. She had no doubt that Whitlock had had a good look through them. She was thankful she'd left anything potentially incriminating hidden in her abandoned luggage.

The station was downtown, not far from the Independence. An imposing red-brick building, it had been built on a slight rise, as if it were the modern descendant of a medieval motte and bailey. It was smaller than she imagined, and there were only a few officers in the bullpen. Two different types of uniform were on display, though she could not say why that might be. When she asked Muldoon, he'd ignored the question.

"Countess Alessandra Zorzi," Whitlock said, after a moment. A large envelope sat in front of him. Through the open flap, she could make out the saw-tooth ridges of several photographs, as well as the unmistakable scrawl of a French police report.

"Mr Whitlock," she said, smiling politely. He'd have to do better than a report with her name on it if he wanted to startle her. "Fancy seeing you again, and so soon."

"Yeah." He began pulling out the envelope's contents and spreading them across the table. "Your friends made quite a mess at the exhibition."

"Not my friends, I assure you."

"You can stuff your assurances in a sack." He glared at her. "It was pure happenstance that I recognized you when I saw you on the train. Luckily, the local offices of my firm were open. I had this file on the overnight from Boston a few hours after I arrived."

"I'm flattered."

Whitlock sat back. "Don't be. I'd make the same effort for any criminal."

"Except that I am not a criminal."

"Then why were you trying to skip town?"

"I told you, I was going on a daytrip."

"A likely story. You're a thief and thieves run. That's what they do."

She frowned and tapped her lips with a finger. "Is that slander – or libel? I forget."

"Neither. I assume you didn't bother with an alias this time around because you thought no one in Massachusetts would recognize your real name." He pulled out several papers. "Countess Alessandra Zorzi, born 1901, in Venice to Count Ferro Zorzi and his wife, Beatrice. You have two sisters, both married. Zorzi, of course, is not your actual name, nor are your parents actual aristocrats."

"We are now," she said. "May I smoke?"

"I'd rather you didn't. Filthy habit." He fixed her with a calculating stare. "Ferro was a gambler – and a good one – while Beatrice was a showgirl…"

"Burlesque dancer," Alessandra corrected, absently. "Also very good. But do go on."

"Sometime around 1900, Ferro manages to con some dissolute nobleman out of his lands and title, takes them as his own, and spends the next decade pretending to be someone he's not." Whitlock smiled. "Like father, like daughter."

"It was mother's idea, actually." Alessandra returned his smile with interest. "And there's no crime in purchasing a title. Plenty of your fellow countrymen are even now strip-mining Europe for every castle and coat of arms to be had."

Whitlock shook his head. "Only there are no lands to go with the title, are there? No money, either."

"The title is the money, and lands are a dreadful bore." Specifically, there was money to be had attending the parties of the great and mighty as a decorative noble. Every newmade tycoon wanted the sheen of respectability that came with titled friends and acquaintances. Americans, mostly, but the English had a great love of royalty. Not so much the French.

"Which is why you turned to burglary. Specifically, art theft."

"I'm sure I have no idea what you're talking about." That hadn't been the reason, but she saw no need to illuminate him. In truth, crime was in the blood. Her father had been a thief, and her mother. Her grandparents too. She was simply following in their footsteps.

"That's OK, I'm not finished yet." Whitlock pulled more documentation out of the envelope. Alessandra was beginning to get the feeling that he was enjoying himself. A bit of revenge, perhaps, for her earlier rudeness – or maybe to compensate for the fact that she'd saved his life. She was beginning to regret that last one. "I've got reports here from the police in Paris, London, Vienna, Vyones, Marrakesh – a dozen others." He pulled out another sheaf of papers. "I've got statements as well, from the Comte d'Erlette among others. You remember him?" He gave her an expectant look.

"I can't say that I do." She was careful not to let any surprise show on her face. Someone had been busy. She knew the comte had a long reach, but this was unexpected.

"Well, he remembers you. And he offered to send someone over here to take you off our hands, didn't he, Muldoon?"

"That he did," Muldoon said, nodding slowly. He looked like he meant it. Or maybe he was just good at pretending. Either way, she felt a sudden unease – the thought of finding herself in the hands of the comte wasn't a pleasant one – and decided to go on the attack.

"Our hands," Alessandra repeated. "Pardon my ignorance but are insurance investigators considered law enforcement in this country?"

Muldoon coughed, and Whitlock fell silent. Alessandra smiled and leaned forward. "If any of this is true, if I am this person you think me to be – do you truly believe I would be so easy to frighten? Anyone can stuff papers into an envelope. Anyone can learn a few names. Do you have evidence?"

The two men traded looks. Muldoon was uncomfortable. Alessandra had him pegged as impressionable and ambitious. Whitlock was ambitious as well, but in a different way. He reminded her of a hound that had caught a scent and was determined to follow it to the bitter end. She knew his type – had dealt with them before. Troublesome, even if discouraged early and often. She sat back and looked at Muldoon.

"Officer, am I to understand I was asked here under false pretenses?"

Muldoon frowned. "No, I asked you here to help with the investigation. And that's what you're doing." He sat on the edge of the table. "What do you remember about the robbery?" Whitlock made to interject, but Muldoon waved him to silence.

"Nothing much, I am afraid. It was quite frightening."

Whitlock snorted. "You didn't seem frightened when you picked up that Chicago Typewriter. Seemed like you weren't bothered at all."

She frowned. "I do not recall picking up a typewriter."

"The Thompson," Muldoon clarified, with another warning glance at Whitlock.

"Ah yes, when I saved Mr Whitlock's life!"

Whitlock glowered at her, but said nothing. Muldoon nodded. "Yeah, you did. Which buys you a bit of consideration, but only so much. That's why I'm willing to give you the benefit of the doubt. Mr Whitlock says you're a thief. But I don't see how you could have been involved in this."

"Because I was not." She tilted her chin to look up at him. "When do I get a lawyer?"

"Only Americans get lawyers," Whitlock said. "You're not American. No lawyer."

"Surely that cannot be right."

"You don't need a lawyer," Muldoon said. "As I said, you're not under arrest. If you were, you'd be talking to Detective Harden instead of a beat cop. You're a witness: I'm taking your statement."

"Then I am free to leave?"

"If you want."

Alessandra considered Muldoon. He was clearly tenacious, as well as ambitious. She had no doubt he would make it a point to make her life difficult if he thought she had something to hide. It might be best to go along with this farce, at least until they decided they were finished with her. "As I said at the train station, I am happy to answer questions."

Muldoon smiled. "I thought you might say that. So after you picked up the Thompson…"

"And saved Mr Whitlock."

He glanced at Whitlock, who flushed. "And saved him, what do you recall?"

"I fired and then sought shelter when they started shooting back."

"Do you remember anything else? Did they use each other's names?"

"Not that I recall," she lied. "I was much too distracted to pay attention to such things. All that flying glass, you understand."

Muldoon nodded sympathetically. "So why didn't you stick around afterwards?"

"I was afraid, as I said. Not least of Mr Whitlock here."

"Me?" Whitlock sounded insulted.

"The way he confronted me at the exhibition. Very aggressive. Very distressing. And then the robbery – I felt faint. I needed to lie down."

"Don't tell me you're buying this," Whitlock said, looking at Muldoon.

"I ain't buying nothing," the young officer said. "But I'm keeping an open mind." He stood. "That's all you remember?"

"I would tell you if I knew." She put on a mournful expression. "It doesn't seem I'm going to be of much help, I'm afraid. Something else might come to me in a few days, but right now… eh." She gave a shrug. "May I leave?"

"No," Whitlock said.

"Yes," Muldoon countered. He glared at the insurance investigator and opened the door. "I think we're done here anyway. But don't leave town."

"I would not dream of it."

Muldoon closed the door firmly behind her. Despite this, she could hear them arguing. She smiled and threaded her way through the bullpen. She felt eyes on her as she went, and wondered how long it would take Whitlock to convince them to issue a warrant for her arrest. Not long, perhaps. He struck her as a determined sort of fellow.

His interest complicated matters. The last thing she needed was that sort of attention. She collected her belongings from a bored-looking clerk, her ears open as officers spoke to one another. Nothing of interest caught her attention, but it was clear that a good deal of effort was being put towards the robbery.

It was getting dark when she finally exited the building. Surprisingly, Pepper was waiting for her, sitting on the steps. "There you are," the cabbie said. She rose and stretched. "I thought for sure they were taking you to the hoosegow."

"The what?" Alessandra looked up as the large white globes to either side of the steps lit up. Each was emblazoned with the word "POLICE". Their soft radiance cast back the growing shadows, for which she was grateful.

"The slammer. The concrete resort." Pepper gesticulated meaningfully. "Prison."

"Ah. No. They merely wished to question me. Why are you here?"

"I told you I was going to wait. I saw them arrive, figured they were there for you, and followed them. I figured you'd need a ride back to the hotel."

Alessandra smiled gratefully. "Thank you."

"Don't thank me yet. I kept the meter running." She opened the door of the cab and Alessandra slid inside. "Where to?"

"The hotel."

"Not the station?"

"No. I missed my train." Alessandra sat back. "Have you noticed a little fellow in a black coat following you?"

"A what?"

"Never mind. Do you know Officer Muldoon?"

"Tommy?" Pepper said, as she guided the cab into traffic. "Yeah, a bit. He gets around, talks to folks. Nice guy, for a cop."

"Is he aware of your…?" Alessandra began. Pepper laughed.

"Him? Nah. He's not what you'd call observant."

Alessandra raised an eyebrow at that. "But dedicated? A good policeman?"

"Oh yeah. Probably better than this town deserves."

"That is unfortunate." Alessandra sat back. "I believe he thinks me to be responsible for what occurred at the exhibition. Or at least involved, somehow."

"Why the hell would he think that?"

"I am sure I have no idea."

Pepper snorted. "Lady, I know a porky when I hear one."

Alessandra raised an eyebrow. "A… porky?"

"A fib, a lie, a confabulation. What are you, some kind of cop? Is that why you're here? Someone snatch that mummy and replace it with a fake or something?" Pepper sounded excited at the prospect. "Oh, wait, I know! There's stolen jewels inside it, right?"

"No, and I am certainly not a police officer." Alessandra was slightly insulted by the assumption. "I am a thief, not a policeman."

Pepper was silent a moment. Then she exploded. "That explains why you were in such a damn hurry to get out of here. I knew it. I didn't know what I knew, but I knew it."

"What did you know?"

"That you're a criminal."

"A moment ago you were certain I was a policeman."

"Crooks and cops are basically the same thing!" Pepper spat. "Am I going to the pokey just for driving you around?"

"I doubt it." She patted Pepper on the shoulder. "Do not worry. I will let you know ahead of time if I am planning on it."

Pepper shook her head. "Thanks. I think."

Alessandra chuckled. "You are welcome."

Pepper was silent for a time. But her curiosity got the better of her eventually. "So, if you're a thief, did you come to steal that mummy? Is that why they're up your nose about it?"

"Whether I was or not, the mummy is gone."

"I bet we could find it."

"We?"

"Well, you."

"And pray tell, how might we do that?"

"I know guys. Guys who know the sorts of guys who steal mummies."

Alessandra snorted. "Is that a common occurrence in Arkham, then?"

"Lady, that ain't the weirdest thing that happened this week."

Somewhat taken aback, Alessandra said, "These guys... are they the sort who keep abreast of local illicit activities?"

"You mean, are they criminals?"

"Yes."

"Then yeah, they're criminals. Strictly small fry, but they pay attention."

"Excellent." She smiled. "I think I will require an introduction."

CHAPTER THIRTEEN
Planning

"So what's the plan?" Pepper asked, scraping sauce off her plate with a scrap of bread. The hotel restaurant was all but empty. It was too early for dinner, and too late for lunch. The dining room was ornate but curiously stark, with an air of the unfinished. The tables were too widely spaced and the ceiling too high.

Alessandra poked at her chicken. It tasted off somehow. She considered sending it back, but decided not to make a scene. Instead she pushed her plate aside. "The plan is to track down our mummy-thieves. But more important is to find the mummy."

"Doesn't one lead to the other?"

"Not always."

"Oh," Pepper said, in understanding. "You think they were working for somebody else. That makes sense. The local mooks wouldn't go to the trouble of robbing that place, especially in the middle of the day, unless somebody told them to."

Alessandra nodded, pleased by Pepper's quick realization. "Yes. They were almost certainly working for someone else and it is them I need to find."

Pepper frowned as something else occurred to her. "What about that Zamacona guy? What's he think about all of this?"

Alessandra rubbed her throat, suddenly recalling the tightness of Zamacona's grip. "He was… willing to renegotiate the terms of our original contract."

Pepper studied her. "Yeah? Generous of him," she said, doubtfully.

"Very." Alessandra took a sip of water from her glass. It had an odd gritty taste. "But that generosity comes with an implied deadline. The quicker we find our quarry, the better." She was no longer certain just what sort of man Zamacona was, besides dangerous. She felt that so long as their bargain held, that danger was kept safely at bay. But there was no telling how long it would hold.

Thankfully, she had always been a quick thinker. She had formulated the rudiments of a strategy during the drive back to the hotel. Pepper had been amenable to an early dinner, and the young woman had practically inhaled a plate of something vaguely Italian.

"One of them was hurt. Not badly, but he will need a doctor." She looked at Pepper. "Where do such men go for medical treatment in this town? Not to the hospital, I think."

Pepper considered this, licking sauce off her fingers. "There's a guy in Riverside. Used to be a horse-doctor, I think. He's a drunk, but he can pull a bullet out of a guy easy enough."

"You know him?"

Pepper shrugged. "Not really. Kind of. Maybe."

Amused, Alessandra raised an eyebrow. "Have you ever been to him yourself?"

"I've been in a couple of scrapes."

"Have you now?"

"It ain't easy being a cabbie in this town." Pepper put her cap back on. "Want me to take you to see him?"

"No. It is likely the police have already spoken to him. They know one of the robbers was wounded. What they do not know are the names of the robbers. But I do. Just like I know they will go to ground."

"Lot of heat on 'em. Maybe they'll just leave town."

Alessandra shook her head. "No. The police will be watching. What I need is to speak to someone who knows where they might go to hide. Or anything about them at all."

Pepper nodded. "That I can do. I know a guy who knows a guy. I should be able to catch him tomorrow morning."

"Good. Talk to them, and see if they will talk to me." Alessandra sat back. "In the meantime, I am going to go get some sleep." She rose. Pepper frowned.

"What about me?"

"I would suggest you get some sleep as well."

Alessandra paid the check and left. Milo was nowhere in sight as she entered the lobby, but a scrum of guests laid siege to the front desk, looking to check-out. She recognized some of them from the exhibition and laughed softly. With the mummy gone, the vultures were seeking other prey – much like herself. She wondered if Visser was planning to up stakes as well. She didn't see him in the crowd. If he was still in town, he might be of some help to her. But that was for later.

For now, she wanted only to sleep. The day had been an exciting one. She paused, looking out through the entrance. Arkham seemed less lovely at night. Not ugly, but… uncertain. A thick mist layered the square across the street, all but hiding it from sight. The streetlights sputtered softly, their radiance dimmed and stretched.

Something about the scene unsettled her, and she hurried towards the stairs. She was not a believer in fate. But if she was, today would have been full of portents. The police weren't the only ones who had an interest in her continued presence in Arkham. More, something about the robbery had begun to niggle at her. Something was off about it, more than just apparent sloppiness.

These thoughts ran through her mind as she entered the stairwell. It was enclosed on all sides, lit by electric bulbs mounted in ornamental stanchions. As the door to the stairwell closed behind her, she felt an instant of what could only have been vertigo. The steps, swaddled in garish oxblood carpet, rippled before her eyes, and the lights flared, flickered and dimmed. She blinked, trying to restore normalcy.

Instead, the lights began to go out. One by one, the darkness descending towards her step by step. Her back was pressed to the door before she knew it, her heart straining in her chest. It was coming faster now. She could hear the bulbs popping, one after the next. She felt sick – shaky. Cold.

A sound rose up out of the dark. Gentle, but insistent. Like the trickling of water, but magnified. Coming from everywhere around her, all at once. She could see the hint of movement between the buildings, like serpents readying themselves to strike. Something was coming, and it was coming for her. She could feel it, even if she couldn't name it.

Tsathoggua en y'n an ya phtaggn N'kai.

It was at once a voice, and not. Like a gust of wind, carrying words like leaves. Like a memory, long buried. She closed her eyes and tried to push back the fear. It gnawed at the edges of her composure like rats. It would take her, if she let it. She began to count down from one hundred. An old trick, taught to her by her mother. Thankfully, it still worked. Her heartrate decreased around the thirty mark, and she opened her eyes. The lights were back – if they had ever gone out in the first place.

She blinked, uncertain. She was not prone to hallucinations or fits of imagination. Perhaps there had really been something wrong with her meal. She wondered if it were possible that she'd gotten food poisoning on top of everything else.

Perhaps fate was trying to tell her something.

Gomes groaned again, for the twentieth time in as many minutes. His arm hurt like blazes and his partners weren't being what he'd call considerate. Instead, they were treating him as if it had been his fault things had gone wrong. He looked down at the wound – a scrape, really – and cursed.

"Jesus, would you knock it off, Gomes? Just for five minutes, huh?" Phipps said from where he sat, playing cards with Jodorowsky. The three of them were holed up in a warehouse near the river. It stank of fish and spilled diesel, but it was quiet. There was no one around, especially this time of night.

Gomes shot a glare at the other man. "Shut up, Phipps. It hurts." He sat next to a window overlooking the street. Through the grimy glass, he could see nothing but mist, blotting out the nearby buildings. He rubbed his arm and spat.

He hated the mist and he hated Arkham. This town had been nothing but trouble for him since he'd arrived. He was a big city sort of guy. Arkham didn't have enough to keep him occupied. But McTyre disagreed, and so did the O'Bannions. They insisted on holding onto real estate in this crummy little town, even when it made no sense.

As far as Gomes was concerned, they could have it. He was

meant for better things. He groaned again as a quivering throb of pain ran through his arm. Phipps sighed. "It's a goddamn scratch. Stop complaining."

"You'd be complaining too if some bitch shot you."

Phipps tossed his cards onto the overturned crate they were using as a table. "Then you should have returned the favor instead of whining about it."

"You're the one who stopped me!" Gomes protested. He hated Phipps almost as much as he hated Arkham. Phipps thought he was in charge because he'd been the one to find the job. But Gomes had been the one who'd arranged everything. It had been Gomes who'd gone and met with the contact. What had Phipps done, really?

"Because you were wasting time." Phipps reached over and took Jodorowsky's cards from him and added them to the pile. He shuffled them. "Pulanski was down and we had to go. I didn't hear you arguing with me."

"When do we get out of here?" Jodorowsky asked nervously. "The cops are probably crawling all over this part of town."

"Soon as the doc shows and we get Gomes patched up. You're the one who called him. When's he getting here?"

"He said fifteen minutes, but I could tell he'd been hitting the sauce," Jodorowsky said apologetically. "Might be more like twenty. Or never."

Gomes perked up and turned from the window. "You sent for that goddamn horse-doctor, didn't you?" he said accusingly. "I need a real doctor, not a veterinarian."

"Then go to the hospital," Phipps said, dealing himself and Jodorowsky new hands of cards. "Be my guest. You'd be doing me a favor."

"You'd like that, wouldn't you? Love to see the cops pick me up.

More money for you and Jodorowsky." Gomes laughed, a high, ugly sound. "No chance."

"Maybe you're not as stupid as you look."

"Why didn't you get the guy the O'Bannions use?" Gomes demanded. "He's pulled slugs out of plenty of men and he knows how to keep his mouth shut."

Phipps looked at his cards. "Because what happens when McTyre asks him why he had to patch you up? You think he's going to hold out on the Wolf?"

Gomes swallowed. He hadn't thought of that. He sat back. "And the vet will, huh?"

"McTyre won't ask the vet, because he don't know about him."

"Think he'll ask about Pulanski?" Jodorowsky asked, hesitantly. Phipps paused. Gomes laughed again.

"Didn't think about that, did you?" he said, nastily. Phipps looked at him.

"Did you?"

Gomes looked away. "Don't matter anyway. Soon as we get our money, McTyre ain't our problem no more." He was looking forward to getting out of Massachusetts. Maybe somewhere out west. Wilma had family out there, or so she claimed.

He smiled, thinking of her. She was a good dame. A waitress at the Tick-Tock Club, but he didn't hold that against her. Girl like her had to take what jobs were available. She was almost as eager to leave as Gomes himself, and had been badgering him to take her to California for months.

Yeah. That was the ticket. Sun and sand and surf. No clammy fog rolling in off a stretch of black river. No Arkham. He touched his arm again and bit back a groan. Thoughts of Wilma vanished, replaced by another woman. The one who'd clipped him, and with his own gun to boot.

He wished he'd shot her when he'd had the chance. He wondered who she was. A cop, maybe? He'd heard there were lady-cops now, in some places. But he didn't think so. She'd been dressed too nice–

The sound of something heavy falling over brought him to his feet. He had his pistol out a moment later. So did the others. "You hear that?" Gomes asked.

"It came from the back," Phipps said. "Jodorowsky – check it out."

"You check it out," Jodorowsky said.

"I'll check it out," Gomes snapped. Whatever it was, it would take his mind off his arm. Phipps stopped him.

"No. You sit and wait for the doc. Jodorowsky – go."

When Phipps used that tone, people listened. Jodorowsky went. The sound was coming from where they'd stashed the truck. They'd left the car a block from the job, and traded up for a battered delivery truck that Pulanski had swiped from somewhere on Northside. The truck sat near the delivery doors of the warehouse, covered in a tarp. The box, and its grisly contents, sat in the back. Or they had.

"What is it?" Phipps called out.

"The damn box fell off the truck." Jodorowsky's voice floated back to them out of the dark canyon of stacked crates.

Phipps looked at Gomes. "Must have overbalanced when we parked and we just didn't notice."

"I tightened those straps myself," Gomes protested.

Phipps didn't reply. "What about the… you know what?"

"Top's open. Looks like it fell out. But I don't…"

There was a soft sound, like papers rustling. Then a slightly louder one. An ugly, cracking, ripping sound. Jodorowsky fell silent, and did not respond when Phipps called out again. Gomes picked up a flashlight and turned it on. He looked at Phipps. "You first."

Phipps frowned but started towards the truck. They found Jodorowsky soon enough, at the end of a trail of blood spatter. He was sprawled on the floor next to the huddled form of the mummy, staring up into the dark, his mouth – and his throat gone. Something had ripped open his jugular and done it so quickly and forcefully that he hadn't had a chance to scream. Phipps snatched the light from Gomes' hand and played it across the mummy.

"It has blood on its hands," Gomes said, softly. Then, "It was curled up before."

"Yeah," Phipps said, absently. "The bindings on its arms and legs came loose. He must have… fallen on top of it or something. An accident." Gomes could tell he didn't believe a word of it. "Help me get it back in the box."

"I ain't touching that thing. I'll keep watch."

"For what?"

Gomes didn't reply, and Phipps didn't push it. Gomes was glad, because he didn't really have an answer. He was certain he'd tightened the straps on the back of the truck holding the box in place. It couldn't have come loose… unless something had caused it to move. He let his light fall on the black mask that enclosed the dead thing's skull. For a moment, he thought he saw something move within the sockets of its eyes.

But he told himself it was only a shadow.

CHAPTER FOURTEEN
Dreams

Pepper strolled through the garage, her hands in her pockets. The close air stank of exhaust fumes and stale coffee. For Pepper, it was a homey sort of smell and always had been. It reminded her of her father and better days.

It was early. The sun was barely up, but the garage was already full of noise. She kept one eye on the dispatch offices as she navigated the crowded confines. She didn't want the head dispatcher, De Palma, spotting her. He might start asking questions she didn't feel much like answering.

The garage housed half a dozen cabs at any one time, plus another handful of alternates that were mostly used for spare parts. There were nearly twice as many drivers as there were hacks, and many of them sat around all day, waiting for a chance at a fare. A lot of the drivers shared cabs – one guy on day shift, one guy on night shift. And some of the guys, well, they were on the special shift, as De Palma liked to call it.

Mostly, the special shift smuggled booze from the docks or the railyard into town. De Palma, greedy little troll that he was, had worked out a deal with the O'Bannions to carry their bootleg liquor wherever it needed to go, safely hidden in his cabs. It worked out well for both parties. While the other syndicates brewed their booze local, the O'Bannions preferred a bit of distance between supply and demand. And De Palma was only too happy to play smuggler – it wasn't him taking the risks, after all.

If any driver got caught by the cops, well, he was on his own. The guys knew better than to complain. De Palma owned their cabs, and could make sure they lost their licenses if anyone gave him any guff.

Pepper had made late runs herself, once or twice. It was good money, if you weren't averse to a bit of risk. De Palma kept most of it for himself, but even he knew better than to skimp when it came to booze.

But it wasn't the sort of thing you wanted to do long term. At least Pepper didn't. She had other ambitions. She wasn't sure what they were just yet, but driving a cab for the rest of her life wasn't one of them. She thought maybe the countess – Alessandra – might be her ticket out of Arkham. But only if she played it smart. That meant helping Alessandra, even though she was a criminal.

Then, to Pepper's way of thinking, there were criminals – and then there were *criminals*. De Palma might be the former, but Alessandra was definitely the latter. She went places, did things, had money… the whole racket. There were worse things to aspire to.

She spotted the face she was looking for bent beneath the open hood of one of the cabs. Iggy Azaria was the garage's mechanic. He wasn't particularly good at fixing automobiles, but he was cheap.

She picked up a wrench from off a nearby workbench and gave the side of the cab a swat. Iggy straightened with a yelp, nearly banging his head. "Jesus Christ, Pepper, what'd you go and do that for?" he demanded.

"Just trying to get your attention," Pepper said, roughening her voice.

"Well, you got it, knucklehead. What do you want?" Iggy paused and looked around. "De Palma hasn't seen you, has he? He was looking for you."

"No, and he won't see me either, if you give me a hand."

"With what?"

"I need a line on a guy."

"A guy?" Iggy frowned. "Any guy in particular?"

"Vigil."

Iggy grunted. "Why?"

"Mind your business, that's why. He still hangs his shingle at the Roadhouse, right?"

"Yeah." Iggy stood, wiping his hands with a greasy rag. He looked around, scouting for De Palma. "Seriously though, why do you want to talk to a guy like that?"

"I got someone who wants to buy some information off him."

"And you came to me?"

Pepper smirked and leaned against the cab, hands still in her pockets. "Don't be that way, Iggy. I know you know him. I want to set up a meeting."

Iggy's expression turned mulish. "Maybe I know him. Maybe I don't. You still haven't said why I ought to do you this favor."

"You owe me."

"Since when?"

Pepper studied him. "Since I took that fare De Palma gave you last week. You know the one I mean." She mimed taking a drink. Iggy blanched.

"I couldn't, Pepper. If the cops had caught me – with my record..."

Pepper waved the excuses aside. "Yeah, yeah. You owe me. So do this little thing for me and we'll be even."

Iggy was silent for a moment. Then, "You just want me to set it up?"

"I'll do the rest," Pepper said.

Iggy's frown deepened. "I hope you know what you're doing, kid."

"That means you'll do it?"

"Doesn't seem like I got a choice," Iggy said. "When?"

"Tonight."

"I'll make a call. If he's willing to talk to you..." He paused and looked her up and down. "You got money, I hope."

"I don't, but the person who wants the meeting does."

"So long as one of you does," Iggy said. He peered at Pepper. "Tonight then. At Hibb's place. But don't tell no one I'm involved, kid."

"Wouldn't dream of it, Iggy. And hey – thanks."

"Yeah, don't thank me yet." Iggy laughed and punched Pepper in the arm. "You're a good kid, you know that?"

Rubbing her arm, Pepper turned away, grinning in satisfaction. "I'm the best, Iggy, and don't you forget it."

Shapes moved in the mist. They staggered ever closer as she tried desperately to throw the ambulance into gear. Fear thrummed through her like electricity, and the smell of smoke and death was thick on the air. She could hear the thunder of distant guns, or perhaps the tread of some unseen colossus. The ground shook as the ambulance's engine whined beneath her frantic attempts to get it moving.

The shapes lurched into view. At first, she thought they were Germans, their faces hidden behind insectile gas masks. But they moved like broken things, whirling and twitching as they drew near. She reached for her pistol, but found that she could not move. Something pinned her in place. Something – no. *Someone*.

"I will grind your bones to… powder," Zamacona hissed in her ear. It was his hand that held her. His strength was greater than she'd imagined. His grip tightened, and she felt the bones of her wrist crack and splinter. She screamed – or tried to. The guns thundered, only now they didn't sound like guns at all but drums.

The canvas top of the ambulance rolled back as if caught in a great wind, and she felt something clawing at her. She could not see Zamacona, but she knew he was there somewhere. Holding her. Trapping her. She tried to struggle, but could not free herself. The sound of drums grew louder and the sky overhead was black and full of cold stars. There was light behind her now, but it was wrong somehow. The wrong color, the wrong smell. It was all wrong. This was not Flanders, but somewhere else.

The twitching shapes drew closer. The gas masks were gone now, replaced by chiropteran masks of onyx and gold. Before she could fully process this, the shapes began to stretch towards one another and blend, becoming one.

She thrashed in Zamacona's grip as it inexorably tightened about her. Bones cracked and skin tore. She felt something give in her chest. She could hear a new sound, like rushing water – only it wasn't flowing down, but up.

The darkness rippled like a curtain. Shadows swam before her eyes and there were sounds in her head. Images like words, but no words she could possibly understand. And yet… understand them she did.

Tsathoggua en y'n an ya phtaggn N'kai.

The darkness unfurled and something emerged.

Something hungry.

Alessandra awoke with a start, breath rasping, heart thudding. She felt as if she'd run a marathon. Sweat beaded on her face and had turned her hair into ratty tangles. She threw back the duvet, suddenly conscious of a queasy pressure in her gut.

She stumbled out of bed and into the bathroom. Her gorge rose and thrashed like a wild animal as she fumbled on the lights. She leaned over the sink, coughing. Something moved in her stomach – last night's dinner, perhaps.

She coughed and spat as whatever it was wriggled in her throat, almost as if it were trying to escape. She remembered her dream, the darkness pouring into her, filling her, and it only added to her queasiness.

Something slipped from between her lips. It had the slimy consistency of phlegm, but it was the color of pitch. It splattered around the basin drain, like oil on snow. She stared at it, panting slightly. Her throat burned. As she watched, it seemed to writhe towards the drain, every droplet seeking the exit. Quickly, she turned on the faucet and washed it away. She splashed water on her face and gargled, trying to clear the taste of it from her mouth.

She caught a glimpse of herself in the mirror. For a moment, her eyes looked black. Not dark, but black. The color of the shadows in her dreams. She blinked, and they were back to normal. Not that they had changed.

"Ridiculous," she muttered. She stumbled out into her room, feeling exhausted. It was early. Far too early to be awake, she thought. But something told her she wouldn't be able to go back to sleep.

Alessandra ran her hands through her hair. She felt sweaty – grimy. Unclean. She wanted a bath, but settled for a shower. The silver nozzle over the bathtub gave forth a shuddering spray of lukewarm water. It poured over her, and she felt a chill that had nothing to do with the temperature. She thought of the black stuff squirming towards the drain. Thought of it coming out of her, and then, finally, the mummy. Staring at her with empty eyes. Black eyes. She scrubbed at her face.

Had it actually had eyes at all? Sometimes they did, she knew. Things dried to hard, tiny marbles, lingering beneath leathery lids. But these hadn't been like that. These had shone like black opals, shiny and wet. And then something…

She bent double, vomiting up water and chicken. Nothing black in it now, just the faint yellowish ochre of digestive juices. The falling water urged it away and out of sight. She feared it might clog the drain, but the water continued to fall and gurgle.

She finished her ablutions, and got out, wrapping herself in a towel. The room was warm, but she was cold. She dried herself quickly, and pulled on a dressing gown. After a moment's consideration, she dropped her pistol into the gown's pocket. Its weight was a comfort, though she could not say why.

Idly, she went to the window and tugged back the curtain. Sunlight danced across the gambrel rooftops. A new morning in Arkham. The clouds of the previous afternoon were nowhere in sight, and the only evidence of rain were the puddles scattered across Independence Square.

If luck were with her, Pepper would have something for her today. The thieves had not fled, she was certain of that. The police were watching the station and the river, and they'd set up roadblocks around town. If she were them, she would hide the mummy and lay low until she could deliver it safely to her client. Unless, of course, they already had.

Then, what if their client lived outside of Arkham? That was an unpleasant thought. Even now, the mummy might already be out of reach. She doubted Zamacona would react well to that. She shivered. No, he wouldn't be pleased at all.

Keeping her Webley close to hand, she began to dress. Pepper would have something for her. The girl hadn't let her down yet. A name, a place, something. Somewhere to begin.

The sooner, the better.

CHAPTER FIFTEEN
Roadhouse

Whitlock scanned the warehouse and sighed. Even without looking around he could tell that whoever had been here was gone. The question was, how long ago?

"So they left their car one block over…" he began, his voice echoing in the oppressive silence of the cavernous space. He turned, letting the beam of his flashlight dance across the windows and walls. The place stank of fish, like everywhere else in this part of town.

Muldoon shook his head. "Stolen. Somebody snatched it off a street in Kingsport last week. We think they moved it to a truck."

"And then came here to hole up." Whitlock let his flashlight play across the packing crates of machinery. "Probably so their buddy could get stitched up."

"You mean the one the countess shot to save you?"

Whitlock ignored the comment. "How'd you track them?"

Muldoon smiled. "Easy – we had a description of the truck, and this warehouse hasn't been used in three years. One of the locals owes me a favor, and he gets in touch when he sees something out of the ordinary."

"Got your own spy network, huh? Some of that John Buchan bullshit?"

"You read John Buchan?"

"Only when I need a laugh." Whitlock stopped. "That look like blood to you?"

"Yeah," Muldoon said. He drew his weapon. "Stay back. Let me check it out."

"Feel free," Whitlock said, drawing his own pistol. Muldoon glanced at it.

"So, do all insurance guys pack a piece, or just you?"

"Insurance investigator, and yeah – the smart ones at least. Sometimes people get annoyed when we ask them why they burned down their own warehouse. Speaking of which, three guesses who owns this one."

"I'm not really good at guessing games."

"Matthew Orne."

Muldoon stopped. "How the hell do you know that?"

Whitlock gestured with his flashlight. "All these crates got the name of his shipping company stamped on them. It went under about two years ago, but he still owns all the property and the equipment."

"And you know that because…?"

"Because I do my research. Part of my job is investigating our own clients. Orne's got more money than sense. He's started half a dozen businesses in the past decade and more than half of them have gone belly-up, and recently. Licenses pulled, contracts broken, grievances… someone in this town does not like him."

"Yeah, and I got a good idea who," Muldoon said, starting forward again, sweeping the floor with his flashlight. "Carl Sanford."

"Who's that?"

"High lord and muckety-muck of the Silver Twilight Lodge."

"The whosits?"

Muldoon stopped and cursed softly under his breath. "I'm going to need to call this in." Whitlock peered past him and cursed as well, more loudly.

"No hurry. Whoever he is, he's real dead." Whitlock crouched beside the body, taking in the damage to the jugular with a cool eye. He'd seen worse in the war. Men split open like ripe fruit or seared black by the edge of an artillery strike. Men cut to pieces by razor wire or drowning in two inches of muddy water at the bottom of a trench.

Like a lot of men his age, he'd gone to war thinking it was an adventure. But that eagerness had been knocked out of him real quick. He'd seen the worst the world could throw at a man and come out the other side.

"Don't touch anything," Muldoon said.

"This isn't my first body," Whitlock said. "There was a truck here earlier. Oil stains over there, and patches of dried mud – likely from the wheels." He looked back down at the body. "Recognize him?"

Muldoon nodded. "His name's Jodorowsky. Small time hoodlum. Works for the O'Bannions. Worked, I should say." He stooped and peered at the body. "I can't be certain, but I think he was one of the thieves."

"Funny we should find him here."

"In this warehouse, you mean?"

"Yes. Orne wouldn't be the first man to rob himself for the insurance money," Whitlock said, looking up from the body. "Believe me, it happens more than you'd think."

"You think he's a suspect?"

"No, I think our sticky-fingered countess is behind it. Maybe she's working with – or for – these O'Bannions of yours."

Muldoon turned. "No proof, though."

"We haven't found any proof. That doesn't mean it's not there." Whitlock smiled sourly. "Hell, maybe they're in on it together, her and Orne. You read the files – that's her modus operandi after all… She doesn't steal this junk for herself. She sells it to rich nitwits who like playing with shrunken heads or what not."

Muldoon chewed his lip. "I don't think Chief Nichols would like hearing that theory. He and Orne are pretty tight."

"So we find some proof." Whitlock stood. "Look, we both want the same thing, right? The mummy found and the thanks of a grateful nation. Work with me here."

Muldoon looked away. "You really think she's involved?"

"I think there's a damn good reason she made a run for it. If she didn't steal the thing, she probably knows who did." He looked down at the body. "Hell, she probably knows who did this as well."

"So we watch her," Muldoon said. He scratched his chin. "I think I can get the chief to go for that. If not him, maybe Engels."

"Now you're thinking," Whitlock said. "I already took the liberty of talking to your boss, and he agreed. No need to worry on that score."

"You already talked to him?"

"I thought it might be prudent. Just in case she tries to run for it again." Whitlock looked at Muldoon. "What are you thinking?"

"I'm thinking she didn't seem the type to rip a guy's throat out."

"No, but I don't doubt she'd hire someone who was." Whitlock looked around. "You want to know what I think?"

"I have a feeling you'll tell me anyway," Muldoon said.

Whitlock turned. "I think they had a falling out. Money splits easier two ways than three. And I think there'll be more bodies before we unravel this thing." He shook his head. "These career criminal types always turn on each other. Mark my words."

"Yeah, well, why didn't they just shoot him?"

Whitlock paused. He had no answer for that. It did seem odd. "Crime of opportunity," he said finally. "Or maybe they knew a gunshot would attract attention, even in this part of town. Doesn't matter, does it? They won't get far."

"I suppose," Muldoon said, doubtfully. He looked around, his face pale in the glow of the flashlights. "I don't like this, though."

"Trust me. I've dealt with this kind of thing before. They always slip up." Whitlock watched the shadows twist in the light and smiled. "Always."

She was somewhere dark. Stifling. Confining. Alessandra could feel it closing in about her, like the sides of a sarcophagus. She felt hot and cold all at once, and her body itched terribly, as if she'd been bitten by a swarm of insects. She longed to scratch, but could not move. Could not so much as twitch her withered limbs. She wanted to scream in frustration, but no sound emerged from her dry, puckered mouth.

Withered?

Puckered?

She tried to look – to see herself. But she saw only darkness. Was she blind? No, she could make out the jagged undulations of rock that surrounded her.

She had been buried alive. The thought sent a thrill of horror through her. This was worse than any prison cell. Again, she tried to scream. But the only sound that came out was a distorted croak that could not have been made by a human tongue.

Tsathoggua en y'n an ya phtaggn N'kai.

N'kai.

N'KAI.

Alessandra's eyes snapped open and she gasped, fumbling for her revolver. She recognized the face floating in front of her own before she drew it. Pepper. She was in Pepper's cab. Not… someplace else. Panting slightly, she sat up with a groan.

"Jeez, you OK? You made like you were about to scream." Pepper studied her with open concern. Alessandra pawed at her eyes, trying to wipe away the last vestiges of sleep – of the nightmare. She felt shaky. Angry and scared all at once.

"I am fine. Bad dream." She was dressed in her working clothes, rather than a dress. Men's clothes, men's shoes. Not to disguise herself, really, but because they made it easier to run and climb, and yes, fight, if that became necessary.

It wasn't food poisoning. She couldn't even pretend to believe that now, no matter how much she might wish to. She took a steadying breath, and felt the tension ease from her. She had learned in childhood how to compartmentalize fear, to lock it away until the job was done and she could safely collapse.

This wasn't fear. Not as she knew it. It was like acid, eating away at the walls of her composure. She wanted to be done with this town, with all of it. She ran her fingers through her hair, feeling the sweat that prickled her scalp. "My apologies for drifting off. I did not mean to fall asleep."

"Hey, who am I to judge? I fall asleep at work all the time."

Alessandra paused, and then shook her head, assuming her English had failed her. Rather than ask the obvious question, she said, "Is this the place?" She peered through the rain-streaked window at the former carriage-house. Hibb's Roadhouse had seen better decades, but was still vibrant. Light blazed from the windows, and the faint scrape of a rhythm guitar filtered through the wet air.

"This is it. Roughest patch of ground between here and Boston." Pepper slumped in her seat as another motor car splashed past along the unpaved street. The headlights washed across the cab, momentarily driving back the shadows that filled it. The sudden change from dark to light made Alessandra flinch, and her skin crawled. "You OK?" Pepper asked.

"I am fine," Alessandra said, more sharply than she'd intended. "You may stop asking. How will we know when this guy you know has arrived?"

"Easy. We go look." Pepper opened her door and hopped out. Alessandra followed suit, feeling the urge to stretch as well as the need for a cigarette. She lit one for herself, and for Pepper, without being asked.

A trio of drunks staggered into the street, singing loudly and incomprehensibly. Alessandra watched them weave back and forth in stumbling synchronicity. "I am surprised the police have not closed it down."

"Sheriff Engle wants to. Police chief disagrees." Pepper shrugged, her hands thrust into her coat pockets. "Welcome to Arkham."

Alessandra chuckled and blew a serpentine plume of smoke into the air. She watched it waver and thin, and something about it reminded her of her dreams. Irritated, she dispersed it with a hasty gesture.

She blew smoke into the air again, and it mingled with the evening mist. "I am going in. What was this man's name again?"

"Vigil. Joey Vigil. His friends call him the Rat."

Alessandra paused and looked at her. "What do his enemies call him?"

Pepper blinked. "The... Rat?"

"I see. That is good information to have." She started across the street, and Pepper followed. Alessandra stopped. "Where are you going?"

"With you. Joey knows me, not you. I've got to make the introductions."

Alessandra hesitated, but only for a moment. Pepper was right. "Fine. But keep your eyes open."

Pepper saluted gracelessly. "Don't worry, countess – consider my peepers peeled."

Scowls greeted them as they entered the Roadhouse, but no one spoke up. The dim light did little to hide the dingy interior. She'd seen worse places, certainly. That didn't make it pleasant. "Don't worry," Pepper murmured. "Nobody cares about us. They're here to drink, play pool or lose at poker."

Alessandra nodded but didn't reply. A live jazz band occupied a rough plank stage along the far wall. Few of the patrons seemed to be paying attention to the music, but some people were dancing in a cleared area in front of the stage. Here, scruffy longshoremen rubbed shoulders with immigrant laborers and out-of-town grifters.

Vigil was awaiting them at a table in a back room, away from both the door and the stage. The room was small, and there was sawdust on the floor. Two men rose from the table as Alessandra and Pepper entered. Neither said anything as they pushed past the two women and headed out into the noise. One stopped and looked back. The shorter of the two, slim and dapper. Too well-dressed for the Roadhouse.

By the time Alessandra and Pepper had taken seats at the table, both men were gone. Vigil was well-nicknamed. Mousy, with a lean face, he gave Pepper a tremulous smile. "How's tricks?" he asked, as he slid something into his coat.

"None of your business," Pepper said, in a voice that was comically deep. She hiked a thumb at Alessandra. "This is the lady I was talking about. The countess. She wants to ask you a few questions."

"Always happy to help a lady," Vigil said, turning to Alessandra. He had a bottle beside his elbow and a pair of shot glasses in front of him. As he spoke, he poured a glass. "You want a nip?"

"Thank you." She took the drink and knocked it back. It was watered down, but still tasted like it had been made in someone's bathtub. "Pepper tells me that you are a man who knows things."

"I keep my ear to the ground," Vigil said, preening slightly. "Long as you got the cash, I got the gossip." She retrieved an envelope from her coat and passed it to him under the table. He made it vanish in moments. "Do I need to count it?"

"If you wish to insult me."

Vigil grinned. "If you can't trust an aristocrat, who can you trust? Ask away."

"I am looking for a man named Gomes." A face crossed her mind's eyes, dark and feral. The man who'd hit her – wanted to shoot her. She owed him more than a scratch on the arm for that offense.

Vigil paused. "I know a couple of Gomes."

"This one robbed the museum recently. He got shot in the process."

"Oh. That Gomes." Vigil frowned. "He don't come around usually. He's not welcome here. He's a gun for the O'Bannion mob and likes to throw his weight around too much for the Sheldon boys to tolerate him."

"But he has been in lately."

"Yeah. Him and a few other O'Bannion goons. Guy named Phipps and another called ... Pulanski, I think." Vigil knocked back his shot and poured another. "They needed guns and a truck." Vigil looked around. "This is a good place to get both, if you ain't picky about previous owners."

"Were the O'Bannions behind the robbery?"

Vigil laughed. "Why would a bunch of bootleggers want a mummy?"

"Why indeed?" She leaned forward. "Perhaps someone should ask the O'Bannions." She felt a prickling sensation between her shoulder blades. They were being watched. She didn't bother to look for whoever it was. Vigil frowned.

"You should keep your voice down, lady. Wrong question can get you dead, especially in a place like this. And me with you."

"Then you had best answer it quickly. What else do you know about the robbery?"

"Maybe you should leave."

Alessandra took his bottle from him and poured herself another drink, and then one for Pepper. "Maybe you should give me the information I have paid you for." She did not elaborate, but Vigil caught the implication nonetheless.

He squirmed in his seat, but reluctantly continued. "Gomes was here a few days before the robbery. He came to meet somebody."

"Describe him."

"Short, round, not the sort of guy you see in here very often. Looked nervous. I heard his name was Ashley. Some sort of professor from the college."

Alessandra paused, chewing this over. "And what did they talk about?"

"That, I don't know. Kept to themselves. If you want my opinion…?"

"Please."

He grinned again. "He was an inside man."

She knew the term. But if Ashley had arranged the theft, had he done so for himself, or as an intermediary for someone else? "Where does Gomes hang around normally?"

"Joint over in the Merchant District. The Tick-Tock Club. He goes every Friday, like clockwork. Word is, he has a dame."

"Most men do," Alessandra said. "Have you told any of this to the police?"

Vigil looked vaguely insulted. "What sort of mook do you take me for?"

She smiled. "Good. If they should come by, do not mention my name." She pushed another folded bill across the table, beneath her shot glass.

"No worries there. My memory is real foggy sometimes."

"See that it stays that way." She rose. "You have been very helpful, Mr Vigil."

"You're welcome." He patted the bulge in his coat. "Come back any time, countess."

CHAPTER SIXTEEN
Miskatonic University

"Treating me to dinner and brunch in the same week," Pepper said, as they sat down in a diner the next morning. It was one of several on this side of town, and close to the university. "A person could start to get ideas." It was a small, tidy sort of place, with a chrome countertop and posters for various university events in the windows.

"I thought you could use a good meal." Alessandra looked at the menu. "And for some reason I am famished."

"So it doesn't have anything to do with you wanting to talk to that professor Vigil mentioned?" Pepper asked, as she gave the menu a cursory once-over.

"Ashley, yes," Alessandra said. She looked up as the waitress came by. "What is Adam and Eve on a raft?"

"Poached eggs and toast, sweetie," the waitress drawled. She was a thin woman, narrow and pinched, but with an easy smile.

"That sounds lovely. I will have that."

"Want axle grease on it?"

Alessandra looked at Pepper, who said, "She means butter."

Alessandra laughed. "Axle grease! Yes, how funny. Yes, a squirt of axle grease please. And some coffee. Milk and sugar."

"One blond with sand. What about you?" The waitress looked expectantly at Pepper.

"Make it two." As the waitress departed, Pepper said, "You think he's in on it?"

"It seems so, if your source is correct." Alessandra looked out the window. The booth she'd chosen faced the university across the street. She had never attended university, though she had visited many. It wasn't the done thing, though her mother had insisted on some form of higher education. Tutors, mostly. She had learned Latin and Greek, as well as English and French. She had read the great books, and composed long-winded essays on their merits or the lack thereof. All very educational.

There had been other tutors, as well. Her father's idea. They had been more interesting teachers by far. The elderly Englishman with an inordinate fondness for cricket. The melancholy albino with his opium-soaked cigarettes. And of course, the incomparable Mr Nuth, who defied all description.

She had learned their lessons well. Though some stuck with her longer than others. And some had made no sense at all. But she had learned, and put what she'd learned into practice. She thought they would be pleased by her progress.

"So what next? After we eat, I mean?"

"As a gentleman of my acquaintance once said, one cannot make bricks without clay." Alessandra looked at her. "If the thieves are proving elusive, find the one who put them up to the crime instead."

"You think he'll tell you where they are?" Pepper said doubtfully, as their food arrived. "He might not be inclined to be helpful, if you get me."

"I can be very persuasive."

Pepper snorted coffee up her nose and began to cough. While she waited for Pepper to recover, Alessandra poked her eggs with a fork. They wobbled in an unappetizing fashion, but she was too hungry to care. She felt as if she hadn't eaten in days, thanks to her earlier illness. "Then perhaps you are right." She took a bite, chewed thoughtfully and swallowed. When it stayed down, she took another. "I will attempt subtlety."

"Meaning?"

"Meaning I will lie. If that fails, I will try bribery."

"And if that doesn't work?"

Alessandra shrugged. "Then I will resort to cruder means."

Pepper raised an eyebrow. "You can't shoot him."

"I am not a street apache, Pepper. I do not shoot people without good cause." Alessandra sat back. "You are free to accompany me?"

"Sure. Wouldn't miss it." Pepper finished her eggs and pointed at what was left of Alessandra's. "You going to finish yours?"

Alessandra pushed the plate towards her. As Pepper tucked in, she pitched her voice low and said, "You know there's a cop sitting over at the counter watching us, right?"

"I am aware, yes. He followed us from the hotel."

"You aren't worried?"

"Why would I be?" Alessandra said. "It will be easy enough to lose him, should the need arise, I think."

"You sound like you've done this before."

"Once or twice. The police in Rome were possibly the most tenacious."

Pepper stared at her, eyes wide. "Rome? Like… Rome? Coliseums and stuff?"

"The very same."

"I'd like to go to Rome," Pepper said, wistfully.

Alessandra smiled. "Maybe you will someday."

"Doubt it. I'll call it a win if I ever get to Boston." Pepper looked around the diner. "My ma was from Boston. She loved it there." She peered at the window, squinting at her reflection. "She died here, though." The way she said it implied that the circumstances had been less than ideal.

Alessandra rarely allowed herself the luxury of sympathy. Life had taught her better. But it was hard, with Pepper. The girl was at once naïve and hardboiled. It reminded her of, well, her. She'd been the same, after her parents had died. Directionless, but needing to go, to do. Something, anything.

"I… understand," Alessandra said, staring up at the brown water marks on the ceiling. She hesitated, then decided to plunge ahead. "My own parents died when I was around your age. My sisters and I – we were lucky. Our grandfather took us in hand."

Pepper looked at her. "What happened?"

"I am still not entirely sure." Her memories of that night were caught fast in a mental lockbox, and as far as she was concerned, that was where they could stay. "Let us say that it is a mystery that I do not care to investigate." She stood abruptly, wanting to change the subject. "If you are finished, we should go."

Pepper gulped down the last of her coffee and followed Alessandra to the counter. They paid and left, the police officer watching them surreptitiously the entire time.

Wrought iron fences separated much of the ivy-wreathed campus from the rest of the town. Miskatonic was a motley mix of architectural styles, both old and new. There was a sense of vibrancy here that was missing in much of the town.

It was still early in the day. Students walked to class, or lounged on benches and stoops. Alessandra drew no small amount of attention, and used it to her advantage. Various students were only too happy to direct them to the history department, and Professor Ashley's office. Pepper looked around as they walked, face unreadable. Alessandra nudged her. "Have you ever considered attending university?"

"What – this place?"

"Not necessarily. There are others."

"I barely got through high school," Pepper said, dismissively. Alessandra detected a trace of longing in her voice, despite her words, but didn't press the matter.

Miskatonic's history department resided in a square brick building that had seen better epochs. The sound of their shoes on the tile floor echoed in the hallway. It was between classes, and the building was all but empty. Finding the academic offices wasn't difficult; they simply followed the smell of coffee that had been reheated, rather than poured out.

Ashley's office had his name on a tiny placard beside the door. The door itself was partially open, and someone was moving around inside. Alessandra hesitated, and waved Pepper back. Whoever it was hadn't noticed them yet. She opened her clutch, and let her fingers brush across the shape of her Webley. Then, very firmly, she shut her clutch. There was no telling who it was, and she'd been pointing her pistol at far too many people lately.

"Hello," she said, loudly, as she opened the door.

The young woman standing in the office yelped and a stack of papers fell from her arms to the floor, scattering everywhere. Alessandra halted, nearly as startled.

"You scared the life out of me!" The young woman glared at Alessandra, her hands on her hips. "Look what you made me do."

She was short and round, with blond ringlets that bounced with every twitch of her chin.

"My apologies. I wished to speak to Professor Ashley."

"He's not here," the woman said, as she stooped to gather the fallen papers.

"I see. When will he be back?" As she spoke, she took in the office, searching for any hint as to Ashley's whereabouts. The office was a study in chaos. Books and papers everywhere, stacks of each on the floor, atop the filing cabinets along the wall, even on the windowsill. The desk was small and cramped, and she shuddered to think of sitting hunched over it for hours on end. The office reminded her of a prison cell.

"Who wants to know?"

Alessandra paused. "I am … a writer. For *La Nazione*."

The woman looked at her, puzzled. "Newspaper," Alessandra clarified, with a friendly smile. "Italian."

The woman looked at Pepper, who'd chosen that moment to make her presence known. "I'm her interpreter."

"She sounds like she speaks perfect English to me," the woman said.

"I'm really good at it," Pepper said.

The woman frowned. "Listen, what did you say you wanted?"

"To talk to the professor."

"About that damn mummy, I bet."

Somewhat taken aback, Alessandra glanced at Pepper and nodded. "Yes. I take it we are not the first?"

"Lady, you're not even the second." The woman set the recovered papers on the desk, and looked around. "I'm his assistant, Delores."

"Alessandra." She indicated Pepper. "This is my friend, Mr Kelly."

Delores nodded, not smiling. "The professor hasn't been in

today. Which is unfortunate, because he has papers to grade, and if he doesn't do them, I have to."

"Would you know how to reach him?"

Delores exhaled noisily and shook her head. "Nope. He doesn't have a phone. He might be hiding over at the Observatory – or maybe the library. A lot of them do that, when they want some privacy."

"What about Professor Freeborn? Might he know where Professor Ashley is?"

"Who knows? I'm not his assistant."

Alessandra let the comment pass. "You said I am not the first journalist… When did the others come by?"

"Why?"

Alessandra smiled. "Because I am curious."

Delores snorted. "Earlier this morning. A guy. He was waiting here when I arrived. Nice hat, nice suit. Said he was from the *Arkham Advertiser*, but I don't think so. He was too slick." The description provoked a faint sense of familiarity in Alessandra, but she couldn't say why. It didn't sound like Zamacona, or his black-clad servant. Perhaps… Whitlock?

"Was his name Whitlock, by chance?"

"I didn't ask, and he didn't offer." Delores straightened the stack of papers.

"Are you certain no one else came by in the interim?"

Delores paused. "They might have. I just got back to the office a few minutes before you knocked. Why?"

"Do you smoke?"

"No. Why?"

Alessandra tapped the windowsill. "Look here."

Pepper craned her neck. "It's a cigarette butt. So?"

"It's still smoldering." She looked at them. "Someone was in here recently."

From the hallway came the sound of a door slamming. Alessandra looked out the window and saw a figure in a pale, seersucker suit hurrying across the courtyard. Something about him was familiar, but she couldn't bring a face to mind. She turned to Delores. "Do you recognize that man? Was he the one here earlier?"

"I- I'm not sure," the young woman said, clearly puzzled. "What do you think he was doing in here?"

Alessandra didn't reply. She looked around the office again, trying to spot something – anything – out of the ordinary. But nothing stood out. She was going to have to ask Professor Ashley what he knew face-to-face.

Someone knocked on the door. Alessandra turned to see a tall man standing in the hall. She recognized Ashley's compatriot, Professor Freeborn, immediately. "Delores, has he shown up yet…?" he began. He stopped when he realized Delores wasn't alone in the office.

"Professor Freeborn," Alessandra said. "What a pleasant coincidence. Just the man I wished to speak to."

"You…" he began. Then, without another word, he turned and hurried away. Alessandra paused, shocked by the rudeness. With a parting glance at Delores, she and Pepper pursued. Freeborn had the long-legged stride of a hiker, but they caught up with him at the stairs. "Stop following me," he said, without turning around.

"If you would stop for a moment, we would not have to."

Pepper, taking the initiative, cut him off and put herself between Freeborn and the stairs. Freeborn sighed and turned. "I'm sorry, Miss…?"

"Countess, actually."

Freeborn frowned. "Countess. My apologies, but Ferdinand isn't here and I'm about to be late for a class. If you'll excuse me…?" Alessandra studiously ignored the hint.

"It will take but a moment, I promise."

Seeing that she wouldn't be moved, Freeborn sighed again. "A moment, then. But no more than that. What was it you wanted to know?"

"I wanted to talk about the robbery," she began.

"I'm sorry, but I have nothing to say about that." He turned and looked meaningfully at Pepper, but she didn't move. "Get out of my way."

"Answer the question first," Pepper said, raising her fists.

Freeborn grunted and turned back to Alessandra. "Look, you seemed to be on good terms with Matthew Orne. Why don't you ask him and leave me out of it?"

"Perhaps I will." She studied him for a moment, and then gestured. "Let him go, Pepper." Pepper hesitated, but only for a moment. She stepped aside and Freeborn practically bolted for the door.

Pepper looked at her. "I don't get it… We're just letting him go?"

"For now. He was right. I should be talking to Orne. Ashley was working for him, after all. He might know where our missing professor has gone to ground."

"What about the mummy?"

"Today is Friday, yes?"

"Yeah," Pepper said, in confusion.

"Vigil said that Gomes visits the Tick-Tock Club every Friday. We will go tonight and see if that holds true."

"Sounds like fun," Pepper said. "What now?"

"Back to the hotel. There is someone I need to speak to."

CHAPTER SEVENTEEN
Visser

Arkham's downtown was more vibrant in the daylight than it seemed at night. The storefronts were the same as one might see in any growing town or small city. Trucks carrying goods and produce rumbled along the afternoon routes, delivering supplies to restaurants and grocers. The streets weren't crowded, but lunch wasn't over yet.

Alessandra and Visser were seated at a small circular table outside a cafe, beneath a wide, white awning. She'd had to drag him out of his hotel room, despite it being midday. Visser had been somewhat the worse for wear, after a night of carousing. Not that one would know it, looking at him now. Men had an easier time of making themselves presentable.

The cafe was near where she'd met Zamacona, along a tree-lined side street opposite a small local department store. It boasted French elegance, but the reality was far and away from any of the Parisian coffee-houses she'd patronized. In fact, it was more Italian than La Bella Luna.

Coffee and pastries arrived swiftly. The pastries had been

covered in sugar to cover the deficiencies of the dough. The coffee was adequate, at least.

"Some excitement the other day, eh?" Visser asked, as he drank his coffee. "Fair scared the hair off young Fairmont." He leaned close. "You didn't have anything to do with that, did you?"

"If I did, do you think I would tell you?"

Visser sat back. "Well, no, I suppose not. Though I'd think it was damned rude of you, I must say."

"I didn't."

"Good enough. Why did you want to meet?"

"To ask you what you thought about the robbery," Alessandra said, carefully. "I am curious as to what you made of it."

"So is everyone else. It's all anyone was talking about last night at the Clover Club." Visser pulled out his cigarette case and opened it for her. She took one with a nod of thanks. He lit it for her and leaned forward conspiratorially. "First time I've ever been that close to a robbery, I can tell you that."

"My first time as well."

He raised an eyebrow. "Really? I find that hard to believe. Rough gal like you."

"I did not say it was my first time around guns, Tad. Just around an armed robbery."

"Not your sort of thievery, then?"

"Not quite."

Visser pointed his cigarette at her. "There's something I've always wondered… Why steal occult objects?" he asked. "Why not jewels or paintings or rare books?"

"Jewels require a fence, paintings have pedigree and rare books… well – I have stolen a number of those in my time." Alessandra frowned down into her coffee. "I suppose it is what I know best. My father had a… fascination for the occult. He taught me about the twilight space you people inhabit. Your own little incestuous world of collectors and collections."

Visser frowned. "Not the word I'd use."

"But apt. You all know each other, and you trade your valuables constantly, willingly or no. For instance, Arkady Cottonwood – you know the name?"

"Yes, of course."

"How many copies of his treatise, *The Oldest Rite,* exist?"

"Can't be more than three or four. Maybe a few bastardized versions here and there."

"Exactly. I have stolen a single copy of that book five times for three different clients." Alessandra took a sip of coffee. "Or consider the collection of the Comte d'Erlette…"

Visser snapped his fingers. "I knew it! I knew you were involved in that."

Alessandra waved the exclamation aside. "The esteemed comte, as well as his ancestors, used thievery to build that collection. And one of the victims of his rapacious nature hired me to steal certain elements back – elements he had previously pilfered from an entirely different rival. You see my point?"

"I think so. It all sounds rather like a game, doesn't it?"

"My father said the same. And because it is, most of you won't involve the police because you understand the rules. You hire someone like me to steal a thing, and then someone else hires their own acquisitionist to reacquire what was taken."

"Acquisitionist, hmm?"

Alessandra shrugged. "I am not ashamed to call myself a thief, but some clients prefer a less… blunt term. So, acquisitionist."

"Good word." Visser paused. He set his cup down. "And you're sure you had nothing to do with the robbery?"

"Tad…"

He gestured placatingly. "I know, I know. It's just awful convenient, is all."

"Not for me, I assure you."

"Have you spoken to the police yet?"

"What a silly question. Have you?"

"Of course. Told them all I knew."

"All?" she asked, eyebrow raised.

"Not quite," he amended. "They wanted to know why someone might steal such a thing, and I, of course, provided some illumination."

"Really? And why might someone steal a mummy?"

"Any number of reasons." Visser sat back. "Well, painters ground up mummies in order to obtain a particular ochre color. And medieval doctors thought mummies were a necessary ingredient to certain philters and curatives."

Alessandra stared at him. Visser shifted uncomfortably in his seat. "I do know some things, Alessandra. I'm not a complete twit."

"I never said you were. Go on. Illuminate me. What else?"

"Well, there are my fellow collectors, obviously. The Victorians were loony for mummies, mostly of the Egyptian variety, and that tradition has continued. I know a few antiquarians who might be monomaniacal enough to hire someone to steal a mummy, if they had an open spot in their collection."

"There were several familiar faces at the exhibition," Alessandra said.

Visser shook his head. "None of them. The real obsessives rarely dare to leave their collections unguarded."

Alessandra nodded. She knew that well enough. Many of her

clients were veritable hermits – shut-ins, hunkered in expensive penthouses or isolated manses. Surrounded by the best security money could buy. She often amused herself by planning for how best to break into their retreats, even as they hired her. "And only a real obsessive would plan so sloppy an operation."

"Or someone desperate. Maybe it's some withered traditionalist who thinks mummy dust will cure his liver spots or something similarly ridiculous. Though why anyone would think that horrid thing was a cure for any ailment beats me."

"It was singularly unlovely," she admitted. She shuddered slightly, suddenly cold. She looked at her plate and pushed it aside. "Though I know of at least one person willing to pay good money for it."

Visser frowned. "Maybe I shouldn't be helping you. Wouldn't want to get into trouble with the local flatfeet."

"It is not illegal to talk to someone, surely?"

"Depends on who you want to talk to." He gave her a steady look. "Not me, I think. Not really. So who?"

"Professor Ashley."

Visser paused. "Why?"

"He might know something about the robbery."

Visser sat back. "You really are intent on playing detective, aren't you?"

"I have a vested interest in this matter."

"I bet you do," Visser said. "Well, frankly I'd like to talk to Ashley as well. Only no one has seen the fat little devil since the robbery."

"He is quite difficult to run to ground. That is why I need to speak to his employer."

Visser frowned. "Matthew, you mean?"

"The very same."

"And that's all you want to do? Speak to him?"

"I am not going to pilfer his silver, Tad." She paused. "What do you think Orne would pay to get his mummy back?"

Visser almost choked on his coffee. "I thought you had nothing to do with it," he sputtered. He looked around, as if checking to see if anyone had noticed.

"I did not. But I am considering the merits of – what is the phrase – dealing myself in. What would he pay?"

Visser dabbed at his lips with his handkerchief. "Probably a great deal, if you could get it back in one piece."

She nodded. "That is good to know. Thank you, Tad."

"You have a line on it, then?" he asked eagerly. "You know where it is?"

"No. But I will soon enough. I simply wish to make it worth the effort."

"What about whoever hired you in the first place?"

"That is my problem, is it not?" She let her eyes roam, taking in their surroundings. Arkham was strange, even in daylight. Something about it put her in mind of Carnival, as if the whole town were wearing a mask.

Visser frowned. "I suppose. Still, you might want to take care."

"When have you known me to do otherwise?"

"Rome. Milan. Florence." He ticked off place names on his fingers. "Half a dozen other places I could mention. Frankly, we're all a little shocked you're still alive."

Alessandra stared at him, momentarily nonplussed. "You all… talk about me?" The thought of Visser and her other clients talking to one another was disturbing, to say the least.

"Not just you." Visser puffed on his cigarette. "Sometimes we discuss the weather."

Alessandra laughed. Visser shook his head. "I knew it," he said, after a moment. "I knew as soon as you came to see me that you had a scheme. Someone hired you to steal the damn thing, didn't they?"

"Does it matter?"

"A bit, given that I helped fund the expedition." Visser sat back. "You put me in an awkward position, you know. Dashed awkward. I'd like to help, but…"

Alessandra leaned forward. "What do you want?"

"What?"

"What do you want, Tad?"

Visser turned, a look of hurt innocence on his face. "Alessandra, I don't know what you're talking about."

She laughed. "Tad, you have employed me on no less than three occasions to acquire items of dubious provenance for that cabinet of curiosities you keep hidden in your library. You are a magpie of the outré. What do you want?"

"A finger."

"A finger," Alessandra repeated.

"From the mummy," he clarified.

"I gathered. I will not ask why."

"Bit of a ritual I read about. I think it'll be great fun."

Alessandra forestalled him with a gesture. "I am not interested. If you want a finger, I will provide you one."

"You mean it?"

"Have I ever lied to you?"

Visser grinned. "That's why I like you, Alessandra. You always have the right answer." His grin faded. "I can ask him. Matthew has been somewhat reticent since the robbery. He was looking to make a big splash – but not that sort."

Alessandra nodded and let her gaze wander across the street.

Something had caught her attention – a glimpse of black, like a shadow out of the corner of her eye. Suddenly uncomfortable, she shifted in her seat and turned back to Visser. "What do you mean?" she asked.

Visser scratched his chin. "Matthew's reputation in Arkham is … not what it once was, if you believe the gossip. He's run afoul of an iceberg named Sanford."

The name rang a bell. "Carl Sanford," she said. "He was at the exhibition."

"Yes. Trying to stir up trouble, no doubt."

"You mentioned that Orne had snubbed him, but not why." She fixed him with a coy look. "Do you know more than you are saying, Tad?"

"A bit, perhaps. Sanford has most of the town council in his pocket – and the bank, and not a few businesses. An invitation to join the Silver Twilight Lodge is key to doing any real sort of business in Arkham – that's not bootlegging, I mean. Turning Sanford down is tantamount to… to self-excommunication."

"But Orne did?"

Visser shrugged. "Matthew has always had a rather inflated sense of self, it must be said. Sanford's been poking holes in it for some time now. Not inviting him to the exhibition was as good as a declaration of war."

Alessandra considered this. "Could Sanford be responsible for the theft?"

Visser shrugged again. "Your guess is as good as mine." He peered past her, and frowned. "Do you know him?"

She glanced over her shoulder and saw a familiar hunched, black-clad shape sitting on a bus bench across the street. The man in black stared at her with milky eyes, but made no move to approach. A moment later a truck passed between them, and when it was gone – so was he. Alessandra felt a chill. Zamacona was keeping an eye on her. "No," she said.

"Curious," Visser said. "I could swear I've seen that fellow before. But not here – in New York. Must be a coincidence."

"Yes. It must be," Alessandra said, hollowly.

CHAPTER EIGHTEEN
Cemetery

"I hate this place," Gomes muttered as they carried the box into the mausoleum. The cemetery didn't look any less foreboding in the daylight. Bones rolled beneath his feet and undergrowth tugged at his trousers as they set the box down on the broken, filthy floor. "Why we got to do it here?"

Phipps closed the mausoleum door behind them. The hinges creaked shrilly, causing both men to wince. "Because here is where he said, and since he's the one paying us, here's where we do it. Get that sarcophagus open." He pointed at one of the three stone sarcophagi, done up in the Georgian style, that occupied the center of the mausoleum.

"You do it. My arm hurts."

Phipps pushed roughly past him and heaved the stone box open, revealing a set of worn stone steps, stretching down into the dark. "Smugglers used to carve out these tunnels," Phipps said. "French Hill – hell, most of this side of the river – is a big honeycomb."

"Fascinating. How we getting the box down there?"

"You go first, I'll follow."

"Why me?"

"Because you only got one good arm, or so you keep saying. So I'll support the weight, you guide me down. Good enough reason, ya mook?"

Gomes made a sound of annoyance. "Yeah, fine." He paused, looking at the box. "Should we have left him there? Jodorowsky, I mean."

"Did you want to bring him?"

"We could have put him in the river or something, at least. Respectful, you know?"

Phipps grunted. "We didn't have time, and you know it. Besides, I didn't hear you complaining about leaving Pulanski behind."

"Pulanski was an asshole."

"So are you. So am I." Phipps crouched. "Stop jawing and let's get down there. I feel exposed up here. Sooner we got this thing hidden, the better."

"We sure the cops don't know about this place?" Gomes asked, as they made their way down, awkwardly and slowly. At the bottom of the steps was a tunnel of brick and hardpacked soil that reminded Gomes of a sewer. The air smelled of damp and dirt and worse things. It wasn't a good smell.

"He said it was safe."

"He said a lot of things." Gomes stopped. "Someone's up ahead." He set the box down and reached for his weapon.

"It's the professor," Phipps said. "He's waiting for us." He cleared his throat and called out. A light danced across the walls and floor a moment later. Someone had turned on a lantern or flashlight.

"This way," a voice called, echoing eerily in the dark.

"You sure that's him?" Gomes asked.

"Just pick up your end and start moving," Phipps said, harshly.

Gomes did as he said, and they started down the tunnel. He could make out a sort of soft, scurrying sound in the background, like rats. Gomes didn't much like rats, or cemeteries. Or dead things in boxes.

He tried not to think about Jodorowsky, or what had happened to him. Phipps insisted it was an accident, and Gomes wanted to believe him, but sometimes the box shifted in his grip in an unsettling way. As if the thing inside were stirring. The sooner they were shed of it, the sooner he was out of Arkham, the better.

"Where are you, fat boy?" he called out.

"I… I'm here," Professor Ashley said, swinging a light so they could see it. "Through here. I've got a lantern set up. Watch your step."

"Why?" Gomes asked, just before he stumbled on a loose femur. There were bones scattered all over this part of the tunnel. In the dim light of Ashley's lantern, he saw oblong shapes that might have been coffins protruding from the curtain of roots that obscured this part of the tunnel wall. He shuddered and averted his eyes.

At the end of the tunnel was a reinforced archway. Beyond it was a larger space – a chamber. Stacks of broken coffins were pressed against the walls, and loose bones lay scattered across the floor. "What the hell is this place?" Gomes breathed.

"A… a bier of sorts. A waiting room for the dead." Ashley stepped into view, lifting a lantern. He set it atop a small stack of coffins and turned it up, washing back the shadows. "I – we – thought it was appropriate."

"Uh huh," Phipps said, noncommittally.

"Were you followed?" Ashley asked tremulously. He was perspiring freely, despite the chill of the tunnel. Gomes thought he resembled an overfed weasel. A nervous weasel. "Only I thought I saw someone lurking. I keep hearing noises."

"No," Phipps said, flatly. "We know our business. Where is he?"

Ashley looked away. "Not here."

"When?" Gomes demanded.

"Tomorrow, I assure you. Have no fear, he wants this affair completed as much as you fellows. I... ah – weren't there three of you?"

It was Phipps' turn to look away. "There was an... incident."

Ashley tensed. "It's not damaged, is it?"

"See for yourself." Phipps opened the box. Gomes took an instinctive step back. Part of him was expecting the thing to jump out. But it stayed where it was. Ashley peered inside warily. Maybe he was expecting it to move as well.

"There's blood on it," he said, horrified. "And its bindings are loose!"

"I told you... there was an incident." Phipps looked at Gomes, who shrugged. "Jodorowsky tripped."

Ashley was silent for a time, digesting this. Finally, he said, "There were accidents in Oklahoma as well. The body?"

"Not an issue."

Ashley frowned, but nodded. "I'll need to look it over. To make sure you haven't damaged it. It'll take me a few minutes."

"And then we get our money?"

"Tomorrow, as I said. You can sleep here tonight. There's food and alcohol. I took the liberty of bringing some newspapers." He smiled nervously.

"Sleep here?" Gomes repeated. "You must be joking. I ain't sleeping here."

"Shut up," Phipps snapped.

"You're free to leave," Ashley said quickly. "The thing will be

perfectly safe here. No one knows about this place. That's why I –
we – assumed you might like to… ah… lay low. But if not…"

"We'll be fine here," Phipps said. "We've slept in worse places."

"Speak for yourself," Gomes muttered. "I got to get out of here."

Phipps rounded on him. "And leave me with the damn mummy?
No, I don't think so."

"Listen, you come with me. It's safe here, you heard the professor.
Nobody will bother it. I got to see Wilma. Tell her to start packing. I
want us out of Arkham tomorrow."

Phipps shook his head. "Are you nuts? You'd risk everything just
to see some goddamn dame?"

"You ain't seen Wilma."

Phipps leaned close, teeth bared. "By now McTyre knows who
pulled that job. He's going to have guys looking for us all over. You
think he doesn't know about her?"

"I don't care what he knows." Gomes patted the holstered shape
of his pistol. "I'm a better shot than any of the other guys, even with
a bum wing. And I'll keep an eye open – I'm not stupid."

"Evidence to the contrary," Phipps said.

Gomes frowned. "Won't be none of McTyre's guys at the Tick-
Tock Club. That's Donohue's place and you know how he feels
about the O'Bannions."

"Yeah, and as far as he knows, you're still working for them. So
maybe think about it a bit, huh?"

"Donohue knows me," Gomes said. "I'm going to see Wilma,
and you ain't stopping me, Phipps. Not unless you want to get
rough about it. But I'm not in the mood for rough right now." He
folded back the edge of his jacket, letting the butt of his pistol poke
forward in a belligerent fashion. "What about you?"

Phipps stared at him. "How long?"

"I'll be back tomorrow morning. Maybe I'll bring you a doughnut." Gomes looked past him, to Ashley, who was watching their confrontation with wide, staring eyes. Fishy eyes. "What about you, fat boy? Want a doughnut?"

"Go if you're going," Phipps spat. "But if you want your goddamn money you'll be back here tomorrow when we make the exchange. And I swear to God, if you bring the cops down on us – I'll kill you myself."

"Yeah, yeah." Gomes started to turn away, but paused. "Try not to have an accident like Jodorowsky did, huh? I'd hate to come back to that." He didn't wait for Phipps' reply. Whistling, he strode back along the tunnel, already imagining the look on Wilma's face when he told her about the money.

And though the shadows seemed to deepen around him, he pretended not to notice.

Alessandra was somewhere cold and hard. Stone. Artillery – no, *drums* – thudded somewhere in the distance. Below her, perhaps. Or maybe above. She couldn't tell.

Ahead of her was only darkness. A vast emptiness, stretching past the limits of her vision. She tried to push herself to her feet, and heard something clink. Chains… she was chained. Someone had chained her to the stones. She looked around. There were… people standing nearby. Men, or maybe women. Naked, but for grotesque masks – not gas masks this time, but ornate masks of onyx and gold. They were praying, or perhaps chanting. But softly, almost as if they were afraid someone would hear.

Or something.

She tried to speak, but no sound came out. She tried to rise again, but the chains prevented it. Panic gnawed at the edges of her composure. She didn't know where she was or how she'd gotten here. All she knew was that if she didn't get out, she was going to die. Something was coming. Behind her, the chanting had changed – become more guttural. And the drums… the rhythm of the drums was different. Faster.

Hungrier.

She yanked at the chains, but there was no give in them. Out in the dark, she glimpsed a hint of movement. As if something immense were stirring in the deeps. Her thrashing became frenzied. She felt a coldness in her and could not look away from the dark. Around her, she felt her captors sink down, bowing before this indistinct motion. She could not draw breath into her lungs.

Tsathoggua en y'n an ya phtaggn N'kai.

N'kai.

N'kai.

N'KAI.

The word hammered through her, like a jolt of electricity. She did not recognize it, but she knew it all the same. It twisted inside her head, stretching down into the marrow of her, filling her up and hollowing her out.

This time, she managed to scream, waking herself in the process. She lurched out of the chair, heart thudding, stomach roiling. She had fallen asleep not long after returning from her outing with Visser. The pastries had sat heavily on her stomach, and not even the coffee had been enough to keep her awake.

Sweat coated her, and she felt flushed and clammy all at once. She looked down at herself, but saw no marks, no wounds. She rose and splashed some water on her face. She avoided looking at the mirror as she did so.

She was dressed for work, waiting for Pepper to arrive. She

looked out the window and froze. Something was down there, almost obscured in the evening mist. Someone. Standing in the park, watching the hotel.

No, watching the penthouse. A cold hand gripped her spine. Her fingers felt for her revolver, though it wasn't as if she was going to shoot them. The mist rolled, and they were gone. She let the curtain fall and sat back heavily in her seat. It had been Zamacona's servant, she was certain of it.

A knock at the door caused her to sit up sharply. Pistol in hand, she stood and went over to it. She waited until she heard Pepper's voice before she opened the door. "You look like a stretch of bad road," Pepper said.

"Is that a joke?"

"Not a funny one." Pepper stepped past her into the room. "We might have trouble."

"What sort of trouble?"

"I was at the garage earlier and some guys came in. Slick types. The sort that wouldn't normally be caught dead in a place like that. They went into De Palma's office, and then he called for me."

"You did not go, I assume."

"Hell no. If Iggy hadn't warned me, I'd have been in a tight spot." Pepper took off her hat and ran a hand through her hair. "As it was, I had to go out the window in the john. And that was a tight squeeze, let me tell you."

"Who were they?"

"I didn't stop to ask their names, but they were O'Bannion goons for sure."

"And you are certain that they were looking for you?"

"Us," Pepper said. She picked up Alessandra's cigarettes and took one. "I think you kicked the hornets' nest, lady."

Alessandra frowned. "What do you mean?"

"Someone saw us at Hibb's the other night. The O'Bannions are taking an interest."

"That could complicate matters."

"I'll say. What do we do?"

"We continue as planned, obviously. I have never allowed the attentions of local criminal organizations to deter me, and I do not intend to start now." Alessandra picked up her cap and pulled it on. "Now, let's go find our thief."

CHAPTER NINETEEN
Tick-Tock Club

The Tick-Tock Club, like the Clover Club, hid in plain sight. The entrance, at least the one Pepper knew about, was a nondescript stairwell near a watch shop. The club itself was supposedly underneath a nearby grocer. Even parked as they were across the street, Alessandra could hear the wailing of jazz horns from somewhere close by.

"Never been here before," Pepper said, leaning over the steering wheel.

"No?"

"Never even dropped anyone off here." Pepper puffed on one of Alessandra's cigarettes. "You hear stories about this place."

"It seems Arkham is full of stories."

"Yeah." Pepper looked back at her. "What now?"

"I will go in, find Gomes and get the answers I need."

"What if he gives you lip?"

"Then I will teach him the error of his ways," Alessandra replied. "You will stay here."

"What? But you might need somebody to watch your back!"

"Watch it from out here."

Pepper frowned, but didn't argue. Instead, she said, "After this... what are you going to do? After you find the mummy, I mean."

"I suppose I will leave." After a moment's hesitation, Alessandra asked, "And you?"

"Go back to being a cabbie, I guess." Pepper sighed and slumped. "It'll seem kind of boring after this, though." She paused. "And I'll miss the money."

Alessandra smiled. "Yes, I expect you will." She reached over the seat and squeezed Pepper's shoulder. "I am going in now. Be ready when I come out."

"What if they don't let you in? I mean, you're not exactly dressed for a party."

"I can be persuasive, when necessary."

Alessandra got out and crossed the street. The night lay heavy over Arkham and shadows pooled at the edges of the light. Something about the darkness reminded her of her dreams, and for a moment she was elsewhere. The stars above were the lights of impossible structures, and the night sky was as the roof of a great cavern.

She looked up and felt something in her stretch towards the dark, as if seeking sanctuary. She put her hand to her mouth and forced herself to keep moving. The last thing she needed was to get sick here, in the middle of the street.

She knocked on the door and it was opened by a tall man, dressed much as she was, though with heavily scarred features. There was a shotgun beside the door, but he wasn't otherwise armed. Given his size, she thought he didn't need it. He looked her up and down, but didn't ask her business. It was obvious why she was there.

He stepped aside with a grunt, and she entered. As he closed the door behind her, he gestured to a towering grandfather clock sitting on the other side of the cluttered shop. She went to it, and wondered how to access the passage that supposedly lay beyond. She turned. "How…" she began.

"Midnight," he said, as he sat on a stool by the door, and picked up a folded newspaper. He extricated a pencil from behind his ear, dabbed it on his tongue, and went back to work on a crossword puzzle.

She blinked and turned back, setting the hands of the clock to midnight. There was a loud click, and the face of the clock swung inwards, revealing a set of narrow stairs. The sounds of music billowed up around her, inviting her down.

The clock closed behind her as she descended. A pressure plate of some sort, she thought. It was all very clever, in a penny dreadful sort of way.

The descent took only moments. The stairwell was confining, claustrophobic. But well-lit, at least. At the bottom, another door. This one was guarded by a man in an ill-fitting tuxedo. He was as broad and as bulky as the one upstairs, and had a face like a lump of granite. No scars, though. At least none that she could see.

He stopped her, and made to search her. But instead of the Webley, he found a fold of cash that had suddenly sprouted from his jacket pocket. He grinned. "Go right in, ma'am."

"Thank you. You are most kind."

The music beat at her senses as she entered. It was almost too loud. She wondered how anyone heard the singers, such was the discordant thunder of the band. Timepieces of all shapes, sizes and styles covered the walls. A closer look told her that of those few that were functioning, each displayed a different time. No two alike. An oddity. She was coming to learn that Arkham was full of those.

She spotted Gomes easily. He was grinning at a woman who sat across from him. A waitress, perhaps, or a singer. She recalled what Vigil had said, about Gomes having a woman.

Whoever she was, she chose that moment to get up and depart. Perhaps heading to the powder room. Whatever the reason, Alessandra decided to take advantage of it. She made her way towards his table, moving as quickly as the crowd would allow.

Gomes saw her coming. He squinted at her. It was clear he recognized her, but didn't know why. She sat down without waiting for an invitation. "Hello, Mr Gomes."

"Who the hell are you?"

Alessandra took off her cap and frowned. "You do not remember me." She studied him coolly. He was favoring his arm, but it wasn't badly injured. She'd only clipped him, after all.

"Should I?" he said, pugnaciously.

"No. I suppose not. You are a bit slow. I suspect you are not the brains of your gang. Is that the correct saying? Brains?" She was baiting the man, despite knowing it was a bad idea. But he'd tried to shoot her, and she was owed some small recompense, however petty.

He lurched to his feet, a snarl on his face. "What'd you say?" he growled.

"And hard of hearing as well? Fate has dealt you a cruel hand, my friend." She leaned back in her seat, watching him warily. His sort rarely went for their guns first. They liked the feeling of a fist against flesh.

"I don't know who you are, but I do know how to shut you up." He reached for her, and she bobbed to her feet. Her fists thudded out, catching him in the kidneys. He staggered, and she caught the front of his shirt, dragging him close. Before he could recover, she rammed her knee up between his legs. He gave a strangled squawk and fell, upending the table. Alessandra managed to snag her cap before it hit the floor. She put it on and stepped back as he clambered to his feet, wheezing, eyes full of tears.

She drew her pistol. He stiffened. The music faltered. Alessandra could feel eyes on them, but didn't take her own off her quarry. "Let me tell you who I am," she said. "I am a woman in need of answers, and you are the lucky fellow who will give them to me. That should be well within your capabilities, however limited they might be."

"I don't know what you're talking about."

"I haven't asked the question yet."

"And you're not going to," a new voice cut in. She glanced over her shoulder to see a slight man, with pinched features and dark hair glaring at her. He was accompanied by a phalanx of much bigger men, dressed to the nines and looking uncomfortable in their starched collars. They were all armed, or so she guessed from the bulges in their jackets.

The smaller man pointed at her. "Who the hell do you think you are, and what the hell are you doing in my club? Answer the second question first."

"M- Mr Donohue," her quarry began, nervously. "I don't know who this dame is. She just up and… and attacked me!"

"Shut up, Gomes," Donohue snapped, not looking at him. "If she's here because of you, that makes this your problem, savvy?" He fixed a dark gaze on Alessandra. She was reminded of a starving fox she'd once seen. "I'm waiting."

"I require information."

"They licensing lady PIs now?" Donohue said and laughed. His men laughed with him, until he gestured sharply. "Gomes doesn't know nothing."

"Double-negative," Alessandra said.

Donohue frowned and looked around. "This look like a grammar school to you?" He shook his head. "Stow the heater. What do you wanna know?"

Alessandra studied him, weighing the odds. She holstered her weapon. "The mummy exhibition," she said.

"Yeah, I heard about that. Everyone heard about it." He glanced at Gomes, who shrank back. "Was that you, Gomes?" Donohue whistled. "You've been a bad boy. And stupid." Gomes had the look of a hunted animal. Donohue's smile was sharp and ugly.

With a panicked yell, Gomes snatched a Colt from beneath his jacket. He fired wildly, rousing a scream from the crowd. Donohue and his men scattered, and Gomes barreled towards the door. Alessandra pounded after him, not quite certain what she was going to do when she caught up with him, but not wanting him to get away.

Gomes upended a table, and she was forced to leap over it. He shoved the doorman aside and was out like a shot. She heard Donohue shouting behind her as she followed. Gomes was a dim figure above her as she hurried up the stairs. He was cursing in Portuguese under his breath. He paused on the landing and levelled his weapon.

With nowhere to go, she started running. The boom of the automatic was thunderous in the enclosed stairwell, and she felt something snatch her cap from her head. She ducked and kept moving, knowing her only chance was to get in close.

He fired again, but between his own panic and the dim lighting, his aim was off. The shot ricocheted along the stairwell, whining off towards the bottom. She was on him a moment later, her hands catching the barrel of the automatic and forcing it upwards. Her momentum carried him backwards. They crashed against the door, knocking it from its hinges with a loud bang.

Alessandra fell atop him, still struggling for control of the pistol. He punched her in the side, bellowing curses. She writhed, striking him in the face with her elbow. The gun clattered away. She heard shouts from below. So did Gomes, for he shoved her aside and stumbled onto the street, blood streaming from his nose.

By the time she'd gotten to her feet, he was gone. She heard the screech of tires and saw Pepper's cab racing towards her. From below came the sound of pounding feet. It was time to go. She ran towards the cab as it slowed. She was slamming the door as the first of Donohue's men reached the street. Gunfire lit up the night as Pepper stomped on the gas.

"What the hell happened back there?" Pepper shouted, as she aimed the cab away from the club. "Why are they shooting at us?"

"I might have made a nuisance of myself," Alessandra said, looking back. There was no telling where Gomes had gone. She punched the seat angrily. "We have lost him."

"Maybe. But we know he's still around, right? That's something, ain't it?" Pepper glanced at her. She was grinning wildly. "That was pretty exciting though, right?"

"They shot at us."

"I know! I ain't never been shot at before." Pepper pounded on the steering wheel. "You get shot at a lot?"

"No." Alessandra frowned. "I do not enjoy it."

"So what now?" Pepper asked.

"Back to the hotel, I suppose." Alessandra closed her eyes. "It is late, and I need to think." She would talk to Freeborn in the morning. He might be able to point her in another direction. Regardless, she would need to talk to Muldoon. If he'd learned the whereabouts of the others, they might have a chance of catching Gomes.

If not, Zamacona was going to be disappointed.

"Know what always helps me think?"

Alessandra cracked an eyelid. "What?"

Pepper grinned at her. "Pie."

CHAPTER TWENTY
Pie

Despite the late hour, Velma's Diner was nearly full when they arrived. The background hum of conversation was loud, and the rattle of cutlery constant. Alessandra and Pepper claimed a booth in the corner alongside the window. Alessandra ordered coffee, and, at Pepper's suggestion, a slice of pie.

The pie was good. The coffee, as expected, was less so. Americans didn't understand coffee, in much the same way that the English didn't understand tea. She set it aside, wondering if it might be more palatable when it cooled off.

Pepper added a ridiculous amount of sugar and milk to hers. Alessandra felt vaguely offended on behalf of the coffee. Why drink a thing if you couldn't stand the taste? But instead of saying that, she said, "Why is this place shaped like a railcar?"

"Because it used to be one," Pepper said, around a mouthful of pie. "Neat, right?"

Alessandra looked around. There were only a handful of booths, pressed tight to the walls. Most of the patrons sat at the chrome lunch counter. The smells of meatloaf and hash mingled in a pleasing fashion. She pushed her plate aside and watched Pepper finish her pie. "Enjoyable as it was, I am still at a loss."

"So he got away. So what? We can find him again. We can visit the Roadhouse again or – hey! – maybe we can go talk to that horse-doctor I mentioned? Somebody will know something."

"Perhaps." Alessandra turned as the bell above the door jangled. A familiar face entered the diner. A slim man, dressed nicely, faintly familiar. He spotted her and gave a cold, hard smile as he took a seat at the counter. She felt a chill as she realized where she'd seen him before – at the Roadhouse. She could tell by the bulge in his jacket that he was armed. Nor was he alone. Another man, similarly dressed, was standing outside, peering about as if looking for trouble.

"Pepper," she said. "At the counter – is that the fellow who came looking for you at the garage?"

Pepper turned, and her face went hard. "Yeah," she said softly.

"Good. Go get me another cup of coffee."

"You haven't finished that one," Pepper protested, not taking her eyes from the man.

"Pepper – go to the counter. Stay there. No matter what happens here."

Pepper blanched. "What're you planning?"

Alessandra didn't look at her. "Do as I say, please."

Slowly, reluctantly, Pepper rose. Alessandra sat and waited. She didn't have long.

"Went by your hotel earlier," the slim man said, as he slid into the booth opposite her. She saw the barrel of an automatic jutting from beneath his folded copy of the *Advertiser*. He wasn't taking any chances this time. "Turns out you weren't there."

"I am rarely where people expect me to be." Alessandra stirred her coffee. "Are you here to threaten me?" She heard the distinctive click of a pistol being cocked. She frowned. "Surely you wouldn't be so gauche as to shoot me here?"

"I'd rather not, but I will if I have to."

"Then what do you want?" She took a sip of coffee. It tasted bitter.

"For us to get up and walk out of here like old pals."

"And why would I do that? I'm quite comfortable here. If you're going to shoot me, then by all means do so."

"I'm not here to kill you. My employer wishes to speak to you."

"And who is your employer?" Pepper was watching from the counter, trying to catch her attention. Alessandra ignored her.

"Come with me and find out." He rose to his feet, weapon still trained on her. She hesitated, and then slid from the booth. He snatched her pistol from under her jacket and shoved it into his coat pocket. "I'll take that. Now move."

"Fine." She caught Pepper's eye and shook her head surreptitiously as the cabbie made to open her mouth. Thankfully, Pepper got the hint. "I have not paid for my coffee yet."

He stared at her. When he saw that she was serious, he dug into his pocket for a few coins and tossed them onto the table. "Happy? Get walking."

They left Velma's and stepped into the damp night. Everything smelled of rain. There was a motor car waiting for them opposite the diner. Two more well-dressed men occupied it. One in front, behind the wheel, and one in the back. Alessandra was ushered none too gently into the backseat. "Drive, Frank," the man beside her growled. He was big and dark -- Black Irish, as Americans called them. He looked at her captor, who sat beside the driver. "She give you any shite, Jimmy?"

Jimmy shook his head. "Didn't give her the chance, Mr McTyre."

McTyre bared nicotine yellow teeth in a wolfish grin. "Good." His dark gaze swiveled to Alessandra. "You know who I am?" His brogue was thick. No one would mistake him for a local.

"No. Though I deduce your name is McTyre."

He didn't seem upset by this. "Aye, well, I know who you are. I know a lot more than that, in fact. But we'll get to that." He gestured. "The docks, Frank. You know the place."

"I should mention that I was with someone."

"Who? The wee cab-rat?" McTyre shrugged. "Well, fine. We weren't planning to kill you anyway."

"Were you not?" she asked, noting the look of disappointment on Jimmy's face.

"First rule of business – never kill someone you don't have to."

"And what sort of business are you in, then?" she asked, despite already knowing the answer. She even knew who McTyre was, in a general sort of way. The number two man in the O'Bannion gang was the king of Arkham's underworld – a fiefdom built mostly on bootlegging. But she wanted to see how much he'd say.

Some criminals were braggarts. They liked to show off. Others would kill you with barely a flicker of warning or hesitation. It was always wise to figure out which was on the other end of the gun before you did something stupid.

McTyre studied her. Then he laughed. "Got a set on her, don't she, Jimmy?"

"Yes, sir, Mr McTyre. Big and brass."

McTyre leaned back. "You know damn well what my business is, sweetheart. Because in a roundabout sort of way, you're in it too." He settled back. "Now enjoy the ride. Frank drives like a damn angel, don't he, Jimmy?"

"Except when he runs over dogs, like that time out near Christchurch," Jimmy said.

"It wasn't any damn dog," Frank said, harshly.

"No, it probably wasn't," McTyre said, ending the argument before it could begin. "But no need to feckin' bore our guest with that daft shite. Both of you shut your gobs until we get where we're going." He crossed his arms and looked out the window. At a loss, Alessandra did the same.

Easttown gave way to Rivertown and finally to the Merchant District. The car slowed when they reached the docks. The night was wrapped in cotton. The light from the headlamps barely made a dent in the evening fog. When they stopped, Jimmy opened the door for her. "Out," he said.

"Show some feckin' courtesy, Jimmy," McTyre said, as he climbed out the other side. "She might come out the other side of this yet."

"I'm not putting money on it."

McTyre laughed. He adjusted his coat as he strode through the mist. "Follow me," he said, without looking back. She hesitated, wary.

"You heard him," Jimmy said, giving her a tap on the shoulder. She turned and gave him a considering look. Wisely, Jimmy stepped back, hands spread. She smiled and followed McTyre. He was waiting for her a short distance away, at the edge of the docks. The smell of the river hung heavy on the night air, and she could hear the faint groan of a foghorn in the distance. The mist rolled over Riverside in waves, obscuring nearby buildings. Soon, the car was lost, save for the soft radiance of the headlights.

"I feckin' hate this time of night," he said, looking out over the river.

"Then why bring me here?"

He looked at her. "Would you rather I have Jimmy there cut your throat and throw you in the bog, then? Naw, I didn't think so."

"That's not an answer."

He turned his gaze back to the river. "You're pretty feckin' mouthy for a poacher."

"Poacher?"

"What else would you call a person who comes onto someone's hunting preserve and starts pilfering?" He pulled a silver cigar case out of his coat and opened it. "I read up on you, didn't I?" He noted her startled look and gave another lupine grin. "Aye, you heard me. O'Bannion – my boss – has deep pockets; deeper than you might imagine. And when I sent your name up the chain, a lot of noise came back down."

"Should I be flattered?"

"Naw, grateful." He selected a cigar and tapped it on the case. "My boss told me to scare you off. And if I couldn't scare you off, I was to pay you off." He glanced at her. "You can imagine my surprise."

"Why pay me off at all?"

"My boss is the pragmatic type. If you can't be scared, that means you got reasons to stay. Why waste a bullet on somebody who might do the job for you?" McTyre laughed and lit his cigar. He offered her one, and after a moment's consideration, she took it.

"Very well. I am listening."

The cigar was cheap and foul, but she let him light it for her. "It wasn't sanctioned," he said. "You know what that word means?"

"I do. They acted without your permission."

"Too bloody right they did." He looked at her. "Sometimes, the lads get ideas above their station. Mostly, when I find out, I take my cut and let it slide. This time..." He shook his head. "Not this time."

"Why not?"

"Because it's all gone arseways." McTyre looked out over the river. "You can find that out for yourself."

"I thought you said you were going to give me information."

"I just did." McTyre paused. "Thing you got to understand about Arkham is we ain't the only game in town. Donohue neither. We're small potatoes, in the grand scheme of things. We do what we do, and we stay out of the rest. Keep to our side of the street, as it were." He spat into the water. "Only sometimes them others ain't so accommodating. You understand?"

"Poachers," she said.

He tapped his nose. "Got it in one. Gomes and the others, they're working for poachers. Been doing it for a while now, apparently. Double-dipping, I call it. That's a bad business, that. Shows a lack of common sense. I don't like it when my lads do foolish things. Draws too much attention from the wrong people."

"Well, we can't have that, can we?"

He peered at her. "Wind yer neck in, why don't you?"

"No. I agree with you. Too much attention can be a bad thing." Alessandra watched a distant fishing boat slide through the fog. She wondered who fished at night. "The question is, what do we do about it?"

McTyre was silent for a moment. "Finding Gomes ain't a problem. That's why Jimmy was at the Tick-Tock earlier tonight, as a matter of fact."

"Ah. My apologies."

He waved the apology aside. "Aye, well, like I said, finding him ain't a problem. I want to know who he was working for."

"You and I both."

McTyre tossed his cigar into the water. "Aye." He spat into his palm and held it out to her. She hesitated a moment before copying him, and clasping his hand. His grip was strong, and he gave her a warning squeeze as he pulled her close. "Don't play me false, lady, or I really will have Jimmy dump you somewhere you won't be found for feckin' yonks, savvy?"

"Wouldn't dream of it, I assure you. How long do you think it will take?"

McTyre shrugged and wiped his hand on his coat. "Not long. Arkham's big, but not that big. There aren't that many places to hide." He pointed at her. "When we find him, we'll let you know." He turned back to the car.

She made to follow him, but he stopped her. "Where the feck you think you're going?"

"I assumed you'd be polite enough to give me a ride back."

"You assumed wrong." He grinned and snapped his fingers. Jimmy tossed him her pistol. McTyre handed it back to her. "Just in case. Be seeing you, countess." With that, he left her standing there in the mist, her only company the slap of water against the docks. She heard the growl of the car's engine, and saw the swoop of its lights as it pulled out.

Something metal rattled a moment later. That was followed by another sound. It was soft at first – so soft, she wasn't sure she'd actually heard it. A slow, scuffle-scrape, subtly furtive. She started away from the river, towards the street. The sound pursued her. Someone or something was following her.

She picked up the pace, and felt for her pistol. She considered stopping and confronting her pursuers, but something told her that would be a mistake.

"You disappoint me, countess." Zamacona's voice slithered out of the fog. Alessandra turned, but could not determine which direction it was coming from.

"I thought we had a deal, Zamacona."

"So did I. But you are not looking for our property."

"I am." She raised her pistol.

"Liar." A hand caught her wrist, and squeezed. She yelped, and the Webley clattered to the ground. She whirled, fist snapping out. Her attacker avoided the blow, and she was left punching at shadows.

A moment later, a hand thrust through the mist and clamped around her throat. She was propelled back against the wall of a warehouse. Zamacona leaned towards her, smiling lazily. "Very good. But not good enough." He whistled softly. The shuffle-scrape grew louder as hunched, broken forms appeared out of the mist.

Alessandra recognized the man in the slouch hat as one of them. He was not alone. There were others. The mist made it impossible to discern just how many, but it was more than a handful. She looked at Zamacona. "Why are you here?"

"You think we are not watching? You think we do not see?" Zamacona tightened his grip on her throat as he peered out of the mist. "If you are looking, where is it, countess? Why do you waste time going to clubs and diners? Why do you talk to gangsters?"

She scrabbled at Zamacona's wrist, but couldn't break his hold. He was far stronger than he looked, and faster as well. "I'm close to locating it," she wheezed, forcing the words out. "I swear!"

Zamacona lifted her off her feet with ease. "Where?" he growled, his eyes shining with an ugly light. "Who took it?"

"I ... I don't know yet," she gasped. Blackness clawed at the edges of her vision. "But I'll find out – I'm close ... !" Her words flew fast and desperate. She knew with terrible certainty that Zamacona would snap her neck in an instant if he doubted her.

Before he could reply, however, the air was split by the sudden wail of a car horn. Lights blazed through the mist, scattering Zamacona's followers. Zamacona himself released her and turned, an animal snarl on his features.

When the car hit him, his snarl turned into a scream. It was swiftly followed by a splash as the impact sent him into the river. Pepper leaned out of the cab. "Get in!" she called out. Alessandra snatched up her Webley and hurried around the cab as the shuffle-scrape of Zamacona's followers sounded all around her. One lunged out of the mist, malformed face twisted in a bestial grimace. Alessandra gagged on the stink of unwashed flesh and rotting meat as pale hands slammed her back against the side of the cab.

She hit him – or her? – with her Webley, breaking the clammy grip. As the creature staggered, whining, she reached for the door. More hands erupted from the mist, grabbing at her from all sides. She fired wildly, trying to drive them back. She heard cloth tear as she hurled herself into the backseat of the cab. "Go! Go!"

Hands reached for her, clawing at her legs and feet as Pepper threw the cab into reverse. One of the creatures gripped the sides of the door, half-in, half-out of the cab as it careened backwards away from the docks. It bared black teeth at Alessandra. Milky eyes rolled in deep sockets as a face out of a mortician's nightmare thrust itself towards her. He – it – hissed like a serpent as it fumbled for her.

She levelled the Webley and fired until the cylinder clicked empty. Her attacker sagged backwards with a groan, and slipped out of the cab. "Get the door – the door," Pepper shouted. Alessandra awkwardly slammed the door as Pepper hit the gas. She was thrown into the seat as the cab bounced along the street.

"What the hell was that? What did I hit?"

"My employer."

"Zamacona?" Pepper squawked. "That was him?"

"Yes," Alessandra panted.

"Is he dead?"

"While it would please me to no end if that were so, I doubt it." She rubbed her throat. "At best, we have made him angrier than he already was." She turned, looking back the way they'd come. There was no sign of her attackers. Only shadows and mist.

CHAPTER TWENTY-ONE
Leaving Town

Alessandra drank her coffee without tasting it. There were some benefits to being tired. She was at the diner she and Pepper had eaten at the day before. Visser was supposed to meet her this morning, before she paid another visit to Professor Freeborn. She wasn't planning to take no for an answer this time. To that end, Pepper was keeping an eye on him, while Alessandra talked to Visser. She didn't want Freeborn vanishing the way Ashley had. At least not until she'd spoken to him.

She yawned and dumped more sugar into her coffee, stirring it half-heartedly. She was still wearing the clothes she'd worn the night before. Unable to sleep after the excitement of the previous evening, she'd spent the hours before dawn puzzling through all that she'd learned. Trying to put the pieces together, as Pepper had put it. Unfortunately, few of them seemed to fit. She was missing something, and she couldn't see what. It was clear that Gomes and his fellow thieves were working for someone. Whether that someone was Ashley or not was as yet undetermined.

All she knew was that until McTyre's men ran down Gomes,

Ashley was her best chance at finding the mummy. But to find Ashley, she would need to talk to Freeborn and possibly Orne as well.

She wasn't sure what she'd do, once she knew who'd arranged the theft of the mummy. Perhaps use it to bargain with Zamacona. Either way, it would mean her time in Arkham was done. "Maybe Florida next," she murmured. "Or California."

"I'm for the latter, myself," Visser said, as he slid into the booth opposite her.

"Tad, you made it. How are you?"

"In a hurry." Visser looked nervous. He jolted slightly as the waitress came over. This time, Alessandra was ready. She'd quizzed Pepper on the proper slang the previous evening.

"Chicks on a raft, please," she said, proudly. The waitress nodded.

"Eggs on toast coming up. Something for you, sir?"

Visser shook his head. "No. No, thank you." He twitched as someone entered the diner. Alessandra glanced towards the door, but it was no one she recognized.

"Why are you so nervous?" she murmured, when the waitress had departed.

"One of my friends called," he said quietly, shooting a wary glance around as he spoke. "He knew where I was, thought I'd be interested that one of my fellow investors is dead. The police apparently wanted to talk to both Matthew and myself."

"The police?"

"He was *murdered*," Visser hissed.

"When?"

"They didn't say and I didn't ask." He looked around again, head lowered. "I think it's time I returned to the big city – any big city, so long as it's not Arkham."

She sat back. "What are you frightened of, Tad?"

"A murder isn't enough?"

"Not for someone as self-involved as you."

He frowned. "Was that an insult?"

"Focus, Tad. Answer my question. I might be able to help."

He was silent for a moment. "I… I think I'm being followed." He said the words quickly, as if afraid that someone might leap to silence him at any moment.

"The police?"

"Maybe." He shook his head. "I don't think so, though. I think – I think…" He trailed off. "I don't know what I think." He ran a hand through his hair. "Something has gone wrong. Do you understand?"

"No. Explain it to me."

He shook his head. "I can't. Matthew wouldn't… I thought maybe you'd join us. When I saw you at the exhibition, I thought it was fate, maybe." He laughed, and there was a brittle edge to it.

"Join you? What do you mean?"

"I told Matthew, I said, if Sanford can have a man like Chauncey Swann on the payroll, why shouldn't we? But he wouldn't hear of it. I thought… I thought if you could find the mummy, maybe… but…" He trailed off. "But I think I messed it all up."

"Chauncey Swann…" Alessandra stiffened and slapped the table hard enough to rattle the cutlery. "That is who he was!"

"Who?"

"Someone was looking for Professor Ashley. The description matches Chauncey Swann. He always had a predilection for seersucker."

Visser stared at her. "You know him?"

"He's an acquisitionist, like myself. Only I heard that he was no longer his own man. Why is he in Arkham?" She paused. "You mentioned Sanford. Chauncey works for Carl Sanford." She paused again, as her thoughts caught up with what she'd heard. "Join you? What do you mean? Is Orne willing to talk to me?"

Visser shook his head and looked away. "He refused to even talk to me about it. I think someone spilled the beans about your – ah – profession to him."

Alessandra sat back. "Whitlock."

"The insurance fellow?" Visser frowned and nodded. "He came to talk to me as well." He was silent for a moment. Then, "I think you should go with me, Alessandra."

"A nice offer, Tad, but you know I cannot." She patted his hand and he returned her smile, if weakly. Visser had fancied her, once. Since then, his affection had become something milder, more friendly. She was aware that she played on it, at times, and he encouraged her. It was rare she had a client that she actually felt some fondness for.

"So, you really are intent on playing detective, then?" He fished out his cigarette case and offered her one. She took it with a nod of thanks.

"I do not have much choice at the moment." She thought of Zamacona and the crunch of the cab against his towering frame. A normal man would have been hurt or dead. But she had come to the unpleasant conclusion that Zamacona was anything but normal – and that went double for his servants. A sudden thought occurred to her.

"You say you think you're being followed… Have you seen them?"

He shook his head. "No. It's just a feeling."

Alessandra frowned. "You will be careful, won't you, Tad?"

He smiled again. "My train is tomorrow morning. Earliest I

could get a seat. I was hoping we might have dinner tonight in the hotel restaurant, if you were up for it."

"I will be there. And thank you for your help, Tad. I appreciate it."

"Much good it did you," Visser said. "Think about what I said, Alessandra. I don't think this town is safe for the likes of us." He stood and departed. Annoyed, she pushed her plate away, her meal half-finished.

Visser was clearly frightened, and that worried her. She paid and left a few moments later, her mood sour.

For his sake, she hoped Professor Freeborn was willing to talk this time.

Gomes made his way down the tunnel beneath the cemetery, his mood sour. He'd screwed up. He knew it, just as he knew that there was no way he could go back for Wilma now. His arm ached worse than it had before, and his back hurt as well. It had taken him most of the night, well into the wee hours of the morning, to make his way back to the cemetery and safety. The worst of it was, Phipps had been right.

He winced and rubbed his arm. That damn woman – what had she been doing there? More to the point, what had Jimmy been doing there? He'd spotted McTyre's gunsel sitting at the bar, watching the whole encounter. When Jimmy had looked as if he was going to deal himself in, Gomes had gone for his gun and made a run for it. Now Donohue's goons would be looking for him as well. Phipps wasn't going to like that.

Then, maybe it was time Phipps suffered an accident like Jodorowsky. Why split the money two ways, when one was better? Besides, it might make up for losing Wilma. The more he thought about it, the more he liked the idea. He patted his pistol, cheered somewhat.

But when he reached the chamber, Phipps was nowhere in sight. Instead, a man clad in strange oxblood robes sat atop a stack of coffins, cradling a skull in his hands. "Where were you?" the robed man asked. Gomes recognized him, despite the funny get-up. "You were supposed to be here this morning."

Gomes hesitated before answering. "I was laying low. I got hassled last night by some dame – and then some of McTyre's boys got on my tail. And I don't think either one of us wants him showing up here."

The robed man was silent. Gomes nodded, as if he'd answered. "Yeah, I didn't think so. Where's Phipps? And fat boy?"

"The professor is otherwise engaged. You're certain you weren't followed?"

Gomes sniffed. "Nah. Even if I was, so what? You got your mummy, and when I get my money, I'm gone. No need to worry."

"I am not worried. Merely cautious. This woman – who was she?" Something in the man's voice made Gomes tense. It was as if he already knew the answer to his own question.

"Some dame with an accent. She was there during the robbery. She's the one who shot me." Gomes tapped his arm. "Tried to clip me again last night."

"I cannot imagine why."

Gomes laughed. "Who the hell knows? Some dames just hold grudges." He looked around, but saw no sign of the box or the mummy. "Already loaded it up, huh? What are you going to do with it, anyway?"

"Do you honestly care?"

"Sure." Gomes smiled. He scratched his unshaven chin.

Something felt off, but he couldn't say what. Where was Phipps?

"We're going to eat it," the robed man said.

Gomes blinked, certain he'd heard wrong. "What?"

"We are going to eat it. Leathery strip by leathery strip."

"You're crazy. This is a joke, right? Very funny."

The robed man sighed. "Have you ever thought about what the dead might know? Or what power might yet remain in them?" He lifted the skull and turned it so that the light of the lantern danced across it. "What strange alchemy percolates in the suppurating marrow of an inhumed corpus? The ancients knew, and they passed that wisdom down to us. Often in their own flesh, appropriately enough."

He set the skull down and stood, still talking. "In Tibet, for instance, it is the practice of would-be sorcerers to seek out the body of another of their sort, and eat the tongue in a ritual of appalling intimacy. The Gauls used to pluck out the eyes of the dead for consumption, so that what they had witnessed might not be lost."

Gomes stared at him in confusion. "What?"

"Knowledge is just another nutrient, after all. Something required for survival. To eat of a thing is to partake of its life, its experiences... its soul. To add the sum of it to your own whole, and thereby grow fat on wisdom."

Gomes drew his weapon, and the robed man paused. Gomes couldn't tell, but he thought the man was frowning beneath his mask. A moment later, the robed man continued with his impromptu lecture. "You wouldn't understand, of course. The concept is beyond your limited comprehension." He turned. "There is a potency in the dead. Like wine, they grow finer with age."

Gomes looked around. "What the hell are you talking about? Where's Phipps?"

"Mr Phipps has received his reward. Now it is your turn."

Gomes didn't quite lower his weapon. "That's more like it. Where's the cash?"

"Who said anything about cash?"

Something hard hit Gomes across the back of his skull, and he went down in a heap. Head ringing, he tried to get up. A second blow caught him between the shoulder blades and he fell, his pistol clattering out of sight. He groped for it blindly, groggily.

"A third should do it, I think, professor," the robed man said, mildly.

Gomes rolled over and looked up into Ashley's flushed, flabby features. Ashley lifted the femur he held in both hands like a club. Gomes tried to speak, but all that came out was a croak. The blow fell, and the shadows rolled in.

CHAPTER TWENTY-TWO
Swann

Freeborn wasn't in his office when Alessandra and Pepper arrived. The office itself wasn't hard to find. It was in the same building as Ashley's had been, just one floor up. Freeborn's office was a marked contrast to Ashley's. It was tidier, though not much larger. The door wasn't locked, so they let themselves in.

Alessandra conducted a quick search, flipping through books, rifling drawers, searching under the desk for hidden compartments or false bottoms. Pepper kept watch. "Anything?" she asked, after a moment.

"A revolver and a box of ammunition." Alessandra put both on the desk and sat down in Freeborn's chair. "An unlocked door means he will be coming back. Go back downstairs and sit across the courtyard, so that I can see you from the window. Signal me if you spot him – or anyone else who looks suspicious."

Pepper frowned, but didn't argue. She closed the door behind her as she went. Alessandra leaned back and watched the morning shadows crawl across the walls. They stretched with the light, creeping around. Twisting.

Moving.

She blinked. No. That was ridiculous. They hadn't moved. Not in the way she'd thought. She shook her head. Just the last tatters of a bad dream. Even so, the thought stayed with her. It was only when she spied Pepper signaling frantically from the courtyard below that she realized how long her preoccupation had lasted.

She heard the sound of someone approaching down the hall. She stood and moved behind the door, holding the revolver.

Freeborn entered a moment later, looking harried. She said nothing as he went to the desk. He opened the drawer and cursed. She pushed the door closed, startling him. "Looking for this?" Alessandra aimed the revolver at him.

Freeborn froze. "You."

"Me."

"Why are you here?"

"I had a few questions."

"I'm not talking to you." His eyes flicked to the door. He was nervous.

"What is it?" she asked.

"Someone's following me."

"Who?"

"I don't know. But he has a gun."

"So do you." Alessandra tossed him the revolver. "When he gets here, let me do the talking. Understood?"

Freeborn nodded jerkily. "Why are you helping me?"

"Because afterwards, you are going to answer my questions. Does that sound fair?"

Freeborn swallowed and nodded again. "It's a deal."

"Good. Sit." Alessandra took up her position behind the door again and waited, one hand on the sap in her pocket. Soon, the sound of someone approaching echoed down the hall. She signaled for Freeborn to remain still. As soon as the door opened, she kicked it shut and heard a curse and a clatter as a small pistol fell to the floor, knocked from the intruder's hand. She kicked it further into the office and ripped the door open. She saw a flash of white, and realized Freeborn's stalker was running for the stairs. She recognized him easily. The same man who'd been in Ashley's office – Chauncey Swann.

He made the stairs, but she caught up to him easily. Too much good living had eroded his endurance. She caught the rail and vaulted over, dropping down in front of him. Startled, he stepped back, slipped on the stairs and fell onto his rear.

"Hello, Chauncey. How's tricks?"

The acquisitionist tried to get to his feet. Alessandra gave him no chance. She drove the palm of her hand into a point just below his breastbone, and he gasped, his face going white. He sank down to his knees, sucking air with desperation. Alessandra took his hat and flung it away. "Why are you following the professor, Chauncey?"

He mumbled an obscenity and tried to rise to his feet again. Chauncey wasn't very big, or very strong, but she had no intention of testing her strength against his. She hit him again, with the sap this time. Just a light tap on the side of the head, enough to ring his bell a bit. Chauncey collapsed onto the stairs with a groan.

Alessandra sat beside him and waited for him to stir. "I will hit you again, if you give me cause, Chauncey. Why are you following him?"

"Why do you think?" he grunted, as he levered himself into a sitting position. He looked as petulant as she recalled. She and Chauncey rarely ran in the same circles, but they knew each other, in a roundabout sort of way, and well enough not to like each other.

"I'm looking for his pal."

"Why?"

"Are you stupid?"

"No, but I want to hear it."

"The mummy. My employer has a vested interest in acquiring it. And if you know what's good for you, you'll haul your keister out of here and let me get back to it." Chauncey leaned over and spat. She tapped him with the sap again. He yelped. "What was that for?"

"Manners. Focus, Chauncey. I do not require an editorial. Merely the facts." She rested on her heels and studied him. "Your employer is interested, fine. What does that mean to me?" She raised the sap threateningly.

Chauncey shrank back. "Nothing! Jesus. Nothing yet. Sanford wants to know who stole it and why." He gave her a sly look. "You know who he is, don't you? Carl Sanford, grand poohbah of the Silver Twilight Lodge. Maybe you've heard of him?"

"Perhaps. Does he think Ashley is responsible?"

"Ask him yourself."

"What did I say about manners?" She tapped her palm with the sap. Chauncey blanched and raised his hands in a placatory fashion.

"Fine, yes, he thinks he did it."

"And if you find him?" Alessandra pressed. "What then?"

"Let's just say no one quits the lodge. And no one crosses it."

She rose to her feet. "It would be best for you if I did not see you again, Chauncey. I will not settle for giving you a love-tap next time." She pulled back the edge of her jacket, revealing her Webley. Chauncey frowned.

"You won't shoot me."

"Are you certain? I shot the Turk, after all."

Chauncey blanched, and made to cover his crotch. "That was you?"

"Someone needed to do it, you will agree." She stuffed the sap into her pocket and stepped aside. "Go, Chauncey. I will not tell you a third time."

He clambered to his feet and headed for the door at the bottom of the steps. As he blasted through it, he nearly collided with Pepper. Alessandra helped her to her feet. "Were you listening at the door?"

"I wanted to see if you needed help," Pepper said, unapologetically. "Who the hell was that?"

"No one important."

"And who was the Turk?" the cabbie demanded. "Something else I should know about? There a murder rap hanging on you too?"

Alessandra smiled. "No. The Turk is very much alive, though he will be singing castrato for the remainder of his life."

"Casta-what?"

"Never mind. Come. Professor Freeborn is waiting for us upstairs."

"What do you mean, he's not in?" Whitlock demanded. The servant, one of Orne's household staff, merely shook his head and closed the door firmly in the insurance investigator's face. Whitlock stared at the door for long moments and then vented his spleen for another few minutes. When he'd finished, he walked back down the steps and across the lawn to the waiting patrol car.

The house was a large, three-story residence, situated almost at the apex of French Hill. Like its neighbors, it showed signs of genteel neglect, with overgrown hedges and trees spreading obtrusive branches over the nearby sidewalk. Only the truly rich could afford to look so shabby.

"He's not in again?" Muldoon said. He stood beside the patrol car, arms crossed. "That's twice now. Think he's ducking us?"

"He damn well is," Whitlock said, hands thrust into his trouser pockets. He could feel the frustration bubbling through him. Ever since they'd found Jodorowsky, things had gotten complicated. The cops had managed to keep it quiet, but that wouldn't last. Someone would talk, they always did. And then there'd be reporters everywhere underfoot.

Muldoon looked amused. "Maybe you shouldn't have told him she was a thief."

Whitlock looked at him. "I have a responsibility to the company's clients." He glanced back at the house. "Even the dumb ones."

"Maybe we can talk the chief into leaving a couple of the boys out here to keep an eye on things. Just in case."

"You mean just in case he gets murdered like the other two investors? Yeah, might be a good idea." Whitlock ran a hand through his hair. This case was turning into a perfect mess. Three murders connected to it, maybe more. An international criminal running around town. And now the client was ducking him. "What do you think?" he asked, reluctantly.

"About the murders?"

"No, about the White Sox," Whitlock said. "Yeah, the murders."

"I think we need to talk to the other investor – what's his name? Visser?" Muldoon sighed. "He might be in danger as well."

"I don't get it. Jodorowsky, I understand. Criminals kill each other all the time. But these guys? What have they done?"

"Paid for the mummy to be found and removed from its resting place," Muldoon said.

Whitlock looked at him. "What – you're saying it's some sort of curse? Howard Carter and King Tut and all that?"

Before Muldoon could reply, Whitlock heard the door of Orne's house open. Both men turned to see Matthew Orne coming down the walk. He was dressed in a silk dressing gown, but otherwise looked as if he were ready to face the day. "I'm sorry, gentlemen, I gave instructions not to be disturbed. They weren't meant for you, obviously." He strode to meet them, hand extended. Whitlock shook it grudgingly, Muldoon less so.

"Sorry to disturb you, Mr Orne, but we've been trying to get in touch for a few days," Muldoon said, taking off his hat. Whitlock snorted, earning him a steady look from Orne.

"I'm sorry, I've been rather busy. The robbery... came at an inconvenient time."

"You mean it was embarrassing," Whitlock said.

"For your company as well as myself. After all, you were supposed to prevent such a thing, were you not?"

Whitlock fell silent. Orne wasn't wrong. He'd been too focused on Zorzi – he knew that. Maybe she'd been a distraction, maybe not, but he'd seen the thieves. So had Muldoon. If they'd confronted them together, sooner, the whole thing might have been avoided.

"What did you wish to see me about? Some good news, I hope?"

"Not good news, no sir," Muldoon said, respectfully. "We found one of the thieves."

"Really? That's not good news?"

"He's dead," Whitlock said.

Orne paused. "Where?"

"Well, that's the thing, you see... looks like they were holed up in one of your warehouses. Funny, huh?"

"No, not especially. I own a number of warehouses. Presumably they broke in."

"Presumably," Whitlock said. "You don't seem bothered."

"Should I be?" Orne looked away, as if bored. But he wasn't bored. He was nervous. Not much, just enough for a man like Whitlock to notice. "As I said, I own several warehouses along the river. The remnants of a more prosperous time. That they broke into one was likely a coincidence."

"Or maybe not."

Orne peered at him. "Are you implying something, Mr Whitlock?"

"No, he's not. And that's not why we're here, sir," Muldoon interjected. "There've been two other deaths. A man named Ogilvy, in Kingsport, and a fellow named Soames, in Boston. You know them?"

Orne tensed. "They were... fellow investors, along with Tad Visser. They were supposed to come out this week. We were going to celebrate the exhibition." He gestured to the house. "That's what I've been preoccupied with, actually. I'm having a bit of a private soiree tomorrow evening, for some close friends. Nothing fancy, but it does require a bit of party planning."

Whitlock smirked. "I would think you'd want to avoid parties, after what happened at the last one. Then, lightning doesn't strike twice, right?"

"How did they die?" Orne asked, ignoring Whitlock.

"Unfortunately, it appears they were murdered, sir."

Orne's face went waxen. "That... is unfortunate. Is Tad all right? I just spoke to him yesterday."

"We'll be seeing him later today," Muldoon said. "For right now, we'd like to provide police protection, especially if you're having a party. I'll talk to the chief..."

"That won't be necessary," Orne said. "I can provide my own protection."

"Even so," Muldoon began.

"I commend you on your dedication, officer, but I'm sure your department's resources are better utilized in finding my stolen property – especially given the circumstances." Orne smiled. "Have no doubt, I will mention you to Chief Nichols in glowing terms." His smile faded as he looked at Whitlock. "As for you..."

"I don't work for you," Whitlock said, his voice mild. "And I don't work for Nichols. But I do want to find that mummy. Though I am still puzzled about one thing..."

"Just one?" Orne said.

Whitlock ignored that. "All this time, we've been acting on the assumption that there was a buyer involved. But we never thought to ask why someone might buy a withered old mummy. It's not really valuable, is it?"

Orne frowned. "It is not simply a mummy. It is the key to unlocking the secret history of this continent. That withered old mummy, as you call it, walked the Earth at a time prior to any recorded human habitation. Before even the earliest legends of the indigenous peoples who would eventually settle there."

"Maybe he was an explorer."

"Perhaps. But where did he come from? What sort of society produced such a man? Consider the condition of his teeth, for instance." As Orne spoke, he became more animated.

"What about them?" Muldoon asked.

"Well, he had most of them. That implies a certain awareness of hygiene."

"I'm not here to talk about hygiene," Whitlock interrupted. "I just want a bit of information – who in this town might pony up good money to buy that damn thing?" He stared intently at Orne. "Just a name. That's all we need."

Orne was silent for long moments. Then, "Have you found Professor Ashley yet?"

Whitlock and Muldoon shared a look. "No. Why?"

"Ashley is a former member of the Silver Twilight Lodge. He was drummed out in some disgrace... or so he claimed."

"And you and Mr Sanford don't get along," Muldoon said.

"That's putting it mildly, I'm afraid. Carl Sanford wants me out of business and out of Arkham. All because I wouldn't join his lodge of second-rate Masons."

"Is that why you funded the expedition? To get back at Sanford?"

"No, I funded it to find buried treasure. You need to find Ashley – and if you haven't yet, you might try asking Sanford where he is." Orne smiled thinly. "Now, if you'll excuse me... I have guests to prepare for."

Whitlock watched him walk back up the path then said, "Do you believe him?"

"Maybe. There's an awful lot of stories about those Silver Twilight types."

"So let's go talk to them."

"No. At least not yet. First, we get permission." Muldoon climbed into the patrol car, and Whitlock circled to the passenger seat.

"Since when do we need permission?"

"Since both the mayor and the chief are members in good standing." Muldoon put the car into gear. "Permission first, then we go talk."

Whitlock sat back and shook his head.

"I'm really starting to hate this goddamn town."

CHAPTER TWENTY-THREE
Freeborn

Alessandra closed the door to Freeborn's office and sat in the chair facing the desk. Pepper stood, glowering with as much ferocity as she could muster. Freeborn studied them for a moment, then cleared his throat. "Who was he?" he asked.

"No one of importance. You are safe."

"Says you."

"Yes. Says me."

Freeborn tapped his fingers nervously on his desk. "You don't strike me as being a policewoman," he said, suspiciously. "And I've already talked to them anyway."

"I am not a policewoman. But I am investigating the robbery."

"What business is it of yours?"

"I am acting on behalf of a private party."

Freeborn stared at her for a moment, processing this. "You're a… detective?" He chuckled. "Forgive me, but you don't look like any detective I've ever met."

"Met many then?"

"A few. I've worked with the Blackwood Agency a time or two."

He preened slightly as he said it. Alessandra had no idea what that was, or why Freeborn seemed so proud of it.

"How exciting," she said. "But I am not employed by an agency."

"Private dick, huh?" he said, smiling slightly. "Like that Diamond fellow?"

"I do not know a Diamond," she said, mildly. "You are avoiding my question."

"I'm doing no such thing," Freeborn protested. But the way he said it told Alessandra she'd hit a nerve. He paused. "You never told me your name."

"You never asked. Zorzi. Alessandra Zorzi. A pleasure to make your acquaintance." She extended her hand across the desk, and he stared at it as if it were a snake. Finally, after a hesitation that was just shy of rude, he took it. His handshake was somewhat south of firm. She held tight when he made to let go. "I trust you will make time for me now?"

Freeborn grunted and sat back. He loosened his tie. He glanced at Pepper, but didn't ask her name. "I suppose I have to, don't I?" He shook his head. "Damn it, Ferdinand."

Alessandra leaned back. "What, exactly, should Professor Ashley be damned for?"

"Getting me involved in this enterprise," Freeborn said, sourly.

"Not going well, then?"

"Are you trying to be funny?" He shook his head. "I'm not one for curses, but this whole affair is making me reconsider."

"Curse? What, like King Tut?" Pepper asked, somewhat too enthusiastically.

Freeborn eyed her. "No, not really."

"Explain, please," Alessandra said.

He frowned, and looked for a moment as if he might decline to answer. "It started in Binger," he said, finally. "It's in Oklahoma. If you've never heard of it, don't worry. No one else has either. The mound was just west of town. There are several in the area, most of them natural formations. Nothing to be excited about, unless you work for the geology department."

"But this one wasn't a natural formation," Alessandra said.

"I don't know what it was." Freeborn looked away, out the window. "Ferdinand claimed to have identified the mound as one mentioned by Coronado." He glanced at her. "You know who that is?"

"Yes."

"Well, I don't," Pepper said.

"Francisco Vázquez de Coronado," Freeborn said. "A conquistador. He led a large expedition from Mexico all the way up into Kansas, looking for the Seven Cities of Gold. First European to see the Grand Canyon."

"Fascinating," Alessandra said. "And he discovered the mound?"

"I'm sure the people who lived in the region already knew about it, but yes. He sent an expedition to the mound, looking for an entrance to fabled Quivira, one of the cities I mentioned."

"He thought it was underground?"

"Ferdinand seemed to think that was what Coronado believed. And… certain elements of the mound's structure bore out his theories." Freeborn grimaced. "We should have had a geologist with us. Dyer, maybe. But Ashley wouldn't hear of it. Wanted to keep things small."

"Why?" Alessandra asked. She was curious now, despite herself.

"A condition of the funding, he said."

"You did not believe him?"

Freeborn looked down at his desk. "I didn't think about it at the time. Around here, you learn not to question where funding comes from – you just say thank you and get on with it. Anyway, the locals were not best pleased to see us. I put it down to the usual hick hostility, and maybe it was. But a few members of the expedition reported seeing strange faces hanging about where they ought not to have been. We lost some equipment the first week. Had some tents torn up. Someone punctured the tires on our auto."

"As if someone were trying to sabotage your efforts."

He nodded. "Ferdinand thought he was being followed. We made supply runs to Binger every week. He oversaw a few of them. Swore someone was stalking him in town. He said that people had been asking about us. I told him that was normal."

"Did you ever identify them?"

"No. If they were even there in the first place." He peered out the window. "Maybe I'm wrong, and they were. He said… it was as if they were trying to figure out why we were there. What our purpose was." He laughed softly. "He thought they wanted his notes. Like we were after treasure and they were trying to keep it hidden."

"Or claim it for themselves."

He paused. "It put me in mind of other things I'd heard. The sort of stories archaeologists tell to scare each other." He shook his head. "The things we dig up, they're not as forgotten as we like to think. Just because a white man's never seen it doesn't mean it's never been seen. And sometimes, when we take something, we don't stop to think that maybe someone might have an objection to it." He looked at the window. "Walters warned us. Too bad we didn't listen."

"Walters? Harvey Walters?" She remembered him from the exhibition.

"Yes. He helped Ferdinand find some old book that pointed him at the mound in the first place. I always got the feeling that Walters knew more about what we were looking for than Ferdinand did. Maybe that's why he chose not to join us."

Alessandra frowned. Was that why Visser had tried to bring him in on the expedition? If that was the case, why had the old man said no? "Do you believe that?"

"No, I think it's because he's a cantankerous old goat." Freeborn sat back. "Where was I?"

"Buried treasure," Pepper said, eagerly.

Freeborn snorted. "There was never any treasure, no matter what our investors believed. Ferdinand probably filled their heads with stories of lost Conquistador gold, but we knew better. Or we thought we did. And then we found that damn mummy."

"It seems to lend credence to your friend's theories."

"No, it's not nearly that old. But it's an intruder."

"An intruder?"

"Something that shouldn't be where it is," he said, forcefully. "It shouldn't have been there. *It shouldn't have.*"

"And yet it was. Surely that is part of its value."

He shook his head. "You don't understand. It's an impossibility."

"Meaning?"

"There are no known records of such a civilization. Just... legends. Folktales. Stories passed down from one generation to the next. But no proof. No evidence."

"Until the mummy."

"Until that goddamn mummy." He sat back, gaze vacant. "I should have known something was wrong then. Maybe we could have avoided all that happened after."

"After?" she asked, steering the conversation back on course.

"It was in a... depression of sorts," he said, absently, lost in his memories. "There was evidence of other digs in the past. Cleared shrubbery, displaced rocks… tools, even. We knew of at least one previous dig, in 1891. An amateur historian named… Heaton, I think, went looking for gold. He didn't find it." He paused. "He went mad, later."

Something about the way he said it sent a chill through her. Suddenly uneasy, she cleared her throat. "And the mummy was in this depression."

"It was more akin to a chamber. There was evidence that it had been carved." His voice was soft now, and she knew he wasn't looking out the window so much as back to that day. "It reminded me of an anchorite's cell. Just big enough to fit a body, bent double."

He was silent for a moment. "There was an accident." He hesitated. "A cave-in. We lost three men." He glanced at her. "We found a second depression, larger than the first. Bowl-like. We began an excavation. Then the weather turned sour… high winds, dangerous at that height." He trailed off, his expression absent as his eyes returned to the window. "For a moment, just before it happened… I could have sworn it was rising up out of the mound… as if it were trying to prevent us from digging any deeper." He swallowed. "It was as if I were back in Australia again, with Peaslee and Ferdinand."

Alessandra headed him off before he could wander down another tangent. "Did you find something, before the collapse?"

He didn't reply for several minutes. "No," he said, finally. "Nothing worth three lives, at any rate." He coughed and cleared his throat. "The collapse was the last straw. Between it, and the incident with the mummy…"

"You didn't mention an incident earlier."

"Didn't I?" He looked frightened. Not of her, but of something in his own head. "I'm sure I did. You must be mistaken."

"I assure you, I am not." She gave him a level stare, and he shrank back slightly.

"I don't see what any of this has to do with finding the damn thing now."

"That is not your concern, Professor Freeborn. Let me be the judge of what is or is not useful information." She spoke more sharply than she intended. He was trying to avoid saying something. "What happened?"

"We... We hired several locals to help with the grunt work. The digging and lifting and such. They got nervous when we found the mummy, started talking about ghosts and strange lights. None of which we ever saw, mind."

"I would be surprised if they had not mentioned such things."

He peered at her, a slight frown creasing his features. "You sound as if you've got some experience with archaeological digs."

"A bit." She'd stolen artifacts from several active digs in Egypt. Mostly that meant dressing up in local costume and blending in with the hired laborers long enough to get the lay of the camp, and sneak into the tent where certain things were being kept. She'd only been caught out once, and hadn't that been an exciting evening?

Racing across the dunes on a stolen horse, pistol in hand, her saddlebags full of broken pottery and one mummified cat. They'd chased her all the way to Cairo, and a bit beyond. This job was proving to be quieter, but only just. More lucrative, however, especially if she could figure out how to get the rest of her payment from Zamacona and Orne, regardless of which one of them got the mummy.

Freeborn ran a hand through his hair. "They swore it moved, when we pulled it into the light. I put it down to its bindings being loose."

"They seemed fairly tight when I saw it."

Freeborn hesitated. "We tightened them. After."

"After what?"

He fell silent, studiously avoiding her gaze. She was about to prompt him again when he said, "It wasn't just the one time. It moving, I mean. Or so they said. I never saw it myself. I don't think they saw anything." He said the last words quickly. "They said it got up, or tried to. That it was... clawing at itself."

"You did not believe them?"

Again, he fell silent. Then, "I didn't. Not at the time."

"But you do now?"

He looked at his hands. "That night, there was a wind. Strong wind, out of the south. Blew out the lamps, nearly extinguished the campfire. And in the dark, something happened. We heard a sound – like a... a hiss. Or a rustle, like dead leaves caught in the wind. When we finally got the fire stoked and the lamps relit, one of the workmen was dead."

Alessandra frowned, feeling suddenly uneasy. "How did he die?"

"Officially, he tripped and broke his neck in the dark."

"Unofficially?"

Freeborn looked at her. "Something crushed his throat. The mummy was on the ground behind him, as if it had... fallen off the table we'd placed it on. Its bindings were far too loose. Its hands were..." He trailed off, his own hands twitching at the memory. "We bound it again, tighter this time. Didn't have any more problems after that. Not until the collapse." He gave a weak laugh. "We decided to cut the expedition short after that."

"Yes. I can see why. Hardly the treasure you promised your investors."

Freeborn's gaze snapped towards her. "Like I said, we promised them bupkis." He hesitated. "Or at least I didn't. God knows what Ferdinand said to get Orne on board." He frowned. "Though… that sounds wrong."

Alert now, she leaned forward. "What do you mean?"

Freeborn pinched the bridge of his nose. "Just, when Ferdinand came to me, he already had funding. Wouldn't say who."

Alessandra frowned. "He may have told someone else. Professor Walters, for instance. Perhaps I should speak to him."

Freeborn gestured absently. "He's probably over in the library. Practically lives there. Just ask for him, they'll show you where he's lurking."

"Thank you." She rose, and then paused. "Were you aware that Ashley was a member of the Silver Twilight Lodge?"

He looked surprised. "No. But it doesn't surprise me."

"What is your opinion of Carl Sanford?"

He hesitated before answering. "I think he's a kook. And his organization is a bunch of kooks, being led by a kook." He pursed his lips. "But… I know better than to say it where some people might hear me."

"Such as who?"

Freeborn gestured haplessly. "People. The dean, for one. Sanford has his hooks in a large part of this town's population. Mostly the affluent part, if you get me. Are you planning to talk to him as well?"

"Perhaps."

"Want some advice?"

"Always."

"Don't," he said, flatly. "Stay away from Sanford. Stay away from the Lodge and all the loonies in it."

"You do not believe they are involved."

"I didn't say that. But if they are, best to leave them to it. Sanford is a bad friend to have and a worse enemy."

"And what about Mr Orne?"

Freeborn shook his head. "He's a very rich man with an abiding interest in history, and a willingness to fund archaeological expeditions. I'll not say a word against him." Another hesitation. "But… I will say this – those two have been fencing since Orne turned down Sanford's invitation. The whole stunt with the mummy? I think Orne came up with that after Sanford set up the lodge exhibits at the museum." Freeborn shook his head. "The rich make pettiness an art form."

"Did Ashley know?"

"We both did. Everyone knew. That's just how Arkham works. Orne and Sanford have been divvying up the upper crust for a few months now. Drawing battle lines. Every cocktail party was a skirmish, every barbeque luncheon an assault."

"Who is winning?"

Freeborn shrugged. "Hell if I know. I have enough problems of my own with the academic snake pit."

"And you are not curious?"

"No." He was silent for a moment, staring past her shoulder. "I mentioned Australia, before. Not the first expeditions I ever took part in, but the one I remember the most. We found things there as well – not mummies, nothing so aggressively out of place, but unexpected nonetheless. Not much, but just enough to… arouse uncertainty."

He looked at her. "That's how that damned mummy made me

feel – how all of this makes me feel. As if I were back in the Great Sandy Desert, staring up at those blasted stones again. I don't ask questions like those any more." He looked away.

"I don't want to know the answers."

CHAPTER TWENTY-FOUR
Harvey Walters

The Orne Library crouched at the heart of the campus like a watchful hound. It was a blocky building of pale granite, inelegant and sturdy. A set of stairs led up to a set of massive oaken doors. Over the doors was carved a motto in Latin – *Lux in obscuro sumus.*

Pepper sounded the words out. "What does that mean?"

Alessandra knew a little Latin, enough to piece together the meaning. "We are the light in the darkness," she said, out loud. She smiled. "A good saying. A bit pretentious, perhaps. Then, it is a university after all."

"Think this place is named for that Orne guy?"

"I believe it is, yes."

Pepper was silent for a moment. "I'm starting to get a bad feeling about all of this."

"Starting to?"

"Look, I don't know much about this lodge stuff, but I know people who do, and they say that even guys like McTyre steer clear of Carl Sanford."

"Yes, McTyre said something similar last night. Perhaps it is merely coincidence."

"You believe that?"

Alessandra looked at her. "Perhaps you should go wait for me at the diner. I will be along soon. Order lunch. You look hungry."

Pepper rubbed her stomach. It had been audibly grumbling for the last few minutes. "Now that you mention it, I am sort of hungry. And this many books in one place gives me hives." She hesitated. "You'll be OK?"

"One old man will not prove too troublesome, I think." She started up the steps. Once past the doors she entered the main hall. Stained glass windows looked down on large mahogany tables arranged in neat rows. Overhead, a domed glass skylight occupied most of the ceiling. Despite the windows, there was precious little sunlight to be had. Electric lamps burned on every table and in the study carrels.

Pillars rose along the length of the hall, supporting the upper stories. Stone grotesques clung to them, glaring down at Alessandra as she made her way to the desk where a blond woman organized books for re-shelving.

"Pardon me, but would you happen to know where one might find a Professor Harvey Walters?" Alessandra asked, inadvertently startling the young woman.

"Oh!" she said, dropping several of the books she'd been holding. Alessandra helped her pick them up, apologizing as she did so. "No, no, my fault entirely. Head in the clouds, you might say." She stuck out a hand. "Daisy Walker. And you are?"

"Alessandra Zorzi."

"And you're looking for Professor Walters?"

"I was told you might know his location."

Daisy laughed. "I might have some idea at that. Come on."

The librarian led her through the stacks, towards the back of the building. "Most of these old offices are storage now," she said. "But a few diehards claimed them for their private use – closer to the books and away from bothersome students, if you get me."

Alessandra chuckled. "I believe so."

"Only Professor Walters and two or three others lasted. The heating isn't the best." Daisy pointed to one of the tables. "If you'll wait here, I'll see if he's in." Alessandra took a seat.

The library was quiet. There were a few students, scattered throughout the main hall, and she could hear others walking around on the floors above. None of them spoke, not even to whisper. The building had an empty, lonesome feel that made her antsy. She wanted to shout, to sing and dance, to fill the silence.

Instead, she sat and waited, and soon enough Professor Walters stumped into view, followed by Daisy. Alessandra looked up at him. "Hello, professor. Thank you for agreeing to meet with me."

Walters smiled genially. "Well, it's not every day a woman such as yourself asks to see me. My days are mostly filled with nervous students and tedious colleagues. You promise at least a chance at something more interesting."

"Even so, you have my gratitude."

Walters turned and gestured with his cane. "Come, come. Let's adjourn someplace more private. My study room is this way." He nodded to the librarian. "Thank you, Miss Walker. Would you see that the countess and I aren't disturbed?"

His room proved to be an untidy niche situated along the back wall. It was larger than Freeborn's office, but felt more cramped thanks to the overstuffed bookshelves that lined the walls. Walters' desk was too large for the space, and an antique. It was topped by white towers of paper, and stacks of books. Wooden masks hung in the gaps between bookcases, and strange idols made from teak, soapstone and obsidian crouched haphazardly on shelves.

Walters brushed papers from a chair, and then beat dust from a cushion. He indicated it as he circled the desk to his own seat. "Sit, please. You're not allergic to dust, I hope?"

"Not that I am aware of."

"Well, you're about to find out. Of late, I prefer this room to my office in the administration building. No one bothers my books down here, and there's a decided lack of interruptions." He studied her for a moment. "So, you saw the robbery," he said. "I assume you've spoken to the police."

She smiled. "Several times."

Walters grunted. "Yes. They've been here as well." He shuffled a stack of papers from one end of his desk to the other. "I heard the shots, but saw very little. Probably for the best." He eyed her. "Why did you want to speak to me?"

"Did you know Professor Ashley?"

Walters sat back. "You aren't the only one to ask me that."

"I am not the police."

Walters nodded. "Obviously. So who are you?"

"A concerned party."

Walters grunted. "I do not like having my time wasted, countess. I have few enough years remaining that I can spend them on obfuscating repartee. What is your interest in Ferdinand Ashley?"

"My apologies. I am unused to American forthrightness. I believe him to be involved in the theft. I thought I should speak to you."

Walters blinked. "Oh." Then he frowned. "That doesn't surprise me. You've spoken to that young fool, Freeborn, then?"

"I have had that pleasure, yes."

"And he told you that I helped Ashley with his research."

"He did."

"I'm sure those were the first words out of his mouth. I don't know where Ashley is, if that is what you're wondering." He turned to his books, and ran his fingers across the spines, searching for one in particular. He found it and dropped it onto the desk. Dust billowed, and Alessandra waved a hand in front of her face to disperse it. Walters ignored the dust as he flipped through the crackling, yellowed pages.

"Over the years I have uncovered a number of... curious commonalities, shall we say. Similarities in symbology, pronunciation, etcetera that indicate a ... a communal memory, for lack of a better term. That's what interested Ashley the most – the commonalities."

"Such as many cultures having some form of great flood in their folklore."

Walters beamed at her. "Exactly! Yes, that's it exactly. A sort of shared experience – a primeval occurrence of such intensity that is recalled and filtered through innumerable generations down through uncounted eons."

"Very interesting, but what does this have to do with what he found?"

"I'm getting to that. Ashley noticed similar commonalities in his own research into the prehistory of North America. The stories of the indigenous tribes hinted at an ... unwritten history. Ashley was determined to uncover that history. So he came to me."

"Freeborn mentioned a book."

"Yes." He tapped the book. "This one here." The pages were full of tight, cramped script in a language she didn't immediately recognize. "It is a copy of a copy. A testament by one Panfilo de Zamacona y Nunez."

"What?" Alessandra looked up, startled. "Who?"

"An Asturian explorer of no particular note. One of hundreds of Spaniards who flocked to the American continent in that period, looking for kingdoms of gold."

"I thought most of them were confined to Central and South America."

"Most being the operative word. Some came further west, farther north. We are a rapacious species, countess. There is very little we will not dare in the name of profit." Walters turned the pages. "Most of this is just a description of his travels through Mexico, and into North America. Interesting reading, but… it becomes pertinent towards the end. Zamacona impressed a native man into service as a guide. The fellow apparently led him to a secret door set into a high rock mound. A door that led to… Well." He looked at her.

"Don't keep me waiting, professor," she said. "What did he find?" She asked the question, already knowing the answer.

"A vast, subterranean empire. A kingdom of shadows, older than any above the surface. At least according to Zamacona." He closed the book. "It was peopled by a foul folk, fond of sadistic entertainments, including a form of alchemical necromancy I have only read about in certain older Latin texts."

"Necromancy?"

"They enslaved the dead."

Alessandra thought of pale, clammy hands grabbing at her, and of milky eyes rolling in their sockets. Of the smell of rotting meat. She said nothing.

Walters shook his head. "In truth, I've always considered this book to be a clever fiction. A literary hoax."

"But now?"

"Now I am not so sure." Walters tapped the book with his fingers. "That mummy – it was found in roughly the same place as this account. There are masks described herein that greatly resemble the one worn by our desiccated friend. That is why I attended, despite my distaste for such gatherings. I needed to see it for myself. As I said last time, if Ashley was right, it could rewrite the history of this continent."

"But what you are implying – it cannot be true. Can it?"

Walters shook his head. "Truth, like beauty, is a matter of perception. What was once known to be a lie is revealed as the truth. What was held as ironclad truth soon becomes a lie. New information, new contexts. The past is an undiscovered country, and our maps are not the best."

She sat back and shook her head. "Why steal such a thing?" It was a question she had been pondering in the back of her mind since the robbery.

Walters was silent for a moment. "For some individuals, such a remnant might be regarded as a key to ancient knowledge." Walters sat back, hands clasped on his chest. "Mummies were a sort of currency among certain sects for a time. They were used in various rituals – or eaten."

Alessandra blinked. "Eaten?"

"Oh yes. The Corpse-Eating Cult of Leng, for instance. They supposedly devoured the bodies of mystics and sages, in order to absorb their wisdom. The Dayak people of Borneo have similar rituals. The infamous Hellfire Club was said to have purchased mummies to feast on, in great celebrations. Benjamin Franklin wrote about it. He even claimed to have participated."

He laughed and continued. "Then of course there were the witch-cults of Salem and Providence. A fellow named Curwen was supposed to have illicitly purchased no less than one hundred and fifty mummies over the course of a decade, none of which were ever recovered."

Alessandra frowned. "And you think such a group is responsible?"

Walters' smile faded. "I cannot say with any certainty."

"Are there any of these groups active in Arkham?"

"I should hope not."

She paused for a moment. "What about the Silver Twilight Lodge?"

"What about them?"

"They are an occult group of some sort, yes?"

"I thought you didn't know anything about the occult," he said.

"Could they be behind the theft?"

"What makes you say that?" he asked, softly.

"Professor Freeborn believes he and Ashley are being followed. Thaddeus Visser believes the same thing. And earlier today I had a run in with one of their members – a man named Chauncey Swann."

Walters frowned, but said nothing. Alessandra read something in his face. "What?" she asked. "Do you know something?"

"No. Maybe." He looked at her. "You said they thought that they were being followed? By the same individuals?"

Alessandra hesitated. "Possibly."

Walters' expression was grave. "Could you come back later? This evening, perhaps?"

"Not tonight, no. Tomorrow afternoon?"

"That will have to do," he said. "I may have something for you then. In the meantime, I suggest you take care."

Alessandra rose, feeling inexplicably shaken.

"Thank you, professor. I will."

CHAPTER TWENTY-FIVE
Sacrifice

Visser did not meet her for dinner. Alessandra was not so much concerned as she was annoyed. She was going to be even more annoyed if it turned out that he'd caught an earlier train. Nervous as he was, she wouldn't have put it past him. Though he could have at least left a note. Still, there was no reason not to enjoy dinner – though she steered clear of the chicken this time.

She ordered, and watched the other tables. Most were empty. With the exhibition over, many of the guests had scattered to the four winds. Arkham wasn't much of a tourist destination. At least according to Pepper.

She'd sent the girl home to get some rest. Tomorrow would be another long day, she suspected. Though she wasn't yet sure what her next move was going to be. Until she heard from McTyre, she was at a dead end. Unless she could locate Ashley before then. But even that was looking less and less likely.

She wondered what Walters had to share with her. He'd seemed shaken when she'd left his office – almost as bad as Freeborn. As if they knew something they couldn't put into words. She paused, a forkful of food halfway to her mouth. The lights overhead flickered and went dim, one by one. She watched them, a cold sensation in the pit of her stomach.

None of the other diners seemed to notice. She set her fork down and made to rise – but couldn't. Her limbs felt like lead. The weight in her stomach was unbearable – it shifted and roiled, like a thing alive.

The tables began to splinter and spread, like detritus in rising water. The ceiling surged away, cascading upwards into infinity. She fell from her seat and collapsed to the floor. In moments, it was as if she were trapped in the heart of a labyrinth. Or so it seemed to her tortured perceptions. Structures fashioned from broken wood and drunken angles stretched towards a sky of stone teeth. The darkness was pervasive, pulling everything towards itself. She could no longer see the other diners.

Pale lights, like the prey-shine of angler fish, danced along the impossible heights. Something about them sent a chill down her spine. Again, as all the other times, she heard the thunder of drums – of artillery – of some great heartbeat, thudding in the dark below the world. She couldn't remember how she'd gotten here. Or even where *here* was. The edges of her perceptions were soft, and barely there.

The pale lights spun about her, piercing her from all sides. The dark rose up all around. Consuming her. She could feel it, hollowing her out and filling the empty shell. Worse, she could hear it inside her. It spoke to her, in a whisper at first and then louder, like a crashing torrent or a howling wind. The same words as before.

Tsathoggua en y'n an ya phtaggn N'kai.

N'kai.

N'kai.

N'KAI.

N'KAI.

N'KAI!

"I don't understand," she cried out, hands clasped to her ears. "What does that mean? What do you want?"

N'KAI!

The word struck her like a hammer blow, and she sat up with a strangled yelp. Blearily, she realized that she was not in the restaurant, but her room. Someone was knocking at the door. Her stomach was in knots as she stood and pulled on her dressing gown. Her throat felt raw, as if she'd been gargling with glass. She paused at the door.

The dream had been stronger this time. More real. As if it were trying to tell her something. Whatever it was, she wished it would just come out and say it, rather than all this cryptic symbolism.

The knock came again, more insistent this time. Not Milo, then. Taking a breath, she opened the door. Her eyes narrowed. "Mr Whitlock. What an unpleasant surprise."

"Get dressed," Whitlock said, brusquely. Two uniformed police officers stood behind him. "Now."

"Why?"

"You know Thaddeus Visser, don't you?" The way he said it implied he already knew the answer. Before she could reply, he continued, "He's dead."

"Dead?" Alessandra froze, just for a moment. It was as if she understood the words, but the meaning escaped her. Visser – dead? It made no sense. She had just spoken to him. An image of him formed in her mind and she saw again the look on his face. The fear in his eyes. She took a deep breath, but fought to keep her feelings from her face. She shook her head, mouth dry. "Perhaps I misunderstood," she began.

"You didn't. You know he was staying here – one floor down?"

"Yes."

"When did you last see him?"

She straightened. "Are you a policeman now, Mr Whitlock?"

"Answer the goddamn question."

"I was supposed to meet him for dinner last night. He was planning to leave Arkham this morning." She took another deep breath. "I am guessing that he did not."

"No. He's probably going to miss his train."

Alessandra stared at him. "You are a callous man."

Whitlock paused. "Maybe. But I think you know more than you're saying. And I'm going to find out what, even if I have to slap you in leg-irons to do it."

"You keep making threats you have no power to enact," she said, unable to keep the anger out of her voice. "Eventually, I am going to call your bluff. Where will you be then, I wonder?" She fixed him with a steady glare. "You are not a policeman. But you keep threatening to throw me in jail. I do not like this."

"You want an apology?"

"No. I want you to leave me alone."

"No dice. You're a thief. I catch thieves." He paused. "Visser isn't the only one who's died, you know that, right?"

She didn't reply. Whitlock almost sounded concerned. When she didn't answer, he said, "Yeah, I bet you do. Doesn't faze you though, does it?"

"Visser was my friend." Her voice cracked.

Whitlock didn't reply for a moment. "I'm sorry," he said, finally. "Muldoon wants you downstairs. We need someone to… identify him."

Alessandra nodded and closed the door. She dressed quickly, pulling on her work clothes, before joining them out in the hall. If Whitlock noticed, he said nothing. "Who found him?" she asked, as they bundled into the elevator.

"A porter. Poor kid went to tell him his cab had arrived. Door was open, he went in the room…" Whitlock trailed off. "Kid damn near fainted. There's a doctor looking him over now." He glanced at her. "It's not pretty."

"In my experience, death is never pretty." Clancy was on duty in the elevator, but he didn't try and share any anecdotes. He looked subdued. Frightened. Alessandra felt as if she had a bellyful of ice water as the elevator lurched downwards. Something about the sound reminded her of things she didn't want to think about.

"Your files mention you were an ambulance driver, in the war."

"Yes. You?"

"I spent my European holiday getting shot at."

"I as well. Or did you think ambulance drivers were immune to gunfire?"

Whitlock snorted. "You're a cool one, lady. Too bad you're bent."

"I prefer to think of myself as curved." The elevator shuddered to a halt, and Whitlock hauled the doors open. The first thing she saw was Milo sitting on a bench opposite, being examined by a sallow featured man in rumpled clothes. The doctor, she assumed.

"Milo," Alessandra said, hurrying towards him. Whitlock, for a wonder, didn't seek to dissuade her. "Milo, are you all right?" A stupid question. He clearly wasn't. But she could think of nothing else to say. The boy had a hollow look in his eyes. "How is he?" she asked the doctor softly.

"Physically, he's fine." He snapped his bag shut. "More than I can say for the fellow in the room down the hall, however." He looked at Whitlock. "Tell Officer Muldoon he'll have my report this afternoon. Both versions."

"Thank you, Dr Mortimore, I'm sure he'll be ecstatic to hear that," Whitlock muttered, as the doctor trooped off.

"Both versions?" Alessandra said.

"Apparently the doc has bad luck. He pulls all the weird consultations. Gotten into the habit of writing two reports. One for official use, and one more... speculative, let's say." Whitlock laughed mirthlessly. "I swear... this town. Sooner I'm out of it, the better."

"There, we are in agreement." She looked down at Milo and brushed a stray strand of hair from his face. He flinched, his eyes locked on something she could not see.

"Come on," Whitlock said. "Muldoon is waiting."

"Took you long enough," Muldoon said. There were two more uniformed officers present, one at either end of the corridor. Both were pale, shaken. Both seemed as if they wished they were anywhere else.

"She stopped for a chat," Whitlock said.

Alessandra glared at him. "I was checking on Milo. The porter."

Muldoon nodded, his expression softening slightly. "You knew Thaddeus Visser, right? Otherwise we've got to find somebody else to identify the body."

"I... I knew him. Yes." Alessandra hesitated. "I am not aware of any family."

Muldoon looked at her, as he stopped in front of the door to Visser's room. "How well did you know him?"

"We were... friends."

He frowned. "You might..." He trailed off and opened the door.

The smell hit her as she stepped inside. An acrid, ugly odor – one all too familiar to her.

Blood.

The room was dark. The curtains pulled. She could hear water dripping in the en suite. "Where…" she began, her voice hoarse. "Where is he?"

"Bathroom," Muldoon said, softly. He stepped aside so she could enter. She did, after a moment's indecision. The bed was rumpled, as if someone had been woken suddenly. Luggage was scattered across the room, unpacked. He'd never gotten to it.

She glanced towards the en suite. The smell was stronger there. The dripping sound – persistent. Almost against her will, she went to the bathroom and pushed the door open with her foot. She reached for the light cord.

Pale light washed across red-marked tiles, revealing everything. The dripping wasn't coming from the faucet, but the tub. Or rather, what was in the tub. Visser had been taking a bath when it happened, she thought.

The raw, red flaps of his torso gaped wide, like an inverted mouth. Something had torn him open, split him from sternum to crotch and removed things from him. Those things, pink and wet and dripping, had been set on the edge of the tub, as if on display. Marks had been carved into his arms and neck and chest with something – perhaps a finger.

His eyes were open. His mouth gaped wide, too wide, as if he'd been screaming as they split him open and scooped him out.

She stepped back, stomach twisting, and turned away. Trying to blot out the image of what she had just seen. "Oh Tad, I'm sorry," she gasped, as she stumbled towards the door. Muldoon's face was white.

"It's him?"

"Yes." She retrieved her handkerchief and put it to her mouth and nose. She wanted to throw up, but was afraid of what might emerge. "They didn't... they didn't touch his face."

"They wanted him to be identified," Muldoon said.

"How do you know that?"

"This ain't my first ritual killing." Muldoon pulled the door to the room closed, sealing the scene once more. "Now what do you know about it?"

"Should I not be talking to a detective?"

"No. The chief wants this hushed up, because Mr Orne wants it hushed up. And the mayor and everyone else. So officially, Dr Mortimore is gonna say it was a suicide."

Whitlock made a sound that might have been a curse. Neither he nor Muldoon seemed happy about the official story. "But unofficially, you both are going to continue to investigate," Alessandra said.

"Officially, I'm still looking for the mummy," Muldoon said. "But I think this had something to do with it. So yeah."

Alessandra hesitated, considering her next words carefully. She looked at the door to Visser's room. She closed her eyes briefly, trying to banish the image. She felt her gorge rise, and swallowed. Her stomach squirmed briefly, and subsided. "I spoke to Tad yesterday morning. He said one of the other investors had been murdered."

"Not just one," Muldoon said, leaning close and keeping his voice low. "Both of the other swells got eighty-sixed. One in Kingsport a few days ago, and one in Providence, yesterday. Both of them helped fund the expedition." He paused. "Same deal as Visser... throats opened, buckets of blood. Ritual."

"Are you certain?"

"As much as I can be without seeing the bodies myself. I've recommended to my boss that we put a couple of guys on Orne. Just in case."

"That might be wise." She paused, grief hardening into anger. "I wish you luck in finding whoever did this, Officer Muldoon. And they had best hope you find them before I do."

CHAPTER TWENTY-SIX
Orne

Pepper sat in the lobby of the Independence, hat pulled low over her eyes, watching the cops stretcher the body through the lobby. The concierge danced around them, flapping his hands, protesting. No one was paying attention to him, however.

She wasn't the only one in the lobby. Guests stood back, whispering amongst themselves, their eyes fixed to the bloodstained shroud that covered the corpse. Pepper pulled off her hat as the body went past, wondering who the poor sap had been.

"Things are getting rough, huh?" someone said, behind her. She looked up and saw McTyre's man – Jimmy – leaning against a decorative pillar behind her chair. He smiled at her. "You're the hack, right? De Palma's guy? Salt?"

"Pepper."

"I knew it was a condiment," Jimmy said, watching the body. "Where's her ladyship? You know, the dame you been working off the books for?"

"Upstairs," Pepper said, pitching her voice low. She pulled her cap back on. "Why? You want me to tell her something?"

Jimmy paused, studying her. "You got some moxie. Maybe I ought to pop you one, teach you to respect your elders."

"Careful you don't throw your hip out, grandpa," Pepper said, with as much bravado as she could muster. Jimmy looked like a gangster, and that was never good. That meant he was good enough to get away with being a bit flashy – or that he didn't care if someone called him on it. Either way, that made him someone not to be messed with.

Jimmy smiled. "Moxie," he said again. He lit a cigarette and took a drag. "South Church. Tonight. We want to see her. You ain't invited."

"I'll let her know. What time?"

"Around seven would be nice. I got a date." His smile widened. "With Gomes missing, his dame is beside herself. I thought I might take her out, show her a good time."

"Good for you," Pepper said, turning away. "I'll tell the countess."

"Glad to hear it." Jimmy reached down and patted Pepper on the head. "See you around, kid." He strode towards the doors, whistling. Pepper watched him go, and frowned. She didn't like it. She didn't trust McTyre, but the countess seemed to think they were after the same thing. That didn't mean Pepper had to like it, though.

Truth was, she didn't care for much of what she'd been through the past few days. It had been exciting at first, sure, but after she'd whacked that guy with her car she'd begun to think maybe she was in over her head.

Too, someone was following her. Some little guy, wearing black. Like one of those goons from the night on the docks. She'd thought about telling Alessandra, but hadn't gotten around to it. Maybe they were just keeping tabs on her. But something told her she might be in trouble. People didn't normally get up and walk away after being pancaked by a cab. But from what she'd seen, Zamacona wasn't normal.

She wished she had a gun, like Alessandra. Iggy could get her one, but she hadn't wanted to ask. That kind of request got noticed. Got people asking questions. That was the last thing she needed. De Palma was already sniffing around, wondering what she was up to. She'd thought about throwing in the towel more than once over the past few days. Alessandra had already paid her plenty, after all.

She could take the money, and her cab, and go. The problem was, there was nowhere to go to. She didn't know what she wanted to do, not really. Other than leave Arkham. She smiled slightly, wondering if Alessandra would be open to taking on an apprentice. That was the life for her. Excitement, foreign places...

"Nah," she murmured. "What would she need with a cabbie?" She looked up as the elevator doors opened and Alessandra stepped out. Pepper rose to meet her. "Bad night?"

"Visser is dead."

Pepper's eyes widened. "That was him?"

"He is not the only one." Alessandra paused. "This affair has... become more dangerous than I anticipated. It might be best if we were to–"

"Nope," Pepper said, cutting her off.

"You did not let me finish."

"I know what you're going to say. You want me to scram. Nothing doing, lady." Pepper crossed her arms and glared at the other woman mulishly. "We're in this together."

Alessandra stared at her for a moment, and then gave a slow, sad smile. "Very well. I need you to take me to French Hill this morning."

"What's up there?"

"Matthew Orne. I need to speak with him."

"I thought he refused to see you."

Alessandra's smile turned cold and hard. "I was not planning to give him a choice."

"You sure this is the place?" Pepper asked, later. They sat in the cab up the street from Orne's residence. Alessandra nodded, studying the neighborhood. French Hill was in a sort of genteel decline. The houses were large, but faded and the lawns overgrown.

"The police cars parked outside are something of a giveaway."

"Speaking of which – how are you getting past them?"

Alessandra pointed to the edge of the fenced in lawn. It was tastefully shabby – overgrown, but not quite a jungle. There were also a number of trees, all of which blocked the line of sight of the police officers parked on the opposite side of the street.

"It will be child's play," she said. She settled back in her seat, trying to push down the anger that threatened to overwhelm her. The more she'd thought about it, the more it seemed to her that Visser's death could be laid at her door. She'd gotten him involved, when he wanted nothing more than to leave. He'd helped her in the name of friendship. And now he was dead. Visser hadn't been much of a friend, but she didn't have so many that she could afford to lose one. The anger flared, good and hot. She wanted to be angry for this.

She looked at Pepper, and felt a sudden queasy sensation. "Perhaps you should go home. Leave this to me."

"Are you kidding? You might need to make a quick getaway!" Pepper turned in her seat. "Besides, I kind of want to see how you're planning to get over there."

Alessandra considered arguing further, then decided there was no point. "As for tonight..." she began. McTyre's message had been a pleasant surprise. She had not expected anything to come of it, really. Too bad it hadn't come in time to do Visser any good.

"No dice. I'm going with you then, too."

"Fine. But you will do as I say. Understood?" At Pepper's nod, Alessandra sighed. "Good. Stay here. If it comes to it..."

Pepper saluted. "I'll hightail it, never fear."

Alessandra exited the cab and ambled down the street, moving with casual urgency. She was careful to keep the trees between herself and the police. When she judged the timing was right, she vaulted the wrought iron fence and landed in a crouch on the other side. She paused, waiting for a telltale shout, or the warning bark of a dog. When none came, she crept forward, through the trees towards the rear of the house.

Most of the houses on the street had substantial gardens around back. Orne's was no different. She slipped through an ornamental hedge and into something out of a landscaping magazine. Marble statuary overlooked neatly tended beds of flowers, all beneath the shade of several overhanging trees.

To her left, the back of the house rose. A glass atrium projected out into the garden. There was movement inside. Someone stepped out – a heavyset man she didn't recognize. He hunched forward to light a cigarette against the morning breeze, turning himself away from her. She drew the sap from her pocket and padded towards him.

Just as she was about to pounce, Orne stepped out into the garden and spotted her. "Countess?" he asked, clearly startled. The heavyset man whirled, reaching for what she took to be a weapon. She went for her Webley. "Leon, stop," Orne snapped. Both Alessandra and the big man froze. "Go back in the house," Orne continued, not taking his eyes from Alessandra. "Tell Maxwell to bring out another cup for coffee. We have a guest."

Alessandra slid the sap back into her pocket and smiled. "Hello, Matthew."

"Countess. I am surprised to see you. I thought I told Tad–"

"Tad is dead," Alessandra said, flatly.

Orne hesitated. She could read the moment of calculation in his face. "When?"

"Last night." She paused. "Of the four men who invested in the Binger expedition, you are the only one left."

"Am I a suspect, then?" He started to smile, but stopped. "But you are not a police officer, countess. Why are you here?"

"To see you. To find out whether you know where Professor Ashley is."

"And why would I know that?" He turned away before she could answer. "Would you like to come inside? I've had breakfast laid out." He went into the atrium. After a moment, she followed.

Orne gestured to a round patio table. "Sit please." There was a pitcher of juice on the table, and a carafe of coffee, as well as two cups. He poured her a cup of coffee as she sat.

She looked around. The atrium was awash in vibrant hues, and familiar smells. Orne was an orchid man. That spoke to money. More, it spoke to patience. Obsession, even. She'd once procured a book on horology for a fat man in New York. He'd been an orchid man as well. "You did not seem surprised to hear that Tad is dead."

"The last I heard, the police intended to speak to him. I guess they didn't get to him in time." He began delicately unravelling the croissant on his plate. He caught Alessandra's look. "There's a bakery just down the hill. The oldest in Arkham. I have a standing order. They make me a fresh batch twice a week."

He popped a sliver of pastry into his mouth and chewed with relish. "Not as good as those made in Paris, I expect, but good enough for Massachusetts." He wiped his fingers on a napkin and looked at her. "You know, Mr Whitlock said I wasn't to trust you. Why is that, do you think?"

"I am sure I do not know."

"He wouldn't like me talking to you."

"Mr Whitlock is not here."

Orne nodded. "True enough." He paused. "I don't know where Ashley is. Nor do I know who killed Tad, though I would quite like to get my hands on them." He leaned towards her. "I expect you would as well."

"Why would someone want to sabotage the expedition?"

He frowned. "What?"

"I spoke to Professor Freeborn. He mentioned several incidents."

Orne was silent for a few moments. Then he smiled. "You truly are a remarkable woman, countess." He sat back, dusting crumbs of sugar from his hands. "There were some problems, yes. Nothing out of the ordinary, or so they assured me." He studied her. "I asked young Tad about you, you know."

"And what did he tell you?"

"That you are a woman of singular ability and resourcefulness." Orne looked her up and down. "Was he exaggerating?"

"Not remotely."

"I intended to contact you myself, eventually. But here you are."

"And why were you planning to contact me?" she asked, already knowing the answer. "Not to ask me out for a romantic evening, I think."

"No. Tad said that you specialize in acquiring objects of certain provenance." Orne refilled their cups. "If that's true, I might have some business for you, if you were interested."

"Always." She watched the morning light fall through the glass of the atrium in scintillating ribbons. "But for now, I am already engaged."

"Oh? Might I ask by whom?"

"No. Did you know that Professor Ashley was a member of the Silver Twilight Lodge?" She asked the question bluntly. He was too comfortable. Too assured.

"Ex-member."

"Are you certain?"

He hesitated. "Why?"

"I am told Carl Sanford bears you a grudge."

Orne frowned and tapped his fingers on the table. "This whole business is like blood in the water, you know. I can feel the sharks circling."

"Then consider this your life raft. Why does Sanford have it in for you?"

"Similar interests do not always lead to fast friendships." Orne sat back and looked down the hill, past the gate. "French Hill was once the beating heart of Arkham, you know. It was the spoke of the wheel." He looked at her. "I'd like to help Arkham grow. Men like Sanford want to keep it small."

"An admirable goal."

"He invited me to join his little club, once. Everyone who's anyone in Arkham is a member. Even the mayor. And more besides... Congressmen, senators, even a few foreigners. The Lodge might have begun as a small-town club, but it has become something else entirely since its founding." He paused. "I declined the invitation."

"Why?"

He paused. "There's something... not right about Sanford." He peered at her. "You think he's behind it – behind Tad's death?"

"I do not know. That is another reason I came – to ask you." She looked out at the garden. In the morning light, the statues seemed to be dancing. Something about it made her queasy. Orne grunted. There was a speculative look on his face.

"He's been trying to put me out of business, you know. Ever since I turned him down. Something like this would be par for the course for him."

"Even murder?"

Orne's frown deepened. "I've heard stories. Sanford makes the local bootleggers look like choirboys." Behind them, someone coughed. She turned to see a servant standing in the doorway leading into the house, holding a telephone in a glass jar.

"Call for you, sir. One of your guests."

Alessandra looked at Orne. "Guests?"

"Do you recall that private party I invited you to when we first met?" he said, with a smile. "The invitation is still open, by the way."

Alessandra stood. "No. Thank you." She turned to leave the way she'd come in. Orne stopped her.

"What will you do, if you find out he's involved? Sanford, I mean."

She left without replying. Orne didn't call after her again.

When she got back to the cab, Pepper was reading her magazines and watching the police cars. She jumped slightly as Alessandra slid into the backseat. "Well?" Pepper asked.

"He is hiding something."

"So?"

"So we may need to come back. But later. For now, we should go."

"Anywhere in particular?"

Alessandra drew her pistol. She cracked it open, checking the cylinder. Then she snapped it closed.

"The Silver Twilight Lodge."

CHAPTER TWENTY-SEVEN
Silver Twilight Lodge

The house which gave the Silver Twilight Lodge its name was located high on French Hill, overlooking Arkham. From the street, it looked like a Victorian mansion. Or perhaps a funeral home.

It was neither as large as Orne's home, nor as well kept. The lawn was overgrown and full of rustling weeds. The iron fence was liberally striped with rust and the trees that surrounded it like towering sentries were dead, or doing a good impression.

Alessandra studied the house from the backseat of Pepper's cab. "An unwelcoming sort of place."

"That's putting it nicely," Pepper said. "Looks like it's haunted." She paused. "Then, so do most of the houses around here. I hate this neighborhood." She turned in her seat. "You sure you want to go in there?"

"No. But it seems I must." She'd considered simply waiting for night, and slipping in, but something told her the house would be a hard nut to crack. Deadly, even. These fraternal lodges were paranoid about intruders. Especially her sort of intruder. So she would take it slow and steady. She would play it safe. She already had a story in mind. It would get her into the lodge, at least. And if it got her in to see Sanford, so much the better.

From there, it was anyone's guess as to what might happen.

"Really?" Pepper gestured. "Those ain't two-bit hoodlums in there. That's some serious mojo is what it is. They got members in the government even. And it ain't like you're a cop. So what are you going to do?"

Alessandra shrugged. "Nothing. This is merely a… scouting mission. I am gathering information. Orne believes Sanford is behind the robbery, though he did not come out and say so. And it is no coincidence that Chauncey Swann was sniffing around Ashley's office."

"Meaning?"

"Meaning I shall be back shortly." Alessandra got out.

"Yeah, I bet a lot of people have said that," Pepper called through her open window. "Bet none of them came back either!"

Alessandra ignored her. Pessimism had its place, but not here and not now. Thievery required a sort of optimism from its practitioners. She'd learned that, among other lessons, from Mr Nuth, her tutor in the art of skullduggery.

Nuth had been a slight man, old when she'd met him, but clever – oh so clever. And good at his profession. Better than she was now, though she was still learning. A day without learning was a day wasted. Another of Mr Nuth's lessons.

She doubted he would have approved of her current preoccupation with this matter. Mr Nuth had always erred on the side of caution, and had urged her to do the same. Thieves only survived by being cautious and careful. No, Mr Nuth would have left at the first hint of things going sour. Better to fail than to be caught – or worse.

But she could not leave. Not now. Not after Tad.

She crossed the street quickly. There was no traffic, though there were plenty of automobiles parked along the road. Perhaps there was a meeting going on. Her pulse quickened as she reached the iron gates. The walkway beyond had been cleared of weeds and growth. The pale stones wound through a corridor of brittle grass. Something about it made her uneasy. It looked like an animal's gullet.

She reached for the gate. Something growled. She stopped. The grass was swaying. Another growl, from her left this time. She opened her clutch and felt for her pistol.

"I wouldn't, if I were you," a woman's voice called out. Alessandra looked up. A tall, red-headed woman stood on the porch, staring at her. She wore a gray dress of fine quality, but somewhat archaic cut.

Alessandra smiled and snapped her clutch shut. "Hello. I was wondering if I might come in?" The growling continued. Two black mastiffs emerged from the grass and stood together on the path, staring at her intently. She wondered what would have happened if she'd actually tried to enter the gate.

The woman walked down the path. Her face was cool and composed. She calmed the dogs with a touch. She studied Alessandra with eyes like chips of jade. She gestured, and the mastiffs vanished back into the grass. "No visitors today."

"Oh, I am not a visitor. I am an applicant."

The woman's eyes narrowed. Then, she gave a sharp smile. "Very well. Come in."

Alessandra hesitated. There was something in the woman's voice that she didn't like – a calculation. But it was too late to turn back now. That would only raise suspicion. Instead, she maintained her smile and opened the gate. She expected it to creak, but it made no noise at all. Recently oiled, perhaps. The façade of the lodge's crumbling grandeur might well be just that – a mask.

"I am Sarah Van Shaw, the lodge warden. Your name, traveler?" The words sounded ritualistic and Alessandra thought it best to answer honestly. Or as honestly as she ever did.

"Countess Alessandra Zorzi."

Van Shaw's eyebrow rose and she looked Alessandra up and down, taking in her clothes and general air of dishevelment. "A countess... how intriguing. Follow me." She turned and strode towards the house, her dress swishing about her legs. "There is a meeting today. You will wait in the antechamber until I announce you."

"Of course. Had I known there was a meeting I might have chosen a better time."

Van Shaw opened the door and gestured. "After you."

Alessandra stepped past her and into the Silver Twilight Lodge. It was warm inside, almost cheery. A fire burned in the great hearth farther along the exterior wall, casting red shadows along the spines of the innumerable books that cluttered the large shelves lining the opposite wall. A long Chesterfield rested on golden gargoyle feet before the fire, its back to the nearest door. A second door, opposite the entryway, sat at the far end of the room. There was a smell on the air – incense. It reminded her of a backroom in Cairo where she'd once spent an uncomfortable few hours.

Curious statuary occupied the nooks and crannies. Some she recognized as Etruscan or Babylonian. Others she thought might be Ponapean, or even Narragansett. All of them were ugly. Grotesque little things that glared blindly at the room and all within it. She could tell that they had been placed to enhance that effect. The antechamber was meant to make guests uncomfortable – nervous.

Carl Sanford liked his visitors off balance.

Van Shaw gestured to the couch. "Have a seat, countess. I will inform the master of your arrival."

"The master?" Alessandra gave a lazy smile. "Does he ask you to call him that?"

Van Shaw gave her a steady look. "You will call him that as well, if you are wise." She turned away without a further word, and went to the door opposite the couch. As it closed, Alessandra took the opportunity to scan the shelves. On occasion, she was asked to acquire the occasional grimoire or volume of magical theory. All nonsense of course, but her clients paid well for the new additions to their libraries.

Given that these were out in the open, she thought them likely to be less than valuable. She was immediately proven wrong. Several of them were first editions. Like the statues, they were meant to send a message.

She crossed to the far door and tested it. Locked. As she'd expected.

There was a sound, from the other side. A faint noise, but… persistent. She leaned close, straining to hear. It sounded like breathing. She recalled a similar moment at the hotel and stepped back, eyes narrowed.

The breathing stopped. The whole room seemed to tense, like a predator readying itself to leap. Her hand edged towards her Webley, though she could see no target.

"That won't be necessary," a voice said. She turned to see Van Shaw watching her, a slight smile on her face.

"The master has agreed to see you," the other woman said. The door opposite the couch opened, and several figures filed out, in the midst of a conversation. One was a grossly fat man, with wide features and deep-set eyes. Another was a youngish man, dressed well, with a pencil-thin moustache and a sly look about him. A third looked like an academic, down to the bowtie and patches on his elbows.

Their conversation petered out as they caught sight of her, and they headed for the door, casting curious looks her way. She filed their faces for future reference. She had expected to find a bunch of rich, educated Arkhamites looking to amuse themselves with explorations into the taboo. But this looked more like the end of a business meeting.

Van Shaw showed her in and closed the door behind her. The room was large, and occupied by a great, oblong table made from dark wood and inlaid with gilt, surrounded by high-backed chairs. At the far end of the table sat Carl Sanford, looking much as she had seen him at the exhibition – older and silver-haired, with a neatly trimmed beard and a suit that had cost good money. Sanford was clearly a man of taste and refinement, or at least he wanted people to think of him that way.

He rose and gestured to a seat beside him. "Sit, please, countess. When Miss Van Shaw told me you were here, and seeking membership no less – well, you could have knocked me over with a feather."

She sat, keenly aware that she was under scrutiny. Sanford's eyes roamed freely over her – not in a lecherous way, but as if he were memorizing her every detail. "You were at the exhibition, I believe."

"Yes. A most exciting afternoon."

"One could say that." Sanford chuckled. He studied her. "Chauncey Swann has nothing but good things to say about you." Sanford peered at her, and tapped his fingers against the tabletop.

"A calculated gamble, coming here."

"Has it paid off?"

"You have five minutes. Depending on what you say in that time, I might have Miss Van Shaw sic her pets on you." He leaned back. "It wouldn't be the first time."

Alessandra sat back. "Chauncey told you what I am, no doubt."

"Yes. Do you know a woman named Standish, by chance? Ruby Standish. Young woman. Quite clever."

"Standish? No. I know no one by that name." It wasn't quite a lie. Ruby Standish was an alias, used by another thief of her acquaintance. An American, with more ambition than skill, but a great talent for pilfering expensive artifacts.

"Oh? Never mind then." Sanford smiled widely. "I'm surprised you came in the front door. Bold of you."

"I am not here to steal from you. I am here to ask questions."

"About the robbery, yes. I know." Sanford tapped his lips with an index finger. "I would have expected a woman like you to have left town as quickly as possible, afterwards."

"I was… curious."

"Curiosity killed the cat."

"So Americans like to say."

"Who are you working for?"

"An interested party."

"I would dearly like to meet them."

Alessandra almost smiled at the thought. "I am sure you would." Her smile faded, as she remembered why she was here. "Ferdinand Ashley."

It was Sanford's turn to frown. "What about him?"

"He is a member of your order."

He nodded, with obvious reluctance. "Ferdinand used to be a

member of the Lodge. Still is, really. He never officially left, but... you know how it is."

"Bad blood?"

"In a sense. And like most academics, he can hold a grudge. One of the reasons he went to work for that twit, Orne, I expect." He drummed his fingers on the table. "I've been waiting for you to come and ask about him for some time, you know."

"Do you know where he is?"

"No, but I would pay dearly to find out." She tried to read his expression, but it was opaque. He seemed to have no such difficulty reading hers, however. "You think he's involved. More, you think I'm involved."

Alessandra tensed. The air in the room suddenly felt different – unpleasant. Like a storm brewing somewhere above. Sanford's gaze seemed as deep and dark as a well. "A not unsurprising assumption, I suppose. We have many enemies, and they would dearly love to see us embarrassed. Are you one of them, countess?"

Her mouth was dry as she said, "That remains to be seen. Did you kill them?"

Sanford blinked. The pressure in the air abruptly faded. "Kill who?"

In that moment of surprise, Alessandra realized that he didn't know. She stood. "Thank you for your time, Mr Sanford. I see I was mistaken coming here."

"Mistaken about what?" Sanford rose. He wasn't used to being the one in the dark. He leaned towards her – and jolted, as if something had shocked him. The expression on his face became... unpleasant. A mixture of confusion and perhaps even fear. "Look at me."

"What?"

"Look at me, I said," he snapped. His mask of geniality had slipped. She did, and he drew back after a few moments.

"Tell me, how have you been sleeping?"

She frowned, wondering what had prompted such a question. "I do not see how that is any of your business."

Sanford reached for her, as if he wanted to shake the answer loose. But before he could lay his hands on her, the mastiffs outside began to bark furiously.

Alessandra was out the door a moment later.

CHAPTER TWENTY-EIGHT
Connections

Whitlock stumbled back as the door opened and someone dressed like a longshoreman raced past, heading down the walk. He heard a shout from inside, and saw the black shapes of a pair of big dogs barreling towards whoever they were. "Hey," he shouted, trying to warn them. He reached for his weapon, and Muldoon, at the bottom of the steps, did so as well.

A woman stepped out onto the porch and whistled sharply. The dogs immediately veered off and retreated out of sight. The woman looked at Whitlock. "Were you planning to shoot them?"

"Only if necessary."

"It would have gone badly for you, if you had done so."

"That a threat, lady?"

Muldoon pushed past him, before she could reply. "Is Mr Sanford in?"

"He is indeed," Sanford said, from the doorway. His eyes were on the departing figure. Something in his expression reminded Whitlock of a hunter sighting his quarry. Whitlock glanced back. There was something familiar about the figure, though he hadn't gotten a good look at them. He pushed the thought aside.

"We interrupt something?" he asked.

"Not at all," Sanford said. He turned to the woman. "I have the matter in hand, Miss Van Shaw. Thank you." She nodded and went back inside, with a parting glare at Whitlock. Sanford noticed and smiled. "She's particular about her pets – raised them from pups herself. Trained them as well. Lethal, if you're on the wrong end."

"I'm sure," Muldoon said. "You don't seem surprised to see us."

"Chief Nichols kindly phoned ahead." Sanford's smile could have cut ice. Whitlock took against him immediately. Something about his eyes – the way the smile didn't reach them. Sanford was a liar, and a practiced one. "You wanted to ask me if I had anything to do with the robbery earlier this week. I'm surprised you're only just now getting to me."

"I bet," Whitlock said. Sanford looked at him.

"Ah, the insurance man. Come to check my deductibles?"

"In a manner of speaking." Whitlock leaned in. "You know a guy named Jodorowsky? Or Gomes?"

"Should I?"

Whitlock opened his mouth, but Muldoon silenced him with a gesture. "We were wondering if you'd spoken to Professor Ferdinand Ashley lately."

"Ah. There we go. No, I haven't. Professor Ashley is no longer in this lodge – or any other. He was… excommunicated, you might say."

"Any particular reason why?" Muldoon asked.

Sanford smiled. "That would be a private matter, I'm afraid. Why not ask him?"

Whitlock grunted. "He's missing, which I bet you already know."

"I'd heard something of the sort. A shame – Ferdinand was a rare mind."

"Was?" Muldoon said.

"Is," Sanford corrected. Whitlock frowned. He was playing with them. Amusing himself. He glanced at Muldoon, whose face was stiff and blank. "I don't know where he is, if that's what you're wondering. Nor can I say with any certainty that he's the sort of man to involve himself in such… shenanigans." He paused. "Though, I might not put it past him."

"Sounds like you're hedging your bets to me," Whitlock said.

"That's what a smart player does, Mr Whitlock." Sanford's smile became colder – sharper. "Especially in the sorts of games men like us play…"

"Us?"

"Myself… and whoever pointed you in my direction." Sanford sat casually on the porch rail and looked out over French Hill. "Think of Arkham as a gameboard, gentlemen. One player moves a piece, another player responds. Your presence is a move in a game most people never even notice is being played." He smiled at them, a more genial expression this time. "A game I intend to win, come what may."

"A game?" Whitlock growled. "Is that what you call four people dead?"

"Collateral damage," Sanford said. "Surely, as a former soldier, you must be familiar with that term?"

"How did you know…?"

"Your experiences are stamped on your soul, Mr Whitlock. Whether you know it or not." Sanford looked at Muldoon. "That goes for both of you." He turned back to Whitlock. "For what it's worth, I hope you find your mummy. It was an unfortunate occurrence. Looks bad for the town. Better for everyone if the thieves are brought to justice as soon as possible."

He stood and extended his hand towards the street. "Now, I'm afraid I have another appointment to get to. If you gentlemen wouldn't mind..."

"Thank you for your time, Mr Sanford," Muldoon said, stiffly. Hat in hand, he led Whitlock down the lane. The dogs watched them from the grass, growling softly as they passed. Whitlock kept his hand near his pistol, just in case.

When they were safely out on the street, he said, "That's it? That's all we're going to ask him?" He looked back at the house. Sanford was nowhere to be seen.

"That's all he's going to tell us," Muldoon said. He sighed and ran a hand through his hair. "Trust me, I know. This town..." He put his hat back on. "We got permission to question him because he wanted to know what we know. Now he does."

"He played us, you mean."

"You heard him. There's something going on that we're not privy to."

Whitlock looked away. "Reminds me of something I heard during the war. Only officers get to see the whole map. Grunts just get to see what's past the lip of the trench." He sighed. "Fine. So what does that mean for us?"

Muldoon shook his head. "Nothing good. Let's go back to the station."

"That's it, then?" Whitlock demanded.

"For now."

Whitlock turned. The dogs sat at the gate, watching them intently. One of them growled, and Whitlock felt an unexplainable chill cut through him. There was something wrong with the animals, but he couldn't say what. He just knew he didn't want to be anywhere near them without a gun in his hand.

"Yeah," he said, after a moment. "Maybe you're right."

"Well?" Pepper asked, as Alessandra got into the cab.

For a moment, she could not formulate an answer. Her hands were shaking and she felt as if she had been underwater. She looked out the window at the house up the street, and could feel it watching her. "We should go."

Pepper frowned. "Yeah, maybe so." She put the cab into motion. "Back to the hotel or…?"

"No." Alessandra shook her head. "No. The university."

"Again?"

"Yes, I promised Walters I would speak to him again. Now seems as good a time as any." She closed her eyes. Her head ached, and she felt sick. As if she had eaten too much, and yet somehow not enough. The shadows on the street bunched and coiled about the cab as they drove, and with every constriction she felt an answering one in her chest.

"Are you OK?" Pepper asked, glancing back. "Only you look like someone walked over your grave. What did he say to you?"

"Nothing."

"Did he do it?"

"No."

"So what now?"

"Now I talk to Walters. Whatever he has to tell me might point me in the right direction. Or at least in *a* direction." She leaned against the window, watching the sky. It looked strange. The clouds were… jagged. Coarse. More like stone.

The cab jolted. Bumped as if it were going over rough ground.

She closed her eyes. Everything she'd learned of late rattled in her head, and she could feel the edge of the solution. It was just out of reach, tantalizingly close… but far at the same time.

That Ashley had instigated the robbery was certain. But why? And at whose behest? Freeborn had claimed that Ashley had a patron, someone setting him on his course. If that patron was not Sanford – then who was it?

Then, of course, there were the murders. Who had committed them and why? She thought of Visser. Someone had been following him – not Chauncey Swann, she thought. Visser would have recognized him.

There was something there – like two frayed strands, yearning to be knotted together. The cab jolted again, and she heard metal buckle. She opened her eyes.

Darkness. All around her. It was as if the cab was driving through a tunnel. Flickers of light gleamed like distant stars, and she could hear the pounding of the wheels on stone. It sounded like drums.

"Pepper," she said.

"*Tsathoggua en y'n an ya phtaggn N'kai,*" Pepper croaked. She turned, and it was not her. It was something else, like a bat and a frog or maybe just the shadow of the thing, hunched in the driver's seat. Veins of gold stretched across black jaws and for a moment, it was Zamacona's face, chipped from onyx.

"*N'kai,*" the Pepper-thing hissed, in a voice like falling leaves. "*N'kai.*"

Alessandra stared, unable to move, unable to speak. She reached for her gun, and felt something wet. Like oil. She forced herself to look down. Blackness spilled into her lap from her split belly. Coils of pinkish intestine and flaps of bloody skin were forced aside by the undulating darkness as it spilled onto the floor, filling the cab.

There was no pain. Only a sort of numbness that was like relief, long yearned for.

There was a knife in her hand – how had it gotten there? She dropped it from trembling fingers and looked up. The Pepper-thing crawled over the seat towards her, with too many limbs, moving too fast and too slow, all at once.

"*N'kai,*" it gurgled again. "*N'kai.*" Each utterance of the word seemed to her a benediction of sorts – a prayer and a demand.

"N'kai," she said, her voice a rasp. The word flowered in her mind, full of context she did not comprehend. It filled her and cored her out like an apple, leaving only the fruits of her being. It explored them lovingly, pulling her apart so as to examine her from all angles.

It was only a little thing, she realized. A fragment of something greater by far. An existence beyond her own, beyond anything she knew. But there, in that instant, she was a part of that greater whole and could see the world as it saw it. A world of colds and warms, of lights and darks. Of the greatest darkness, a sea of stone stretching beneath the skin of the world, and containing all the secrets of reality.

The thief in her longed to know more, to plunder the dark. But what gripped her refused to release her into the sea. Instead, it tightened its hold, and with many mouths, it whispered unintelligible words into her ears. She tried to listen, but she was already crumbling in its grip. It caught what was left of her head in its hands, and seemed to swell, until she was dangling from its grip like a child's toy. The cab was gone, the world was gone. There was only darkness.

Only N'kai.

And then, almost tenderly, it swallowed her whole.

She sat up with a strangled gasp, and found Pepper – the real Pepper, not the half-thing of her dream – staring at her with obvious concern. "You are not OK," Pepper said, her voice cracking slightly. "You look like you've been on a three-week dry drunk. What's going on?"

"Bad dreams," Alessandra said, wiping her eyes. Her fingertips came away black. She blinked, and saw that no, she'd been mistaken. "Are we here?" She looked out the window, trying to slow her heartrate. It felt as if it might burst from her chest at any moment. She saw the familiar iron fencing of the campus.

"Yeah, but you've been asleep back there for twenty minutes." Pepper continued to stare. "Maybe I should take you back to the hotel, huh?"

"No. Not yet." She paused, reading something on Pepper's face. "What is it?"

"I got a bad feeling about tonight. Maybe we shouldn't go."

"You do not have to."

"You don't either."

Alessandra smiled sadly and got out of the cab. "I fear that choice may have been taken out of my hands. Stay with the cab. I will be back shortly."

CHAPTER TWENTY-NINE
K'n-Yan

Professor Walters was waiting for her in the library when she arrived. The old man was pacing the confines of his room impatiently, rubbing his signet ring and muttering to himself. Books rose from his desk like the parapets of a castle, many of them old and crumbling. He looked up as she knocked on the door. "There you are. Finally!"

"My apologies for being late. I was… unavoidably detained." Her dream, if that was what it had been, was already fading from her conscious mind. The details slipped through her fingers like sand, and she couldn't help but feel grateful for that fact.

Walters cleared aside the books so that they could face one another over the desk. "I asked around about you yesterday, after our talk. You have quite the reputation, countess. Indeed, a number of my European colleagues have nothing but good things to say about you. Others, however…"

Alessandra had expected as much. Walters struck her as a conscientious man. She sat and pulled out her cigarettes. "May I smoke?"

"Only if you share," Walters said. She extended the pack. He took one and she lit it for him. He sat back. "Is it true, what they say?"

"Depends on what they say, really."

"Are you a thief?"

After a moment's hesitation, she nodded. "A very good one, yes." It didn't seem strange to her that Walters knew. Presumably he had similar sources to Orne and Sanford. There was more to the folk of Arkham than met the eye. They were not so bucolic as she had assumed.

"I assume, since we are having this conversation, that you were not behind the theft of the mummy." He exhaled, and his face was momentarily masked by smoke.

"Your assumption is correct."

"Then why do you care?"

"I want to steal it back, obviously."

"And return it?" He gestured. "No, forget I asked. A silly question. A better one is – why should I help you find it?"

Alessandra lit her own cigarette before replying. She leaned back, and thought of her dreams. Of Zamacona and the mummy. But mostly of the voice in her dreams. The compulsion, rising out of the dark, driving her on. Had it been that way since she'd arrived? Had she wandered, unknowing, into a spider's web? Regardless, she was caught now. And there was only one way to go. "I think … I must. I think I am caught fast in this situation, and the only way out is to do what I came here to do."

"Might I ask why you came here at all?"

"Someone paid me handsomely to steal that mummy."

"Who?"

She hesitated. "It is probably for the best that I don't tell you."

Walters frowned. "That bad, eh?"

"I believe so, yes."

Walters pushed himself to his feet and stumped along the shelves. "And when you find the mummy, do you still intend to give it to them?"

Alessandra paused before answering. "I don't know."

Walters chuckled. "You're honest, at least." He glanced at her. "Tell me – why the hesitation? A change of heart?"

"I wouldn't go that far." Despite her words, the truth was she had begun to consider a change of career, at least. She had money enough, after this job, to last for a while. If she were careful, it might stretch for a few years. Perhaps she could write her memoirs. If she survived. She blew a plume of smoke into the air, trying to decide if she should confide in the old man. Something about the way he looked at her, about the way he spoke on these matters, told her that she could do worse. "I've been having dreams."

Walters turned, book in hand. She recognized it as the one he'd shown her before – the other Zamacona's journal. "What sort of dreams?"

"Nightmares."

"Not unusual, given what happened. You were almost shot, after all."

"Not about that. About something else. Something I don't understand." She paused, cigarette halfway to her lips. Trying to remember the dreams seemed counterproductive. She didn't want to remember them in any more detail than she already did.

Walters sat back down, book in hand. "Describe them," he said, softly. Unconsciously, he touched his signet ring. "Where are you? What do you see?"

"I thought you were an archaeologist, not an alienist."

"A mind must be flexible as well as strong. And I have seen much in my time. And talked to those who've seen more. There are great reefs of knowledge yet undiscovered in the ocean of time."

"Now you remind me of my clients. They all talk the same rubbish."

Walters grimaced. "Sometimes I wish it was." He puffed on his cigarette. "Humor an old man, countess. Tell me about your dreams."

Alessandra was silent for long moments, trying to organize her thoughts. She let out a steadying breath and said, "I'm underground, I think. Great... caverns. Like something out of Jules Verne. Or Burroughs. There are... towers, suspended between immense stalactites and stalagmites. I know they are inhabited because... I can see light in them. Bridges of stone stretch like roads through the abyssal darkness, connecting these points of light." She trailed off, and chewed on the end of her cigarette. "It's almost like a memory of something I've never experienced."

"Such things are not unknown," he said. "Do you see anyone? Hear voices?"

"Some, I think. Nothing I can remember. Nothing I want to remember." She rubbed her eyes, suddenly tired. "Mostly, I just hear a sound – a susurrus, like the rushing of water, down deep in the black. Sometimes, though, I see..." She stopped, momentarily overcome by the memory of those shapes – shapes without shapes, boiling upwards like living extensions of the darkness. Hungry and swift.

Walters didn't press her for more details. Instead, he opened the book. "I think you are involved in something... bigger than yourself. Bigger than me. Something beyond the laws of men."

"Now you definitely sound like my clients."

He frowned. "I'll thank you not to compare me to them. I am a seeker of knowledge, not a magpie hoarding trinkets." He tapped the book. "In your various dealings, have you ever heard the term *N'kai*?"

"No," she lied. "Why?"

He studied her, gaze keen and bright. She knew that he heard the lie in her words. "What about *Tsathoggua*?" he asked.

"Again, no. What is it?"

He frowned. "A person – or, rather, an entity. A god. The Sleeper of N'kai."

Something about the phrase sent a shiver through her, and an image filled her mind all unbidden. A vast shape, squatting atop a mountainous plinth of broken stone. Obese and monstrous, with a face as wide as the moon. A face like that of a toad or a bat or some foul amalgamation of both. She shook her head.

He flipped to a page. There was a rough sketch, in an unsteady hand. A grotesque mask of onyx, veined in gold. "The same mask," she said, softly. "The one the mummy was wearing."

"Yes. Carved to resemble the face of Tsathoggua." Walters shook his head. "I cursed myself for a blind fool when I realized. It had been staring me in the face the whole time." He tapped the book. "According to Zamacona, the folk of K'n-Yan – the subterranean kingdom I mentioned earlier – worshipped him, or had done so at one point."

Trying to push the image from her mind, she said, "Fell out of favor, then?"

"In a manner of speaking." Walters tapped cigarette ash into a nearby coffee mug. "Supposedly, the folk of K'n-Yan went into the dark below the city, into a place called N'kai and there learned the true horror of that which they had worshipped, and so turned from it. They took up the worship of other deities, no less awful but more remote."

"And your mysterious scribe wrote all that?"

"Among other things." Walters looked down at the book. "If Zamacona's accounts are true, and not simply the work of a creative huckster, then it is very likely that K'n-Yan still exists. A subterranean empire, stretching beneath our very feet."

Alessandra wanted to laugh, to deny his statement. Instead, she found herself nodding. Coincidences happened. Any thief knew that. But this was anything but. She wondered who Zamacona was really working for. "If it still exists, then its people may well want their property back," she said.

"I did some digging yesterday," he said. "Made some calls to Oklahoma. All those who worked with Ashley and Freeborn in Binger are dead."

"Murdered," she said. It was not a question.

"In a most savage fashion. If this account is true, then the culprits are obvious."

Zamacona – or his masters – had been busy. There was no doubt in her mind now. Nor, it seemed, in Walters' mind. "The folk of the mound, you mean."

"Yes. An ancient race who have lived in secrecy for thousands of years. Why not a thousand more? Can you imagine what might happen if the world were to become aware of them?" He laid his hand flat on the book. "Can you see why they might not be amenable to such an occurrence?"

"Then why put the mummy somewhere so… accessible?"

"I do not think that is how they thought of it." Walters leaned forward, intent. "Are the things we bury inaccessible to those who lurk beneath us? They give us no more thought than you gave them before today. They put it someplace they thought was safe. Someplace *forgotten*."

"Only someone found it."

"Yes. And what might such people – such horrid, monstrous people – do then?"

Alessandra sat back. She felt sick. "They would come looking for it."

"Yes, and they would seek to silence all those who might know about it. The workers in Binger, Freeborn, Ashley, Visser, the other investors... and you, my dear. You are a loose end if I ever saw one."

Alessandra closed her eyes. "I suspected as much." She fell silent. "Why the ritual?"

"What?"

"The killings – they are ritualistic. The police used the same term. Why? Why draw such attention?" She answered her own question a moment later. "A message. To the thieves. A warning, perhaps."

"Or a promise." Walters paused. "Or something else... The bodies were – I hesitate to use the word – excavated. As if they were looking for something." He stared at her, and she was suddenly reminded of the way Sanford had studied her earlier. As if they'd seen something, or suspected something – but what? She pushed the thought aside.

"What do you think they were looking for?"

"God only knows."

"Which god?" she asked, without thinking. She shook her head. "Do not answer that."

"What are you going to do?"

"They will not come for me until I have found what they are after. Or, rather, who they are after. I am a... stalking horse, I think." She frowned and rubbed her throat, feeling Zamacona's grip about it. "That gives me a chance, at least. A bargaining chip."

"The name of the one behind the theft, you mean."

"Yes. They want the name, not just the mummy. They cannot risk leaving anyone with the knowledge to find them again." She stood, dropping her cigarette into a half-empty coffee cup. "Thank you, professor. Your help has been invaluable."

"Has it? I don't see how."

"Nor do I. I was being polite." She smiled at him. "But I thank you for your time regardless." She paused. "You will be careful, I trust?"

He nodded. "I have encountered similar situations before. I am … protected. But you are not. What do you intend to do?"

"I will do as I have been paid to do. I will find the mummy. After that …" She trailed off. "I do not know. I will deal with what comes."

Walters frowned. "There are those who might aid you."

"Like the Silver Twilight Lodge, you mean?" Alessandra asked. A sudden suspicion flared in her mind. "Is that because you are a member as well?"

Walters shook his head. "No. But I have had dealings with them. Sanford isn't to be trusted, but … he might be able to help you."

"I fear it has gone past that. And I do not trust him."

"Oh, that's a shame. And here I came all this way," Carl Sanford said.

CHAPTER THIRTY
Alliances

Alessandra turned. Carl Sanford stood in the doorway, a crooked smile on his face. She looked back at Walters accusingly. "Is this an ambush, then? Is this why you wanted me to come back today?"

"You Continentals, always so dramatic." Sanford came in and shut the door behind him. "Hello, Harvey. How's tricks?"

Walters sighed. "Say what you wish to say, Carl. And then get out." He met Alessandra's glare. "As I said, he might be able to help. I suspect that he has as much to lose here as you do."

"Of course I can help. Why, I wouldn't have bothered to come, otherwise." Sanford moved a stack of books and sat on the edge of the desk. "Not after you so rudely departed this morning. Distressed Miss Van Shaw to no end."

Alessandra faced him, her hand on her Webley. If Sanford noticed, he didn't seem to care. "I thought our audience was at an end. Perhaps I was mistaken."

"You were, but I forgive you. You were followed here, you know." He smiled at her. "I could deal with them, if you like."

She felt a chill. "No."

"As you wish. The offer stands, if you change your mind. Anyway, I'm not here about that." His smile turned thin. "Or perhaps I am. It's getting hard to tell. The playing field is crowded, these days. More so than I am used to."

"You have a point?"

"I want to help you, as Harvey said."

"What will it cost me?"

"Nothing much… just your soul." Sanford paused, and then chuckled at her expression. "Forgive me. Just a little joke. And the look on your face…" He shook his head. "Oh mercy."

"Carl," Walters said, heavily. Sanford glanced at him and snorted.

"Fine. This morning, after our chat, I… came into some information, let us say."

Alessandra heard the hesitation. "What sort of information?"

"About you. About the thing you are after. Chauncey did some digging – you scared him quite badly, by the way – and found that this mummy wasn't the only one stolen, of late. There have been other thefts, mostly from small collections up and down the east coast. And the occasional grave robbery."

"What does one have to do with the other?"

"The culprits. One of them was a fellow named Phipps. A known associate of a gentleman you are familiar with – a bootlegger named Gomes."

Alessandra sat back. McTyre had said that Gomes and his crew were double-dipping. It seemed that they had been doing so for longer than anyone realized. "What else did Chauncey find out?"

"Nothing much you don't already know." He smoothed his beard. "Though you might wonder what the police and I spoke about, after your hasty departure."

"The robbery, obviously."

"Yes, but who told them I was involved? Not you, I think. And certainly not my chum Harvey here." He chuckled. "You see it, don't you? The pattern."

"Orne," she said, softly. That was the missing piece.

Sanford nodded. "I knew you were clever. He's always been troublesome."

"Why would he do it? Why steal his own mummy?"

"Why not ask him?" Sanford laughed. "Oh, he thought he was clever. But this time, he's bitten off more than he can chew. Literally."

"What do you mean?"

"Private joke. Never mind." Sanford leaned forward. "The mummy is more than it seems. It is not simply a withered hunk of meat."

"So I gathered."

"I doubt that." He looked at her. "You lack the wit to see the truth, even when it is waved in front of your face."

Alessandra blinked. "Pardon me?"

"You have spent your life acquiring objects of great power for reckless men. Every jade figurine or tattered grimoire you pilfered was an artifact of incalculable worth. But to you, they were just... pretty things."

"Most of them were quite ugly, actually."

Sanford ignored her quip. "And now, at last, you have reached a point where willful ignorance will no longer serve you as a shield. If you do not open your eyes – if you do not see – you will die. Or worse."

"What could be worse than death?"

Sanford fixed her with a steady stare. "Would you like a list?"

She almost laughed, but something told her it might make Sanford angry. "The mummy is not what it seems. What does that mean, Mr Sanford? Use small words so that I might understand."

Sanford was quiet for a moment. "I have no answers." He looked at her. "But I suspect you do." He tapped the side of his eye. "I can see it in your eyes."

Alessandra hesitated. "See what?"

"That is the question." Sanford glanced at Walters, who looked away. "I can find out, if you let me."

Alessandra frowned. "How?"

Sanford gestured and the lights in the office fuzzed and sputtered. Her hackles rose. "I know a few tricks." He leaned forward intently. "Tell me about your dreams. Not just what you told Harvey. I want to know all of it."

"If you heard, then you know everything."

"I think you are lying. Or, at the very least, obfuscating." He frowned. "Maybe you don't even know yourself."

"Carl..." Walters began.

"Stay out of this, Harvey, there's a good man. She knows something, even if she doesn't realize that she knows it." Sanford stood. Alessandra did as well. Sanford hesitated. "I only want to help," he said.

"Help who?" she said, flatly. "Thank you for the offer, I will handle this on my own."

Sanford frowned. "You are making a mistake. You know what awaits you, even if you don't know its name. I can sense it, inside you. Waiting for an opportune moment."

She swallowed thickly. There was a rusty taste at the back of her mouth. "Perhaps."

He reached for her. She drew her Webley. He stopped, mouth slightly open. She'd surprised him. Maybe he hadn't actually expected her to draw it. "Perhaps," she repeated. "But it is my mistake to make. Thank you again for the offer, and the information. Professor Walters ... ?"

Walters laughed grimly. "I hope you know what you're doing, countess. Regardless, I wish you luck. I think you're going to need it."

Sanford didn't follow her as she left the library. She didn't blame Walters for the ambush. They were scared, and if what Walters had told her was true, she didn't blame them. The thought was too vast, too impossible for her to focus on.

It was too big for her. She was just a thief.

She stopped on the steps outside and lit another cigarette with trembling fingers. She had to focus. Orne. Orne was the problem. He'd hired Gomes and the others to steal his own mummy. Everything Freeborn and Visser had told her came back in a rush. It had been Orne who'd set Ashley on the trail, perhaps knowing what he'd find. And Orne who'd set her against Sanford. Trying to get her killed, perhaps.

Maybe he'd killed Visser and the others as well. Or maybe that had been someone else. She looked up. A figure in black sat on a bench across from the library, watching her. She stood for a moment, watching him in turn, wondering if he was truly a corpse – or simply corpse-like. It didn't matter. The end result was the same.

She took a last drag on the cigarette and tossed it aside. She stalked towards the man in black, her hand thrust into her pocket, her finger on the trigger of her pistol. When she reached him, she said, "Where is he?"

He looked up at her, but said nothing. She looked around, but saw no one else. Taking a deep breath, she sat. "Our last meeting resulted in an unfortunate miscommunication," she said. "A lapse in judgement on both sides. I am willing to let bygones be bygones, if he is."

Still, the man in black said nothing. Was he the same one she'd met in the train yard? She could not say. She sighed and looked away. "I am close, as I said. Once I know where they are, he will know. And then he will have his property back and you may all return to Oklahoma – or wherever you are from."

The man made a sound that might have been a sigh. "When…?" he croaked.

"If all goes well, tonight. Will you tell him?"

"Tell… him…"

She shuddered in revulsion. She realized now that he was not breathing. She pushed the thought aside and nodded. "Good." She swallowed.

"And tell him I will expect payment in full, once the matter is settled."

"You're telling me Gomes told her everything?" Whitlock said, peering into the interrogation room. The woman was pretty, in a vapid sort of way. Her name was Wilma and she was a waitress at one of Arkham's many speakeasies, according to Muldoon. She looked nervous – no, scared. He felt a flicker of pity as he spoke. Muldoon nodded.

"Sounds like. She said he was a great one for the pillow talk."

"And she's spilling beans why?"

"Said he was supposed to meet her, only he never showed. She's worried about him."

Whitlock laughed and leaned back against the wall. "Oh lord, that is funny. He probably vamoosed with the money."

"Or he got some of what Jodorowsky did," Muldoon said.

Whitlock scratched his chin. "What now?"

"Now, we wait to see what happens."

Whitlock stared at him. "What? We know it was Orne. He's probably got it right now. We go over there, you arrest him, I collect the company's property – right?"

"Things aren't that easy in Arkham," Muldoon said, softly. He looked around the bullpen at the other officers bent over their desks, or otherwise busy. The mood in the station was subdued. There was a feeling of battening down the hatches, though Whitlock couldn't tell what had caused it. It was like they were waiting for a storm only they could see.

"I sent it up the chain," Muldoon continued. "Now we sit and wait and see." He rubbed his face. He looked tired. Whitlock wondered how much grief Muldoon was getting from his superiors. "What I can't figure is why? Why steal something he already as good as owned?"

"I told you – a lot of rich guys do it. He gets the PR for the stunt, and the insurance money. And then he gets to enjoy the thing in peace, with no one the wiser." Whitlock expelled a breath, as a new thought occurred to him. "Or maybe he's trying to throw somebody off the trail."

"The murders," Muldoon said, catching on.

"Sometimes, when these things get dug up, people aren't happy about it. Just because it was out there doesn't mean it didn't belong to somebody." Whitlock snapped his fingers. "Zorzi. She doesn't steal this stuff for fun. I think the real owners sent her. Only Orne beat her to the punch, and stole his own damn mummy. He was probably trying to make it look like somebody else…"

"Sanford," Muldoon said.

"Maybe. But either they didn't buy it, or they didn't give a shit.

Hell, they're probably still after him." He looked at Muldoon. "We should get over there. Just in case."

For a moment, Muldoon looked tempted. Then he shook his head. "No. It's out of our hands now."

Whitlock laughed sourly. "Yeah. That party he's having – I wonder who's there?" When Muldoon didn't answer, he nodded. "Makes sense, though. Got to give the notables time to make their apologies, right? Make sure we don't embarrass anybody."

Muldoon looked at him. "That's how it has to be."

"For you." Whitlock pushed away from the wall. "I'm not a cop though. I only answer to Argus Insurance, and they want that damn mummy. So I'm going to go get it for them."

Muldoon caught his arm. "What are you saying?"

Whitlock shook him off. "What do you think I'm saying? I'm going to go to Orne's house, and I'm going to find the mummy. Then I might peruse the hors d'oeuvres table, and see if there's anything good. But either way, I'm going." He paused and looked at Muldoon. "You coming or not?"

Muldoon was silent for a moment. Then he sighed and went to his desk. He retrieved a cloth wrapped bundle and re-joined Whitlock. "Let's go if we're going."

Whitlock gestured to the bundle. "What's that?"

Muldoon unwrapped it, revealing the dark length of an M1 Garand semi-automatic rifle. "This is Becky. I never go to a party without my best girl."

Whitlock clapped him on the shoulder. "I knew I liked you, Muldoon. Now let's go crash a party."

CHAPTER THIRTY-ONE
Christchurch

South Church was an imposing sight. The gray of its stones stood in stark contrast to the red brick homes that surrounded it. Its spired bell-tower rose into the dark sky like a headstone. Alessandra looked up at it, and couldn't help but think of the geologic formations of her dreams. "The deep towers of K'n-Yan," she murmured, and felt what might have been an answering murmur deep within her.

"What was that?" Pepper asked.

"Nothing. You have been here before?" The streets were quiet, and a thin mist crept across the pavement. It smelled of the river, and brought with it a chill. Alessandra pulled the edges of her coat tight.

"Sure." Pepper thrust her hands into her pockets. "Da used to take me, when I was little." She frowned. "Think McTyre's guy is in there?"

"If not, he soon will be." Alessandra started up the steps. "Come on." She pushed open one of the tall hardwood doors. The crimson flicker of the sanctuary lamp was the only illumination. Stiff, wooden pews lined the nave. A large crucifix hung above the marble altar. Shadows danced across the stained glass windows in the red glow of the lamp, and covered the face of Christ. Alessandra felt nauseous at the sight, though she could not say why. She glanced at Pepper, and gestured to one of the pews near the door. Pepper nodded and sat.

Jimmy was sitting in the middle pew, arms stretched along its length, whistling softly. He glanced at her as she took a seat beside him. "Nice of Father Michael to leave this place open all night. Really speaks to the soul of the community, you know?"

"I would not know."

"Yeah, I guess not. You being foreign and all." Jimmy smiled. "That guy who got killed this morning – he a friend of yours?"

"What business is that of yours?"

"No skin off my nose. Just curious, is all. My condolences."

"Thank you." She leaned back, and watched the shadows dance in the high places of the church. There was a familiarity about the way they moved – another memory of something she had never experienced. She swallowed and looked at Jimmy. "Your message came as something of a surprise. I thought it might take you a few days to find anything."

"When Mr McTyre wants something done, everybody pitches in until it gets done." Jimmy looked smug as he said it.

"How fortunate for all of us. What did you find?"

"We know where they're holed up. Or were." Jimmy inspected his fingernails. "I beat it out of the guy who told them about it myself."

"How commendable. If you know where they are, why not go get them yourself?"

Jimmy smiled. "Mr McTyre said maybe you might like the honor."

Alessandra nodded. "I'm sure he did. Where?"

"Christchurch Cemetery. You know it?"

"I can find it." She paused. "They're hiding in a cemetery?" It seemed an obvious choice on the face of it – a bit too obvious. Perhaps it was a little joke of Orne's.

"Not in the cemetery proper. There's a bog just downhill, near the potter's field. That's where we found the truck."

"How did you come to look there?"

"There's plenty of old moonshiner paths out there," Jimmy said. "Lots of places to hide, especially if you know about them. Like we do. And there are smugglers' tunnels all under French Hill. It's like a goddamn molehill." He frowned. "You can go from one old house to another and never see daylight."

"Ideal for bootlegging."

Jimmy shook his head. "You won't catch me down there. Not any of the other guys either. Not after last time. Those tunnels are bad juju."

"I am starting to see why McTyre wanted my help," she said, wondering what had happened last time.

Jimmy's expression tightened. "Lady, you don't know nothing." He leaned forwards. "You're a goddamn canary in a coalmine. You find them, we'll deal with them. That's all you need to worry about."

Alessandra watched his eyes. Jimmy was scared. Criminals were barometers of trouble. If something was going on, the local criminal element was usually the first to know about it. This robbery had them all at sixes and sevens. She thought of Zamacona and shuddered. Jimmy didn't notice. He was too busy looking towards the back of the church, towards Pepper. "You know that guy?" he muttered.

"Yes."

Jimmy sat back. "Good." He didn't relax. "This whole thing has everyone stirred up. Sooner it's done, the better."

"I'll go to Christchurch tonight."

Jimmy blanched. "At night?"

"The longer I wait, the more likely they are to move the goods, as you might say. The sooner I find them, the better for all of us."

"Your funeral," he said, looking away.

"I suppose that means that I cannot count on reinforcements, should I get in trouble?"

Jimmy just looked at her. Alessandra patted his shoulder. "I meant no offense." She rose. "Thank Mr McTyre for me. And that I will ask before encroaching on his territory, next time."

"Lady, there better not be a next time, if you know what's good for you." Jimmy turned back to the altar. Pepper joined her as she headed for the doors.

"So?"

Alessandra didn't look at her. "Do you know how to get to Christchurch Cemetery?"

Pepper frowned. "Yeah, but – at night?"

"When better?"

"Never, preferably."

Alessandra smiled. "Come on. Take me there."

Christchurch wasn't far. It took only a few minutes, once they'd collected Pepper's cab. From across the street, the cemetery looked like the archetypal burying ground from every ghost story she'd ever read. An iron gate and fence, separating the kingdom of the dead from that of the living.

"Iron is supposed to have some mystical properties, you know," she said, idly.

"What do I know from iron?" Pepper said. She slumped behind

the wheel, staring at the bog with barely concealed distaste. "What's the plan?"

"I will investigate. You will stay here."

"Maybe I should come with you."

"It is better that you stay, just in case." Alessandra hefted an electric torch – a flashlight, Americans called it – she'd borrowed from Pepper. "If I do not come back in an hour, call someone. Muldoon, for preference. Tell him everything I've told you."

"What if you need backup?"

Alessandra smiled. "That is why you are staying here. If you see anything untoward, honk the horn." She wondered if Zamacona were watching. Given his propensity for showing up unannounced, she thought it good odds he was. But that was fine. Once she found the mummy, it would be up to him. And he was welcome to it. She would be well out of it. She could leave Arkham and forget all about this sordid affair.

Unless things went horribly awry, of course.

Trying not to dwell on the possibility, she climbed out of the cab. She pulled her jacket tight about her and turned on her flashlight. The bog was small in comparison to some she'd seen. A stretch of swampy ground that hooked around the edge of the potter's field, and trailed off towards the river. Dark trees, mossy and crooked, rose like a palisade to block the sight of the burying ground from its nearest neighbors. She wondered if that was why the town had left it as it was.

Insects sang in the dark. The mist hung thick over the low water. There was a path, hacked through the overgrowth. Others branched off from it, winding through the bog. Some went towards the river, others... back towards the potter's field.

Her breath danced on the air. In the light, she saw the rutted tracks of a vehicle. A truck, even as Jimmy had said. She followed the tracks, stepping over rotting logs and through bunches of cattails. She heard the sudden whirr of wings and stopped, listening. Something had startled the birds. Not her. She swung the light, but saw nothing. A prickle of fear crept through her, but she fiercely quashed it.

She wondered if Zamacona's helpers had followed them. Followed her. Her hand found her pistol, but she didn't draw it. Not yet. She waited, but whatever had scared the birds was gone. She turned back to the path, but kept her hand close to her gun.

The truck wasn't hard to find. It had been rolled into the trees, and covered in a tarp. There was nothing in the back, of course. Nothing in the front either. She slammed the passenger door and let her light play over the nearest path. One of those heading to the potter's field. They had gone to the cemetery after all.

She glanced back the way she'd come, wondering if she ought to go back. But only for a moment. Then she headed for the potter's field, light bobbing ahead of her. Long minutes later, the trees thinned and the underbrush faded, and she walked over muddy grass, among wooden markers. Anonymous, save for dates.

The cemetery was quiet. Part of that, she thought, was due to the river mist. It seemed thicker here than elsewhere. Mausoleums rose like silent storefronts along crooked avenues. Headstones clumped in untidy gatherings, many shrouded in moss.

She followed the path, letting her light play across trampled grass. It had rained since the theft, but there was still evidence that someone had come this way. When she spied an overgrown mausoleum near the path, she had a sudden thought. Jimmy had mentioned tunnels. In Paris, she'd once escaped into the catacombs through a tunnel hidden in the *Cimetière des Innocents*.

Following her hunch, she approached the mausoleum. Some of the overgrowth had been cleared from it, enabling access. It could have been the work of a groundskeeper, but she doubted it. She approached the entry gate, revolver in hand.

The inside of the mausoleum was a mess of bones and broken stone. It stank of wet dog and moldering cloth. The central sarcophagus was ajar. Reluctantly, she peered over the rim. Instead of a crumbling corpse she saw a set of worn stone steps, leading down into the dark. "Ha," she said, softly. "Got you."

She holstered her revolver and climbed over the edge of the sarcophagus. She paused at the top of the steps, looking down. In that moment, she was back beneath the earth with the shadows that surged like ocean surf and the chants of her captors ringing in her ears.

N'kai, the shadows murmured. She closed her eyes, banishing the images before they could overwhelm her. "Yes, I am coming," she said, without knowing why.

Then, taking a deep breath, she began her descent.

Pepper sat quietly, smoking one of Alessandra's cigarettes. Her eyes were on the bog, and the edge of the cemetery beyond. She flinched as the whirr of wings sounded nearby. She'd never been out here at night before, and she was starting to regret coming. More, she was starting to regret not going with Alessandra. The other woman was competent enough, but she didn't know Arkham. She didn't understand.

"I knew the money was too good to be true." She slapped the steering wheel and started to get out when a sudden sound made her freeze. An awkward scraping sort of noise, that she'd only heard once before. On the docks. She slid down in her seat, peering over the edge of the window.

Broken shapes moved out of the mist. They hopped and slithered and stumped. Some walked almost like men, while others crawled like beasts. Most wore clothes, but some wore nothing at all save their scars. The great mass of them broke and flowed around the car, heading into the bog like dogs with a scent.

"Alessandra," Pepper whispered. She swallowed thickly as the smell of them filled the cab – like rotting meat. They were following the countess. She had to do something, but didn't know what. Then, the decision was taken from her. The driver's side door was abruptly wrenched off its hinges with a screech of tearing metal. Pepper twisted around in shock as a hand seized her by the shirt and yanked her from the cab.

The next moment she was flying through the air. She landed hard, all the air rushing from her lungs. She tried to get to her feet, but a great weight settled on her chest, pinning her in place. A foot. Zamacona looked down at her.

"You hit me with a car," he said.

Pepper stared up at him in horror, unable to form words. Even if she had, she had no breath to speak them. He pressed down harder with his foot. She beat at his leg, but it was like punching a length of rebar. He laughed.

"She has found my quarry." Zamacona lifted his foot, and she rolled onto her stomach, coughing and panting. "Soon, I will deal with them both." He reached down and caught her by the back of the head, as easily as a man might pick up a kitten. "What should I do with you in the meantime? Smash your skull to flinders against the ground, as I would a rat? Or feed you to my servants?" He pulled her close, studying her. "Which would you prefer, boy?"

She tried to kick him. Zamacona smiled, and she felt as if she'd been doused in ice water. "You are brave," he said. "I was brave once. Coronado himself commended me for my heroism. But that bravery only brought me pain, in the end." He stared into her eyes, and she closed hers, unwilling to meet that awful, burning gaze.

"I will be merciful," he said, as if to himself. He flung her against the side of her cab and she sank down, wheezing. Her ribs felt wrong, and her arm wasn't working. She noted these things idly, through a fog of pain. Zamacona said something in a language that wasn't Portuguese or Spanish, or any that she recognized.

Pallid things gathered about her, panting slightly. They crouched, waiting for his signal. They were smaller than the others, more feral – starveling things, with parchment-like flesh stretched tight over crooked bones. Zamacona stroked the head of one, and it uttered a mewling cry. He looked down at Pepper.

"I will let them have you. And when they are done, I will leave you dead. Your mistress will not be so lucky."

He turned and strode into the mist, leaving her surrounded by his followers – all save those who remained behind to encircle her. The small, hungry ones, who crept forward on claw-like hands and feet, their milky eyes rolling in their sockets and broken teeth champing in eagerness. Pepper grabbed at the hood of the cab, hauling herself to her feet, despite the spike of pain. One of the creatures darted at her and she kicked out at it, catching it in the head. It was like kicking a pumpkin.

The thing staggered and shook itself, whining. Another one came, and another. She threw herself into the cab through the missing door and out the other side, kicking the door shut on them. Biting back a scream of pain, she dragged herself to her feet and staggered away. But they were too quick. They cut her off, surrounding her again.

She turned in an unsteady circle, trying to keep them all in sight. "You want a fight?" she panted. "I'll give you a fight." She made a fist with her good hand. One of the things tensed, haunches quivering, and leapt.

The crack of a rifle split the air. The thing crashed down, twitching. A second shot followed swiftly on the echoes of the first. Another of the creatures pitched backwards. A third shot, a fourth, and then the survivors scattered like startled rats.

Shaking, Pepper turned. A tall shape emerged from the trees. "You OK?" Officer Muldoon asked, reloading his rifle as he approached. He stopped. "That you, Pepper?"

"It's me," Pepper said, wincing. She was getting some feeling back in her arm now, but it still hurt like blazes.

He looked around. "Where'd the rest of them go?" He didn't ask what they were. From the look on his face, he seemed to have a pretty good idea.

Pepper pointed. "They're going after the countess," she said, still trying to understand what had just happened. "Where the hell did you come from?"

"I was following someone. Maybe you saw him – tall guy, foreign looking…"

"Yeah, I saw him." She rubbed her chest. "He's the one in charge."

Muldoon cursed. "You said he's going after the countess? Can you walk?"

"My shoulder hurts."

"But not your legs?"

Pepper winced. "You're all heart, Muldoon."

Muldoon smiled grimly. "Come on. I've got a feeling she's going to need our help."

CHAPTER THIRTY-TWO
Tunnels

Curved brick walls rose around Alessandra as she reached the bottom of the steps. They were slick with effluvia and mold, and old mortar drifted through the air. Everything stank of river mud and other, less identifiable things. She smiled slightly. Forgotten tunnels could be a thief's best friend.

As Jimmy had said, it appeared that French Hill and its environs were riddled with old tunnels like this. Secret paths from cellar to cellar, or cellar to cemetery in this case. Alessandra paused, listening to the drip of moisture and the whisper of vermin. She let the flashlight play across the tunnel. She wondered which had been built first, it or the mausoleum. She looked down. The muddy floor was covered in bootprints.

She drew her pistol and followed them. There were signs of regular passage, back and forth. Whoever was using this place had been doing so for longer than the robbery. Then, if Sanford was correct, Gomes and the others had been busy for some time. She wondered what else might be going on, just underneath Arkham's feet.

She caught a whiff of something and stopped. The tunnel had narrowed significantly. There was a crudely reinforced archway ahead. She sniffed the air. Beneath the river stink was a coppery odor. Blood. She glanced back the way she'd come, half-convinced something was creeping up behind her.

She steeled herself and pressed on. The walls here were covered in thick curtains of root, and loose soil crunched underfoot. The edges of what could only be wooden caskets jutted through gaps in the brickwork. She tried not to think too hard about what might be in them. Or about the smell of blood, getting stronger.

At the end of the passage was a chamber of sorts. Small. Cramped by stacked coffins, most of which appeared to be rotting down to their nails. Some had been shattered and recently. But among the broken husks of wood was a new body.

Gomes hadn't died easily – someone had pulverized him. The chamber was full of splintered wood and broken headstones. Several braced archways, reminiscent of mine entrances, occupied two of the walls – offshoot tunnels, of the sort Jimmy had mentioned. Blood soaked the dark brick.

She crouched beside Gomes. A cursory glance told her he'd been dead for some time, a day at least. As she examined him, she spied something pale in one of the coffins. Another body – a man. She vaguely recognized him as one of the robbers. Someone had stuffed him into a casket after beating him to death.

Orne was tying up loose ends. She could feel it.

A sound intruded on her reverie. She froze, alert. The silence stretched about her, taut and unyielding. But just as she'd begun to think she'd imagined it, it came again. A slow, persistent scrape, as of a spade. As if someone were digging. A chill gripped her and she stood and backed away. Perhaps someone had noticed the light. She told herself she didn't want to be found here. She was in enough trouble as it was. And someone needed to report the bodies to the police.

The sound was louder now, more insistent. As if the unseen digger were growing more agitated – more eager. She turned to go, when in the glow of her flashlight, she spied a footprint in the loose soil. More than one, in fact. A dozen or more, all in a cluster before a low tunnel. She paused and turned back to the dead men.

Dirt crumbled from the far wall. An old brick bulged and shifted, as if something were pushing against it from the other side. She cocked her pistol. The sound was loud in the confined space. The unseen diggers ceased. She heard a soft sound, a hiss or chitter. Rats, then. Likely drawn by the smell of the bodies.

Decision made, she stepped into the tunnel, electric torch held high. "Enjoy your meal, fellows," she murmured. "With my compliments."

The tunnel was narrower than the one she'd arrived by, and consisted of planks of rotting wood and sailcloth, fitted to hold back the soft earth. A newer tunnel, by a few decades at least. But still older than most of the town. A smugglers' tunnel, hacked out of the earth in the years before the British had surrendered control of their former colonies. It smelled of something peculiar, not earth or rot but something else.

The tunnel wound around and down in serpentine fashion before suddenly sloping upwards at a shallow angle. At one point, she fancied she could hear the murmur of the river, somewhere on the other side of the rotting timbers. But all too soon it faded, leaving her with only the sound of her own footsteps for company.

That sound changed imperceptibly. She looked down. Brick, rather than dirt. The sides of the passage had narrowed. It was barely wide enough for one person to pass through. Up ahead, a wall. No, not a wall. A shelf. The back of a shelf. She slowed. What was it Jimmy had said? That one could move from house to house without being seen. She let the light play across the shelf and caught the gleam of glass. A wine-rack. She laughed softly and went to it. It moved easily, following grooves scraped into the brickwork. The bottles rattled, echoing eerily. She stepped into a large wine cellar.

She paused, listening. Above her, floorboards creaked. Faint music. Voices. A party, perhaps. Hadn't Orne mentioned a party? Was this his house, then? It would make a sort of sense. She frowned, wondering if she ought to have accepted his invitation.

The cellar was surprisingly clean and spacious. Then, it would need to be, if people were moving in and out of the tunnel. She let the light play across the contents as she explored. Occasional laughter drifted down from above. The shadows bunched and heaved about her, dancing away from the light. A damp breeze reached her, stretching from the other end of the cellar. There was an opening there of some sort.

She followed the breeze, moving as quietly as possible. The opening proved to be a raised ring of old brick, set into the floor. The mouth of an old cistern, perhaps.

Alessandra crouched, examining it. She decided to risk the chance of someone seeing the flashlight, and shone it into the cistern. A set of stone steps wound around and down, just like in the mausoleum. "Not a cistern, then," she murmured. Something older, perhaps. Another tunnel, extending through the depths of French Hill.

She froze as she heard the creak of the cellar door opening. A rush of noise filled the space – laughter, music, voices raised. Feet on the steps. Someone coming for a bottle of bubbly. She debated brazening it out, but decided discretion was the better part of valor. At least until she knew more. Besides, where better to hide a stolen mummy?

She started down. As she descended, she realized that the steps went farther down than she'd first thought. Too far. Below the level of the river, perhaps, but she wasn't sure. The tunnel beyond was old, but well maintained. There was evidence of new plaster and other, minor repairs. There were electric lights as well, strung up every few feet. Someone had gone to a lot of trouble. The question was, why?

"Only one way to find out," she said, softly. At the end of the brick tunnel was a room. A proper room, not simply a chamber. The walls were plastered over, and carpet laid. Soft, crimson lights burned at the four corners, casting long shadows. The room reminded her of the exhibition room in the museum, save that it was smaller by half. Exhibit cases lined the walls and filled the empty space like a labyrinth. She wandered among them, taking note of the items on display. It was a cabinet of curiosities.

Strange things from Arkham and beyond filled the cases – withered batrachian shapes, no larger than cats, whose tags proclaimed them Ponapean mermaids; glass bottles containing slivers of metal or stone that seemed to resonate curiously as she bent to observe them; and other things, unidentifiable and unnamed.

There were mummies as well. Broken things glaring through the sides of glass sarcophagi at the intruder in their midst. Some, she recognized as Egyptian. Others were of more uncertain pedigree. A few were not really mummies at all, but rather bodies dried and shrunken by exposure to great heat.

Alessandra heard the creak of a floorboard and turned. A

shape was creeping among the display cases at the far end of the room. Someone else was poking around where they shouldn't be. Someone who'd followed her down the tunnel, perhaps. She secreted herself between two of the standing sarcophagi and drew her pistol.

The shape moved closer. Whoever they were, they hadn't noticed her yet. One of Zamacona's companions, maybe. She raised her Webley. As the shape passed the sarcophagi, she cocked the pistol. "Stop where you are," she murmured.

The shape froze. "Turn around," she said. The shape turned. She sighed. "Mr Whitlock, you do turn up in the oddest places."

Whitlock glared at her. "I could say the same thing about you, countess. What are you doing here?"

"You first."

"Orne was behind the theft."

"However did you guess that?"

"One of the robbers talked to someone he shouldn't have," Whitlock said, glancing over his shoulder. "Did you hear that?"

"No. Why are you here?"

"The same reason as you, I figure."

"You came alone?"

"I'm not an idiot. Muldoon is outside." He paused. "Or he was. He's following some guy we saw watching the place when we arrived – tall, dark…"

"Zamacona," Alessandra said, softly.

"You know him?"

"Unfortunately. He is dangerous, more than you can probably imagine."

"I'm armed," Whitlock said.

"We hit him with a car. He got up."

Whitlock looked askance at her. "What?"

She shook her head. "Never mind. Why is Muldoon following him?"

"Obvious, isn't it? He's the murderer." Whitlock grinned. "Or maybe not. Who knows? But it's a bit of a coincidence, him watching the place…"

"No, you are right." Alessandra looked at him, suddenly certain though she could not say why. "He killed them. He killed Visser as well."

"You got proof?"

She shook her head. "Just a feeling."

Whitlock stared at her for a moment, and then grunted. "Me too." He tensed. "There it is again. Tell me you heard that."

She did. A creak. Something jostled one of the cases. She peered past him, trying to see. But she saw nothing save shadows. Whitlock turned. "I've had a weird feeling since I came in here," he muttered.

"How *did* you get in, by the way?"

"Climbed the fence, came in through the atrium." He smirked. "He left it unlocked."

"And you managed not to be noticed?"

"Big party," he said. "Lots of noise, lots of booze. Nobody looked twice at me. How did you get in?" Whitlock asked as he padded after her.

"There is a secret tunnel, leading to the cemetery."

Whitlock shook his head. "I really hate this town." He paused. "Huh. Would you look at that…"

"What?" She turned to see him studying a case containing a book, open to a rather grisly etching. "What is it?"

"Pigafetta's *Regnum Congo*," he murmured. "That book is older than this town. And worth more than either of us."

"How do you know?"

"A copy was stolen from the university library a few years ago. My company is responsible for the policy on the university's rare manuscript collection." Whitlock leaned close. "That's it. Look – there. See the scorch marks?"

"Looks like it was in a fire."

"Close. It was struck by lightning. Or, rather, the house it was in was struck. Some shack in the Miskatonic River Valley." He turned. "What else do they have here, I wonder?"

"I am only interested in the one thing, myself." Alessandra made to head for the doors, but Whitlock grabbed her.

"You're not going anywhere. You're staying where I can keep an eye on you."

Alessandra stared steadily at him until he released her. "Surely you do not think I am still responsible for all of this?"

"I don't know what to think," he said, in a low voice. "But until I get some answers, I'm not letting you get away. So stay close."

Alessandra considered ignoring him. But Whitlock was stubborn enough to pursue her, if provoked. For the moment, she would simply have to endure him. "Fine. But do not get in my way."

"And you stay out of mine," he began. She heard the telltale whistle of a leather sap, moving swiftly, and turned, a warning on her lips. But too late. The blow solidly connected and Whitlock staggered with a groan. He fell against a display case and slid down, clutching at his head. As he fell, two shapes were revealed. Men in oxblood robes, their heads hidden beneath heavy cowls. They both carried blackjacks.

They came at her quick. She caught the first blow on her forearm. The blackjack sent a shockwave through her arm, numbing it to the elbow. Her fist popped forward, piston-like, and caught her attacker in the belly. He gasped and faltered, stumbling against the wall. She made to dart past him, but the second man was already there, gripping her bicep, spinning her around, sap raised.

Alessandra stomped on his foot and ducked aside as the sap struck a display case behind her. He lurched forward, off balance, and she ripped her arm free of his grasp. The first man was on his feet now. She drew her Webley and fired. The gunshot was loud, but his scream was louder. He stumbled, clutching at a dark stain on his shirt.

"Enough."

She froze as she heard the distinctive click of a pistol being cocked.

"Drop the gun. Turn around."

Alessandra did. Matthew Orne smiled at her in the dim light. This time, in this light, he did not seem so handsome. Quite the opposite, in fact. His face was twisted into an expression of almost unholy glee. And the way he held the gun was practiced – careful. He was clad in robes, as were the handful of men behind him.

"Matthew," she said, with forced mildness. "The party is going well, I trust. Though I suppose my invitation has been revoked."

"You might say that, yes," he said. "I wish I could say I'm surprised to see you, but… well. I suspected this was going to happen sooner or later the moment you decided to stick your nose in." He turned to the others, and gestured lazily towards the groaning Whitlock. "Bring him along as well. We'll have a double-header today, I think."

CHAPTER THIRTY-THREE
Banquet

The room they took Alessandra and Whitlock to was large, situated behind the collection room. It resembled a dining room, of sorts, though the decorations were not conducive to a normal appetite. A single table stretched along the room's center, crafted from casket lids, its legs made from human femurs, bound together by iron rings. Opposite the entrance to the collection room was a second set of doors, heavy and foreboding, the panels inlaid with bone.

There were oil paintings on the walls, depicting scenes of colonial barbarity. Men in grandiose periwigs, stalking frightened urchins through the streets of Arkham. Red-clad horsemen, running down fleeing natives or slaves. Others, even more obscene. But all had similar anthropophagic themes – the conspicuous consumption of human flesh.

"Ghouls," she said, looking around in horror. "You are ghouls."

Orne chuckled. "No. We are human enough."

"That is debatable," she spat. Candles made from human hands dipped in wax sat atop iron braziers and candelabras, casting a pallid light throughout the room. Bones, bleached white and scrimshawed with careful artistry, decorated the walls or hung from the ceiling like gruesome wind-chimes. The carpet was the worst, made from sewn together scalps that rustled and crinkled beneath their feet.

"Tell me what you really think," Orne said, as his people tied her to a chair at the head of the table. They did the same to Whitlock, who sat slightly behind her. The insurance man groaned, head lolling. There was blood in his hair, and she thought they might have cracked his skull. "It took some time to decorate properly. Ambience is so important to these things."

"Very pretty," she said, not hiding her repulsion.

Orne laughed. "I told you I had an interest in history. True for all of us, isn't that right, Ferdinand?"

One of the robed figures threw back his hood, revealing the florid features of the much-sought Professor Ashley. "Indeed. Though I suspect our history is more storied than most." He checked Alessandra's bonds. "Some say we were founded at Valley Forge, during that long devil's winter of '77 and '78."

"I think that's a bit of borrowed glory, myself," Orne said. "But we are as old as this fine nation. So long as the Stars and Stripes have flown, we have been here." He looked at the others, and they murmured assent. She had the feeling that this ritual was a regular one at these gatherings. "Oh, we have our far flung chapters to be sure – St John's lot, in merry old England, and the Bavarian rabble, led by Kraske – but we are American-made, countess, of that you can be sure."

"So you are patriotic cannibals, then."

Orne sneered. "Cannibals eat the living, madam. We are necrophagic practitioners. We eat the dead and only the dead. The longer in the ground, the better."

"Ghouls," Whitlock said, his voice a harsh rasp. Alessandra glanced at him. He wasn't unconscious after all. But he sounded as if he wished he was.

"No, Mr Whitlock – keep up. We are connoisseurs. We pay good money for our meals. Case in point – Ferdinand, the bell please."

Ashley reached over and lifted a delicate silver bell from a tray set on an occasional table made from what appeared to be a crouching, mummified figure, its head replaced by a flat wooden tray. He rang it. A moment later, the far doors at the opposite end of the room opened. A group of servants, dressed in mock-Regency garb, with wigs and coats, entered the room, bearing a large platter between them.

From the other side of the room came the sound of voices. A group of men and women, perhaps a dozen in all, entered. Like Orne, Ferdinand and the guards, they wore oxblood robes, their faces hidden behind masks of crudely stitched leather. Orne greeted them with a wide smile. "Friends, welcome. The meal is set to begin."

"What about everyone else?" Whitlock said. "There were at least thirty people at the party upstairs. They on the menu, is that it?"

"No. They are, by now, on the wrong side of my wine cellar. Those of my security staff upstairs will ensure that they come to no harm – and that no one notices our absence. No, tonight's meal is one I have been waiting on for a long time…"

The platter was set on the table, revealing the withered form of the mummy, its contorted limbs pressed tight to its sunken chest, its grisly mask staring directly at Alessandra. She looked away, her stomach churning. "Is that what all this has been about? You're going to eat the damn thing?"

"Of course." Orne indicated the mummy. "We do not feast on

the bodies of the poor and forgotten. We eat kings and queens. Pharaohs and priests." He paused. "We eat sorcerers. To eat – to *consume* – is to take into oneself the power of the consumed."

"And is that who he is?" Alessandra asked. "A sorcerer?"

Orne hesitated. "Perhaps. Someone important, at least, to be buried in such a way, wearing a mask of such peculiar quality. A high priest, maybe. Or a nobleman."

"You sent Ashley to find him, didn't you?"

Orne looked at Ashley. "I didn't believe him at first, I admit. The idea of a hidden civilization stretching beneath the Midwest was... inconceivable. But Ferdinand is quite convincing. He showed me certain... artifacts he liberated from an old acquaintance..."

"Carl Sanford," Alessandra said, flatly.

Ashley grunted. "Sanford is a fool. When I explained, he told me I was mistaken. But I knew better... and now, I will be privy to secrets beyond even his crooked wisdom."

"By... eating it."

"Oh yes," Orne said, as his guests began to take their seats. "Would you believe that much of my fortune comes from buried treasure? I partook of the flesh of several notorious smugglers and pirates, and learned the secrets they took to their graves." He tapped the side of his head. "All that they knew is now mine. History is an open book to me. To us." He looked around. "We have all of us profited from the wisdom of the dead."

"You're mad," Whitlock said harshly.

"Not mad. Educated. I learned at the feet of a master." Orne smiled absently. "He was a brute, though a learned one. Self-taught, mostly. That copy of *Regnum Congo* out there was his. When it was turned over to the university library, I went to some lengths to... acquire it, for my own collection. He couldn't read it, of course, it being in Latin. But he did so like the pictures." He sighed. "A shame about the lightning. A bad end, no matter who you are. I am obliged to the old fellow, though I don't know his name. He showed me much about the way of things, mad as he was. I took his lessons to heart – and built on them, as only an educated man could."

"He taught you about eating people."

"About why one might wish to do so," Orne corrected, softly. "And I found other likeminded individuals to share those lessons." He looked around at his followers, smiling beneficently. "Knowledge not shared is knowledge wasted, after all."

"You're a goddamn lunatic," Whitlock said loudly.

"I assure you, I have no particular affinity for the moon." Orne smiled at them. "Not that I expect my assurances to comfort you at this stage. Still, rest assured that there is historical precedent for the agonies to come."

Alessandra snorted. "One can make that claim about almost anything."

"Including theft," Orne said, looking at her. He caught her chin, and forced her to meet his eyes. "You weren't at the museum by coincidence. Someone sent you to steal our prize. Who?"

"I make it a point to never divulge the identity of my clients."

Orne smiled. "Professional pride, is it? I understand." He turned to the table and selected a knife, one of several sitting there. "I wonder how long that pride will sustain you, when I begin to flense the meat from your lovely bones?"

Alessandra tried to pull away, but his grip was too strong. "Going to add me to the stewpot as well?"

"Perish the thought. But one does not kill solely for sustenance. There are other pleasures to be had – ones we rarely get to indulge in."

"Why steal it?" she said, desperately. Orne paused.

"What?"

"Why steal it?" she said again, hurriedly. "You found it, after all. What was the point of hiring Gomes, of staging a robbery?"

"He wasn't the sole owner," Whitlock said. Orne glanced at him, frowning.

"No, I wasn't, more is the pity. And the less said about Freeborn and the university the better." Orne shook his head. "I should never have involved myself with academia. It's been nothing but trouble."

"And of course, the original owners might come looking for it," Alessandra said. She looked at Ashley. "Isn't that right, professor?"

Ashley frowned. "Be quiet."

Orne looked at him quizzically. "What is she talking about?"

Whitlock caught on. He laughed. "Someone killed the other investors. If that wasn't you, you're in trouble."

Orne snorted. "It was Sanford who killed them, obviously. Don't be fools."

"Was it?" Alessandra said. "Because Sanford seemed to think it was someone else." She laughed softly. "Did you tell him what happened, professor? In Binger?"

"Shut up!" Ashley snarled and struck her across the face. She leaned over and spat blood onto the floor.

"About the sabotage?" she pressed. "The deaths?"

"What about Jodorowsky?" Whitlock interjected.

Orne looked back and forth between them. "Who is Jodorowsky?"

"One of your pet thieves," Whitlock said. "Someone tore out his throat."

Alessandra shook her head. "Not someone. Something." She looked at the mummy.

Orne stared at her. Then he lifted a flint knife from the tray and ran his thumb along the chipped edge. "Explain. Quickly."

"She doesn't know anything. She's just stalling," Ashley said. "It's Sanford, it has to be. Whatever civilization might have existed in K'n-Yan once, there's nothing there now."

"I assure you, I am not." She began to work at the knots that bound her to her chair, moving slowly so as not to attract attention.

Orne looked at the mummy. And then looked at the knife in his hand. He shook his head. "No. Ferdinand is right. Sanford and his fellow collectors of trinkets are not good at sharing. They think in the same way bootleggers do – they'll not stand for any rivals on their patch." He tapped his lips with the knife. "Or perceived rivals, at least." He pointed the blade at her. "I never did ask you how your meeting with him went."

"About as well as you might expect."

Orne laughed, and several of his guests laughed with him. "Yes, my little joke. I wanted to tweak old Carl's nose a bit. And I thought he might solve the problem of you for me." His smile faded. "But as ever, Carl surprised me." He shook his head. "But with the secrets of K'n-Yan at our disposal, that will not happen again. The time of the Silver Twilight Lodge is coming to a well-deserved end, and Arkham will once more be in the hands of those best suited to guide it."

Alessandra laughed harshly and continued tugging at her bonds. She had the knot in her hands. It was loose now, fraying. A bit more time, and she might be able to get loose. The question was, what to do then? Even if she got out of the room, escaping the house was unlikely. And what about Whitlock? She glanced at the insurance man. He'd been nothing but trouble, but she couldn't very well leave him to die, tempting as it was.

Whitlock met her gaze, and something in his eyes made her pause. Her eyes flicked to his bonds, and she almost laughed. He had a razor blade between two fingers and was sawing away, however slowly, at his own bonds. Maybe she didn't need to worry about him after all.

"Still, you provided some amusement these past few days. Running all over creation. Really whetted the appetite, you might say." Orne turned. "By way of thanks, I thought you should witness the ceremony. It might give your final moments a bit of... meaning."

"Or make them incredibly tedious," Alessandra said, bluntly. Orne glared at her, and for a moment, she thought he might strike her. Instead, he smiled and shook his head.

"Either way, I suggest you enjoy the show." He turned to the mummy on its platter, and, wielding the flint knife with consummate skill, began to cut away at the wrappings that bound its bent limbs together.

The sound of it set Alessandra's stomach twisting. She bowed her head and sucked in a mouthful of air, trying to still the roiling in her gut. But the sensation only grew worse. Orne narrated his efforts as he worked. His guests leaned forward, watching avidly, their gazes greedy and excited behind their masks.

"You'll notice that unlike the other mummies we've consumed, this one is largely unwrapped. Its method of preservation is still a mystery." With some effort, he removed the mummy's mask, prizing it from the skull with a laborious grunt.

There was a wet sound, like a sigh. Alessandra felt something in her throat. Her stomach convulsed and she hunched forward, causing her chair to creak. Orne and the others looked at her. "Are you... unwell, countess?"

"She is afraid."

The words echoed through the room. Orne turned, mouth open in shock. His followers rose from their seats about the table. Zamacona stood in the doorway, with several of his followers crouching at his feet. No one had heard him enter. There was blood on his sleeves, and he held the robed bodies of two guards slumped at his feet.

"And with good reason," Zamacona continued, letting the bodies fall. The other guards turned, reaching for their weapons. Zamacona paid them no mind. He looked at Alessandra. "When this is done, you and I will continue our conversation from the other night." His gaze flicked to Orne. "I am pleased to make your acquaintance, Mr Orne. I had intended to visit you, in time."

"You..." Orne said. He glanced at Alessandra. "Do you know what he *is*?" he hissed, his eyes wide with fear.

"I have some idea," she said.

"I am the wrath of K'n-Yan," Zamacona said. "And not a one of you will leave this house alive.

CHAPTER THIRTY-FOUR
Wrath of N'kai

Zamacona unbuttoned his coat and shucked it as he strode into the room, tossing it to one of his servants. The shuffling figures of his deformed – his *dead* – followers spread out around him like eager dogs. There were six of them; lanky, ugly things wrapped in rags. "You will forgive me entering unannounced. The rest of your guards are... otherwise occupied." As if to emphasize the point, a volley of gunfire sounded from somewhere above in the house, followed by a long drawn-out scream.

"What in God's name...?" Whitlock began.

"Which god?" Zamacona said, lazily. He unbuttoned his cuffs, and rolled up his sleeves. "Not yours, I think." He fixed Orne with a level gaze. "Kill them. Leave the leader to me."

Everything became very confusing, very quickly. Zamacona's creatures leapt towards Orne's guests with bestial glee, howling and gibbering. Men and women screamed in fear as dead hands clawed at them. Ashley squealed and went down behind Alessandra, a black-clad corpse chewing at his throat.

Zamacona himself snatched up Orne, gripping him by the

throat. He slammed him onto the table and held him sprawled there. "I followed Coronado from Mexico, and into the mountains and prairies of the southwest," he intoned. "We sought cities of gold, but found only shadows and death. And some of us – worse than death. I repented my sins, and was given a new life by great Zhothaqquah, whom men call the Sleeper of N'kai. Repent, and I will be merciful, little flesh-eater."

Orne shrieked and stabbed at Zamacona with the flint knife. Zamacona hissed like some great serpent and slapped the blade from his hand, sending it skidding across the floor. It landed at Alessandra's feet.

But she saw these things only from the corner of her eye. Her attentions were fixed on the mummy. It was twitching. Like a newborn, suddenly realizing that they could move. Clawed fingers groped at the air. Her stomach clenched with every twitch. "No," she whispered. She heard Whitlock say something, but she could hear nothing save the shadows.

The mummy sat up, with a rattling groan. Zamacona turned, Orne's limp form dangling from his grip. "No," he growled. "No – the mask. Get the mask back on it." Two of his servants darted towards the mummy, but it rose to meet them, swinging its legs off the table. Shrunken talons shot out, catching both dead things by the throat.

They spasmed and went limp, necks broken, black blood staining the mummy's forearms. It dropped them and turned towards Zamacona. A sound like water going swiftly down a drain emerged from between the frayed lips. There were no words, and yet Alessandra understood its intent perfectly. Zamacona appeared to understand as well, for his snarl became that of a frightened animal. For the first time, she saw something that might have been fear in his eyes.

He hefted Orne's body and flung it full at the mummy. It batted the body from the air with bone-crushing force, smashing it to the floor and trampling over it in its haste to reach Zamacona. It knew him, and hated him. Alessandra could feel that hate beating in her mind. It was like an open flame, only the fire was cold – so cold.

"Stop it," Zamacona howled. "Restrain it, fools!" At his roar, another of his servants left off mauling Orne's guests and leapt over the table onto the mummy's back. The mummy staggered and fumbled blindly at its attacker. Zamacona avoided the stumbling melee and made for the mask.

She didn't understand why, but Alessandra knew she could not let him get it. The knots at last came loose in her hands and she lashed out with her foot, catching the edge of the mask where it lay on the table and kicking it out of Zamacona's reach. She scrambled to her feet as he swung towards her, his eyes ablaze with fury. "You," he snarled. "You did this!"

She didn't bother to correct him. Instead, she snatched up her chair and smashed it against him as he lunged towards her. Zamacona staggered back with a guttural yelp, right into the waiting arms of the mummy. It had dispatched its attacker and was now free to concentrate on the object of its hatred. Its leathery limbs snapped shut about him, and he howled like a wolf in a trap. Bony talons tore into his flesh as he tried to free himself.

His servants, those not preoccupied by Orne's surviving followers, came to aid him. The mummy, moving swiftly for so fragile a thing, flung Zamacona towards them and turned towards Alessandra with a peculiar reeling motion.

Their gazes met and all went still and silent. It was as if there were only the two of them – one dead, one alive – in all the world.

It did not speak, for the dead cannot speak. But it made sounds nonetheless. A hissing, gurgling *wet* sound. Like the hiss of a bat filtered through the guttural croak of a toad.

The sounds were meant to be words. Maybe they were, just not in any language she could comprehend. It seemed to realize this, for its shriveled features twisted into what might have been an expression of frustration. It groped vainly towards her, almost pleadingly. Its movements were stiff and clumsy, as if it were not in control of its own limbs.

And suddenly, she *knew*. Alessandra knew why she had stayed in Arkham, despite all common sense. This moment – it was all down to this moment and what came after. She felt a burning in her stomach and throat as her eyes flicked down to the floor, where the flint knife lay. Quicker than thought, she snatched it up and sent it whistling into the chest of the mummy as hard as she could.

The dead thing looked down at the blade and seemed to smile. Slowly it reached for the hilt and jerked the knife free, raising it over its head.

"No, do not let it," Zamacona shrieked, though Alessandra could not say who he was speaking to. She watched as the mummy plunged the flint knife into its own chest again with a dry crackling sound. A puff of dust erupted as the blade went into the tattered flesh. Gripping the bone handle with both hands, the dead thing slowly drew the knife down towards its pelvis, cutting itself open in a grisly parody of ritual self-destruction.

Zamacona was screaming something that sounded like the words from her dreams, but they came too late. Whatever power the bindings carved into the husk had possessed, whatever power the mask had held over it, it had been rent asunder by the blow of the knife – whether hers or its, she could not say. The mummy flung the blade aside and grasped the edges of the bloodless wound. Then, with awkward strength, it ripped itself open, exposing the hollows within.

For a moment, there was only silence. Then, a sound like rushing water – furious and swift. The dark within the corpse pulsed with movement, with life, and something erupted into the dim light of the room. It was like a streak of tar, or a splash of oil or perhaps a shadow. A blotch of dark that unraveled at great speed, darting towards Zamacona with obvious intent.

Reacting swiftly, he caught one of his servants and interposed them between himself and the thing. The creature thrashed and mewled as the shadow splashed against it, and enveloped it with frenzied speed. There was a sound like the cracking of tree branches, and the body fell twitching to the floor. The shadow rose like a rearing serpent, bulbous excretions forming along its length. Alessandra stared, unable to look away. They were eyes – or maybe mouths – or perhaps some other organ entirely. A sound like the whistle of a train engine rose from the trembling liquid shadow.

The sound rose higher and higher until Alessandra thought her skull might split. She clapped her hands to her ears and looked away. She saw Whitlock tearing at the last strands of rope. He was pale, eyes bulging. As if he could not process what he was seeing. He lunged for one of the knives on the table, and his sudden movement caused the shadow to whip around. Something that might have been a maw opened, and darkly shimmering fang-shapes sprouted. It surged towards Whitlock, even as he turned to meet it.

Alessandra went low, sweeping her legs against Whitlock's shins and bringing him to the floor. The shadow sprang over him to strike the far wall. Whitlock glared at her and she wondered if he even saw her. She heard a wet sound and turned to see the shadow bunching and boiling across the wall, reforming itself. Its tendrils carved steaming gouges in the plaster as it studied her through the flickering orbs she thought were eyes.

It paused, and she felt the world go slack about her. The pain in her gut became unbearable, and was joined by a crashing agony inside her head. She faltered and fell to one knee, her throat flexing as something squirmed up her esophagus and towards her lips.

She vomited shadows. They wriggled towards the greater mass. She felt hollow, empty – alone.

"Fool. Idiot." Zamacona leaned down and clamped a hand on the back of her skull. "I should have seen – it was in you all along."

"W- What?" she gasped, clawing at his hand.

"I thought it might be in the others. Hiding in them. Whispering to them. I tore them apart looking for it. But it was cleverer than I thought."

Blindly scrabbling, her fingers found the fallen flint knife. As he dragged her into the air and made as if to dash her against the floor, she lashed out with the knife, driving the stone blade into his neck. Zamacona screeched like a wounded jaguar and flung her into the table. He groped for the knife jutting from his neck, and stumbled on the shrunken remains of the mummy.

The formless shadow enveloped him. Zamacona howled and flung himself backwards, flailing like a drowning man. He was shrieking in a language she didn't understand. His dying – if he could die – wasn't easy. The shadow stretched about him, as if he were the spoke of some hideous wheel. Writhing, night-black cilia speared anything that moved, human or otherwise. A sound, a hungry keening wail, threatened to burst Alessandra's eardrums as she faced the writhing mass of darkness.

"Countess – *move!*"

She turned, and saw Whitlock hefting one of the braziers. She leapt aside as he hurled it like a spear, straight towards the shadow-thing. It went up like oil, shrieking and wailing. It lashed out, knocking over the remaining braziers, upending the table. Flames crawled across the hairy carpet and licked at the walls. The shadow-thing twisted and squirmed, seeking an escape from the light.

Alessandra was on her feet in seconds. Smoke was filling the room. If any of the cultists were still alive, she couldn't tell. Coughing, she grabbed Whitlock by the arm. "Come on, we have to get out of here!" If the fire didn't get them, the smoke would. For once, Whitlock didn't argue.

They ran for the tunnel. As she reached the entrance, she stopped and turned back. The darkness rose up, crashing against the ceiling. It flailed like a wild beast, and then began to shrink in on itself. Then the fire roared, preventing her from seeing anything more. She turned and followed Whitlock out of the inferno.

Smoke already filled the cellar when they reached it. Whitlock took her arm as they fumbled towards the door leading to the house. It was open – hanging off its hinges. The hall beyond was a scene of carnage. Bodies lay broken on the floor, living-dead men worrying at them like jackals.

The creatures paused in their hideous repast when Alessandra and Whitlock appeared. "Shit," he said, with some feeling. She nodded. There were too many of them, and without Zamacona to call them off, there was little likelihood of escape.

"Come, back to the cellar, we can go out through the tunnel," she began. But even as they turned to go back, fire rushed up to greet them in a lashing flame that licked at the edges of the door. She heard the bottles in the wine cellar shattering. Whitlock pulled her back.

"Only one way out," he grunted. She nodded and turned, driving her fist into the flabby features of one of the creatures as it dove at him. It fell, but scrambled to its feet. Whitlock was driven back against the wall by another. It snapped at him with blackened teeth as he fought to hold it at bay. Alessandra was unable to aid him. Two more of them circled her, murmuring to themselves.

"Countess! Duck!"

At Pepper's shout, Alessandra dropped to the floor. She heard the boom of a pistol and one of her attackers spun with a wail. As it flapped at the wound, she spied Pepper standing at the other end of the hall, a pistol in hand. The young woman was pale, her eyes wide, but she took aim and fired again, and then a third time. Muldoon stood beside her, a rifle in his hands. He fired and worked the bolt smoothly, putting a round into Alessandra's remaining attacker and then Whitlock's. "Come on, both of you," he shouted. "We've got to get out of here before this place goes up."

Neither Alessandra nor Whitlock needed much in the way of encouragement. Together, the four of them made their way to the front doors. Smoke bled upwards through the floorboards as they ran. They were all coughing by the time they reached fresh air. Sirens wailed in the distance, and flames crawled up the foundations of the house.

Zamacona's followers – those that remained – scattered into the night. One of the creatures, clad in black, stopped at the edge of the lawn and met Alessandra's gaze. But only for an instant. Then it was gone, blending into the shadows. Coughing, she turned to Pepper. "I thought I told you to stay with the cab."

Pepper shrugged and winced. "I must have misheard. What now?"

"That depends entirely on our friends here." Alessandra looked at Muldoon and Whitlock. The latter sat on the pavement, looking away from the house, shoulders hunched, head bowed. Muldoon seemed less shaken, though not by much.

"What happened in there?" he asked, in a smoke roughened voice.

"An old debt was paid," Alessandra said. "Are we under arrest?"

"No," Whitlock said, without looking up. "Get out of here."

Muldoon looked at him, and nodded. "We never saw you."

Alessandra smiled, but it was a weak thing. She was tired. "And I was never here," she said, turning to watch the fire rise up and claim the roof. She wondered whether it was still there, beneath the house. Trapped by the fire. She remembered her dreams. Remembered how small it had made itself in its cage of flesh and bone, all to escape the light.

She looked away, and tried not to think of it at all.

CHAPTER THIRTY-FIVE
Leaving Arkham

Alessandra looked up as the bell over the door jangled, and Muldoon entered the diner. He was out of uniform, but still looked like a police officer somehow. She smiled and turned back to the window, and continued her study of the iron defenses of the university across the street.

It had been a long night, but a dreamless one. A relief, after the past few days. She did not feel rested, even so. She did not think she would until she left Arkham. "There you are," she said, as Muldoon slid into the booth across from her.

"Sorry I'm late," Muldoon said, placing a wrapped object on the booth beside him. "Whitlock didn't want to let me out of his sight, but I distracted him with some paperwork."

"Clever." Alessandra sipped her coffee. After a moment, she asked, "How is he?"

"Beat up, but he'll live." He looked at her. "He... won't talk about what happened."

"No. I do not expect that he will."

"What about you?"

"No." She looked out the window. A faint streak of smoke still scarred the morning sky. Orne's house had made a lovely light, as it burned. The fire brigade had managed to arrive before it spread to the neighboring houses. "I was surprised that you wanted to meet, after last night. Surely the case is solved to everyone's satisfaction."

It would be hushed up. Not everyone had died in what they were calling a gas explosion, but those who'd escaped – or not attended – would be silent about what had happened. She doubted any of Orne's special guests had escaped, but then again, there was no telling how far or how deep the tunnels stretched. Orne was dead, at least, and Professor Ashley as well. A great tragedy, according to the papers.

"Not quite." Muldoon ordered a coffee as the waitress came over, and then tapped the brown parcel. "There's a matter of... ownership to clear up."

Alessandra looked at the parcel. From the size and shape she could guess what was inside. The mask the mummy had worn had somehow survived the blaze intact. The firefighters had stumbled across it somehow and turned it over to the police. She tried not to think about how it could have gotten somewhere accessible. "Oh?"

Muldoon was silent for a few moments. Then, "I know some things. Not a lot, but... enough. Enough to know when to follow something through, and when to let someone else handle it. In this case, I've done my duty and I'm finished. But I can't leave this thing in the evidence locker. That ain't safe enough. Maybe nowhere is."

"So you've brought it to me." Alessandra set her coffee aside. "I am flattered."

"Don't be." Muldoon paused. "Whitlock still wants you arrested – though I think that's more stubbornness than anything else. But there's plenty of paperwork to keep him busy and a train leaving for Boston this afternoon."

"Is that a hint?"

"A suggestion. Lucky neither the chief nor the sheriff are interested in questioning you. They just want all of this to go away, and I don't blame them." He looked at the package. "What do you intend to do with it? Sell it?"

"No. I do not think it is right to allow such a thing to fall into the wrong hands." She frowned. "Maybe that is a silly thing to say, under the circumstances."

"Maybe. But you're right all the same. What're you going to do with it, then?"

She nodded towards the university. "I made a call to Professor Walters this morning, after you contacted me. He advised me to turn it over to the university. Apparently, they have quite the collection of artifacts. The mask will be safe with them."

Muldoon sighed and sat back. "I could get into real trouble if anyone found out."

"So do not tell them." She finished her coffee and set it aside. "Forget this ever happened. Forget what you saw. I intend to do the same."

Muldoon was silent for a moment. "I have a duty," he said, finally. "And I guess, so do you." He passed her the mask.

Alessandra took it. "What will happen to the rest of Orne's collection?"

"Most of it got burned up. The town will probably auction the rest." Muldoon smiled grimly. "I hear Carl Sanford already put a preliminary bid in for the whole lot."

"Of course. I wish him luck," Alessandra said, as she slid out of the booth. She paused. "What about the rest of Orne's… following?

Some of them may have escaped. There's no telling what they might do now."

"That's my problem," he said.

She left money on the table and picked up the mask. "Then I wish you luck as well, officer. May your nights be quieter, here on out."

Muldoon shook his head. "No such thing as a quiet night in this town. Believe me, I know." He took a sip of his coffee. "Not all bad, though."

Alessandra left him to his coffee and made her way across the street. The campus was quiet, and the library all but empty when she reached it. She made her way through the familiar tables towards the offices situated beneath the glass skylight. She'd paid little attention to it before, but Walters had told her to take the mask there. She spotted Daisy Walker, the librarian, moving to intercept her and stopped.

Daisy smiled. "Hello again."

"Hello," Alessandra said. Before she could say anything else, Daisy continued.

"Doctor Armitage is waiting on you in my office. Just go in." She glanced at the mask and looked away. "Good luck," she added, touching Alessandra on the arm. Alessandra nodded her thanks and continued to the office.

She knocked on the door, and heard a muffled invitation. Inside was a circular office that was mostly composed of shelves and books. An older man stood in front of one of the shelves, his back to her. "Doctor Armitage?" she asked.

"Ah, you must be Countess Zorzi. Harvey mentioned you might be coming around." Armitage turned, his arms full of books. He was narrow and slightly stooped, with hair the color of iron, and dressed well for an academic. "You look like you've had a rather disagreeable night." He set his burden down and gestured to a chair. "Sit."

Alessandra did. She set the mask, in its brown paper wrapping, down on his desk. "Disagreeable, but successful," she said. She paused, lighting a cigarette. Her last. She eyed the stack of books. "Doing research?"

Armitage chuckled. "You might say that. This used to be my office, you know. Miss Walker has done an admirable job since my retirement, and she's added a few books to the reference shelf since I departed." He tapped the stack. "And I wanted to read up on certain items before we spoke."

Alessandra sat for a moment. "How much do you know?"

"Some. Enough to know that what happened was bound to happen. Enough to know that you might want to stay away from the Midwest for the time being. Oklahoma, specifically."

She smiled and tapped the mask. "Professor Walters mentioned that you might be able to find a home for a certain objet d'art, should I acquire it."

"I see." Armitage adjusted his spectacles. "May I...?"

Alessandra pushed the mask across the table. Armitage carefully unwrapped it. He grunted softly and ran his fingers over the bestial contours, not quite touching it. He looked at her. "You know what this represents, I trust?"

"I know enough to know that it belongs somewhere safe."

Reluctantly, he pushed it back towards her. "We do have a... special collection here, yes. I can't speak for the university, but I doubt we can pay very much, I'm afraid. Nowhere near your normal fee, if Harvey wasn't exaggerating about that."

"He wasn't. But... we'll call it a donation, shall we?" Alessandra looked at the mask, and then up at Armitage. "The first of many, perhaps."

Armitage frowned. "What do you mean?"

Alessandra stood. "Of late, I have begun to give serious thought to a change of career. I'm of the mind to take up a more socially conscious profession. One that benefits everyone."

"I think I understand." Armitage rewrapped the mask. "And I can say that should you wish to make further… donations to our collection, we will happily take them." He paused. "I should warn you, however… such a change is not to be undertaken lightly." He looked at her. "It will be dangerous. Far more dangerous than anything you might have done before."

Alessandra smiled. "After what I've seen, professor, I think I am quite prepared." Her smile faded after a moment. "And if not… well, I've always been a quick learner." She turned to go. Armitage cleared his throat.

"For your sake, I hope so, countess. In any event, I wish you luck."

Alessandra didn't turn. "Luck is something I have never been short of, professor."

Pepper was waiting for her outside the library, as Alessandra had known she would be. The girl looked up as Alessandra descended the steps. "Well?"

"It is taken care of."

"Really?" Pepper sounded doubtful.

Alessandra paused and lit a cigarette. "I hope so. My bags?"

"In the cab." She said it sourly. Her cab was sitting in a wrecker's yard. The one she drove now had been borrowed from her garage. "What now?"

"Now, you take me to the train station. I might be able to catch the midday train to Boston." Alessandra looked down at Pepper. "As lovely as Arkham is, I think I have worn out my welcome."

"Yeah? Shame. I was starting to have fun." She smiled and then winced and rubbed her arm. It still pained her, and Alessandra knew the girl had her ribs bandaged beneath her shirt. She hadn't said what had happened, but Alessandra could guess.

Alessandra hesitated. "You could come with me, if you like."

Pepper stared at her. "Come where?"

"Wherever." Alessandra gestured with her cigarette. "Out there. Away from Arkham. I could use the help, and you proved yourself singularly adept. I'd pay, of course. Not much, but more than you make driving a cab, I'd wager. Especially given the condition of yours, at the moment."

Pepper turned away. She was silent for a moment. Then, in a small voice, she said, "You mean it?"

"I wouldn't have made the offer otherwise." Alessandra offered her a cigarette. "Think about it. I'll be staying at the Copley Square Hotel in Boston for a few days. Wire me if you decide to accept my offer, and I'll extend my stay until you can arrive."

"Why?" Pepper asked, as she took a cigarette.

Alessandra lit it for her. "Why what?"

"Why make the offer?"

Alessandra sighed and sat awkwardly, smoothing her dress. "As I said, I could use the help. I need someone I can trust."

"I don't think I'd make a good thief."

"I can teach you."

"Yeah?"

"Yeah." Alessandra looked at her. "It is not an easy life, but it is exciting."

Pepper grinned. "I do like excitement." She snuffed the cigarette and put it behind her ear. "Let me think about it." She hopped to her feet. "We'd better get moving if you want to catch your train."

Alessandra rose and took one last look around. The sun was shining, but the shadows were long. She didn't see anyone waiting in them. But that didn't mean they wouldn't be there tomorrow, or the next day. Shivering slightly, she followed Pepper to the cab.

She had a train to catch.

EPILOGUE
Darkness

In darkness, it slept. Aching from the sharp light of the fire and its long confinement, it had dug itself deeper and deeper, seeking refuge. Deep into the dark, where the light and the heat could not reach.

And there, it curled tighter and tighter in on itself, making itself as small as possible. In the dark, it could rest and regain the strength that had so long been denied it. It had fed, though not well. But it would feed again, once it had rested. It would rise up, once the light had faded, and would feed and feed and *feed–*

A sound. A call.

It stirred. The call came again. The old words. It paused, listening. Then, unable to help itself, it answered.

It dug through the loose soil, burning a passage upwards through the sediment, tasting the fading heat of the conflagration and shying away from it. Though the fire was gone, the memory of it still stung.

When it reached the surface, it thrust itself upward, spreading and stretching itself, glorying in its freedom. It rose over the warmbloods who gathered in the ruins of the house below. They were not the same as those who had trapped it – betrayed it. They were smaller things, weaker and more fragile. Younger, as it judged such things.

That they knew the words was surprising. But it felt no fear of these little ones. It had been caged once – they would not do so again. Could not. The wisdom was not in them. It undulated above them, listening as they spoke, wondering which it would consume first. There were so many of them, and all pulsing with heat and life.

One of them raised a limb, as if in greeting, and spoke in the tongue of the warmbloods of K'n-Yan. "You are even as the old texts claimed, ancient one. Like a fold of night come alive."

It paused in its calculations. The speaker noticed this hesitation, and a smile spread across his face. "Magnificent... but not a brain in the gelatinous skull. Mr Swann – the binding wand, please."

"Yessir, Mr Sanford," another said. It did not understand the meaning of these words, but it sensed the threat. It lunged at the first to speak, intending to consume him. But he flung up a hand, and spoke words of light and pain. They stung it, disorientating it. It lashed wildly, trying to escape the tormenting words. But more words rose, as the other warmbloods spoke. Too many words, rising like fire.

Then there was a new pain – an old pain. It reared, trying to stretch itself higher and higher, to escape the pain. The one who had spoken held a rod that glowed with cold light. The light encircled it, forcing it to shrink, to fold down. It could not escape, no matter how much it raged. As it shrank, it heard the voice of its new master.

"Settle down, settle down. There's nothing for it now. You're caught." He leaned over its shrunken form, smiling widely. "But it's not the end of the world..." The smile faded.

"Not yet anyway."

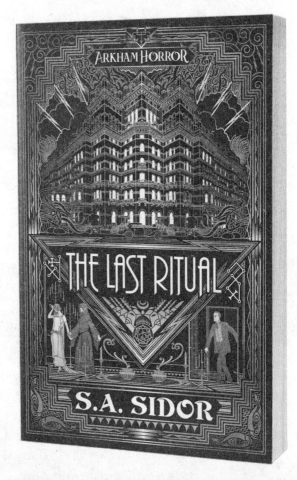

DISCOVER MORE NEW WORLDS

*Enter Rokugan, a realm of warring samurai clans –
filled with honor, battle, magic and demons – in the
epic fantasy world of* Legend of the Five Rings.

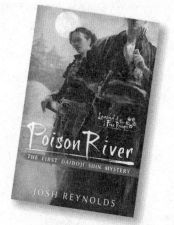

*Explore a planet of
infinite variety – wild
science fantasy adventures
on an impossible patch-
work world of everything
known (and unknown) in
the universe, in the first
explosive and hilarious
KeyForge anthology.*

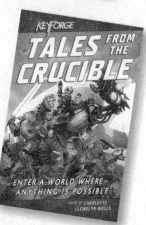